Glad You Came

Glad You Came

CHLOE FORD

An Aria Book

First published in the UK in 2026 by Head of Zeus,
part of Bloomsbury Publishing Plc

9 7 5 3 1 2 4 6 8

A catalogue record for this book is available from the British Library.

ISBN (PB): 9781035922208; ISBN (ePub): 9781035922185

Cover design: Gemma Gorton

Typeset by Lumina Datamatics Ltd
Printed and bound in Great Britain by Clays Ltd, Elcograf S.p.A.

Bloomsbury Publishing Plc
50 Bedford Square, London, WC1B 3DP, UK
Bloomsbury Publishing Ireland Limited,
29 Earlsfort Terrace, Dublin 2, D02 AY28, Ireland

HEAD OF ZEUS LTD
5–8 Hardwick Street
London, EC1R 4RG

To find out more about our authors and books
visit www.headofzeus.com
For product safety related questions contact productsafety@bloomsbury.com

To the eldest sisters who stepped up.

One

The fight-or-flight response has always been a fascination of mine. Partly because, whether through necessity or personality, I've always been quick to fight. I'm a fighter. Well, ok, not in the literal sense (although I once punched a dear friend in the face because he paid me to after one too many tequilas, and I broke a finger). But I am *confrontational*. I bite back when barked at. It's who I am.

So naturally, I don't like this queasy feeling, or the jittery shakes in my fingers. And I'm definitely not enjoying the whirling, anxious thoughts morphing into a full-blown headache.

And worse still, none of it is firing me up for a fight.

No, it's telling me to *run*. And that would be fine.

Totally fine.

It's just a shame it's my wedding day.

I stare at my reflection as a rainbow-coloured dildo passes over my shoulder, mid-flight. The hair stylist flinches as she adds the final bobby pins into my tight bun. Behind me, my younger sisters – Abby, Gemma and Millie – are pure frenetic energy. With their blonde hair styled, make-up pristine, their lovely, dusky pink dresses zipped up, and their heels strapped on, the three of them have grown impatient.

"Watch out!" Abby says, ducking to avoid the dildo as it ricochets off the wall. Millie, my youngest sister, and the culprit, picks it up and wags it in the air. "Really?" I sigh. "Can you not destroy this hotel room, please?"

She spins on me with an eye roll. "It's hardly going to break anything. It's rubber."

"There's no way that's rubber," Abby interjects, shaking her head. Ever the nerd of the family. "If anything, it's soft plastic."

Millie scoffs. "Who the hell made you the expert of dildos?"

"I'm just stating facts."

"*Dildo* facts." Millie grins, the accomplished antagonist that she is.

"Will you both shut up." Gemma steps in, but as always, it's only to press her own agenda. She tilts her head and forces a smile. "Sara, Brad wants to see me before the ceremony. You don't mind, right?"

I let out a slow breath, but it's ragged. Panic tightens my chest. And of course, the extra-large dildo whizzes past my head again. I stifle a scream.

Must remember to pick my battles.

Besides, beyond my gut-wrenching anxiety about today and the tension gathering at the base of my skull, I promised myself I wouldn't morph into bridezilla. I've taken extra precautions to avoid this likelihood, such as, pretending I'm not that fussed about *anything* to do with the wedding.

Wrong flowers arrived? *Oh well.*

Guest no-shows? *Who cares.*

Rain forecast? *That's just as well.*

Signs everywhere? *Who believes in signs?!*

I even hired a wedding planner for this specific reason, and yet wrangling my baby sisters is proving an even bigger job than planning a wedding. I shoot Gemma a look, who shrugs apologetically but turns her attention back to her phone. I know if I ask her to ignore her toxic, too-old-for-her boyfriend until *after* the ceremony, the curtains will come down on that one and I'll be labelled the worst bridezilla to have ever bridezillered.

I can feel myself really starting to spiral when a soft hand squeezes my arm. Hattie, one of my best friends since university and my maid of honour, gives me a reassuring smile before quickly inserting herself.

"Can I see that dildo?" she asks Millie politely, who frowns, reluctantly passing it over for inspection.

Hattie scrunches her nose at it, steps up to the open window and flings it out. Whatever it *is* made of, it certainly lands with a dramatic *thwack*. I can only hope it hasn't hit any guests on its descent.

"Hey!" Millie complains. "That was Sara's wedding gift from me."

"That's so weird," Hattie says, shaking her head. "And Gemma, pass me your phone please."

Gemma eyes me suspiciously as if Hattie and I have some form of telepathy. She regards the window before handing it over. In fairness, I understand her wariness, Hattie has been known to act on impulse – she's as fizzy as her wild, strawberry-blonde hair.

The stylist tuts at my constant movement, and I quietly apologise.

A bead of sweat drips down my back but I'm conscious of not moving again. Instead, I take a deep breath, attempting to push away the sick feeling climbing my throat.

"Deep breaths," Hattie says to me, holding Gemma's phone up to her mouth to record a voice note. "Hi, Brad. Gemma is *really* busy *supporting* her older sister on a *really* big day and so I'm hoping you'll be able to entertain yourself for a moment. Thanks so much, Brad. You're a hero." Her tone drips with sarcasm and I smile – actually *smile* – for the first time today.

"Great, now, where were we?" Hattie asks. Gemma lifts her chin, clearly irritated her phone has been confiscated. She sidesteps Hattie to stand behind me as I'm misted with hairspray without warning.

"All done," the stylist says. "Are you happy with the curls I've done at the front? They'll likely fall out before the reception, but you have such naturally straight hair."

"It's lovely," I say, brushing the strands from my face. The curls feel so intensely trivial right now.

"I think it looked better down," Millie adds, lying back on the bed. Hattie turns and shoots Millie a look. "Never mind. The curls are cute. They definitely don't make you look *more* uptight than usual."

Ah, there it is. The stinger.

I exhale slowly. The thing about being the eldest of four is that you end up taking on responsibilities before you're old enough to do so. I believed I was far more mature and knowledgeable than I actually was. I know I got lots of it wrong: I pushed too hard when their grades were down; spoke out about shitty boyfriends before they were ready to hear it; and I had, *still have*, a serious inability to ignore behaviour that needs calling out.

But I am also the one they call when things get tough – partly because we lost our mother when I was only fourteen and someone had to fill her shoes.

I've bailed Gemma out of credit card debt three times. She dates wealthy, older men, but somehow, always ends up paying for everything.

I've picked Millie up from the side of the road, since she was old enough to go out drinking with her mates, more times than I'm willing to admit.

As for Abby… Well, she's the quietest, brainiest one of the bunch. I never had to worry about her grades – she aced every exam – but I *would* have to worry about whether she'd remembered to eat during revision periods or if she was allowing herself enough rest. She struggled with friendships in a way none of us ever did and, although everything seemed fine on the outside, I'd lie awake at night worrying about her the most.

And so, I'm sorry, I guess, if I come across a little uptight at times.

But if I was relaxed, nothing would get done and the girls wouldn't have anyone to lean on when things get tough.

And that's why I cannot possibly run. Not in front of my sisters. Not in front of family. Not today. I've left it too late. Just the thought of letting them down makes me want to throw up.

Ugh!

Hattie clears her throat, bringing me back to earth. "Come on bride-to-be, let's get you into your dress." She signals to Millie. "And turn the radio up please. I fucking love this song."

The song playing is a familiar chart topper, the kind with a quieter bridge that leads into a big, sweeping chorus. It's that style of song that makes you want to jump around the room, even if you don't know the lyrics. I can never remember the name of the band, but I'll give it to them, they know how to write a hit.

I follow Hattie into the swanky bathroom, Abby trailing behind me. I'm primed for marriage: every inch of me has been waxed and tanned over the past few days. Add in my blonde hair and angular features, I feel almost Barbie-like. But not in a good way.

The dress I chose is a ball gown shape with the sweetheart neckline and lace sleeves. The lady who worked in the shop looked me up and down once, picked it right off the hanger and told me it was the one. And although I tried other dresses, she was right, this was the best shape on me.

Now, of course, I hate it. I wish I'd picked something more daring. More *me*.

I'm not a princess. And I feel like an imposter in it.

But that's starting to feel like a theme these past weeks. Even months. In some ways I've felt like an imposter in my own life, and it's terrifying. But it's not worth dwelling on right this second. I've already decided I'm going through with this wedding. We've been together for five years, it's time. It makes sense. Even if my heart is sagging in my chest.

I shake myself out of it. Everyone is here for a wedding. Some of my family have travelled hours to get here. And I am programmed not to let people down.

I'm going to be the perfect bride.

I am strong enough for this.

Hattie eyes me as I remove my satin dressing gown. I

think she can tell something is on my mind but isn't saying anything. At least not in front of Abby. They team up to lower the dress so I can step in, raising it again as I slide my arms into the sleeves.

"Right. Let's do this," I say, forcing a smile and nodding to Hattie.

Abby moves the mirror, so I have no choice but to look at myself. "You're so pretty," she says, and I can tell by the gentleness of her voice that she really believes it.

"You're even prettier," I remind her, turning the attention away from me.

"Mike is one lucky man," Hattie agrees, coming over to adjust my bodice slightly and apply some skin tape to the front exactly the way the seamstress showed her in the shop at my final fitting only two weeks ago. It feels like so much has happened since then. So much has shifted. "I bet he's nervous too."

I bet he is, I think.

"I'm not nervous." I am very nervous.

I'm terrified I'm about to do something incredibly stupid. And I can't tell if that's marrying the man I'm supposed to love or running away from the man I'm supposed to love.

She sniffs. "Of course you're not. I've never seen you nervous. You're a wolf, not a lamb."

I stare at myself for too long. I look like the woman Mike should be marrying. But I don't look like *me* and with rising dread in the pit of my stomach, I realise I've done this to myself.

I've ignored my doubts all week.

Oh God.

I've ignored my doubts all week!

It's too late to leave.

Is it too late to leave?

I turn to Hattie and take a steadying breath. I'm being irrational and I'm *never* irrational.

This is just cold feet. It will pass!

"Do you think I look too much like a bride?" I ask suddenly. "Like I'm trying *too* hard to look like a bride?" I take fistfuls of the dress in each hand.

Hattie regards me, brow raised. "Hmm. I'm trying to work out how your brain got to that question. I'm pretty sure looking like a bride is the whole point."

"Well, yeah, but…" my voice trails off. I have the urge to step out of my body and look at this from a different perspective.

But I don't have time. Gemma and Millie poke their heads round the door.

"You look bloody perfect," Gemma says, sounding resentful of the fact.

Millie sighs. "Maybe *too* perfect."

This confirms my fears. "Yes! Thank you! I look like I've tried too hard."

"Hair down would've been better," Millie says, hitching her hip like she's just been proven right.

Hattie spins on her. "Sara's hair is *fine*. Stop it."

"It's perfect!" Gemma states again with a sting in her tone.

"Should I mess it up a bit?" I ask, staring at the tight bun it's been rolled into. "I've got time to take it down." I feel manic.

"No, don't you dare!" Hattie says. "The wedding planner will kill us if we mess with her schedule. You are ready and you look absolutely perfect… Er, no… Beautiful… *Regal*. Whatever. Doesn't matter. You're going down the aisle like this!" She shakes her head. "Everyone, get your flowers."

Hattie ushers my sisters out of the bathroom and they scurry towards the door.

"See you out there," Abby says, giving my arm one last squeeze.

"Break a leg!" Millie adds.

"Really?" Gemma frowns.

"What? It's a thing people say!"

"Girls, move it, go, go," Hattie practically shoves them out and closes the door behind them, exhaling. "Ok, let's touch up that make-up one last time."

I pause, turning back towards the mirror to take in my reflection. "More make-up?"

"Just lipstick. Where is it?" she asks.

"Here," I say, fishing through my purse on the side until my fingers close around it. I pass it to Hattie just as my phone vibrates on the nightstand. I lean over to take a look. It's a text from Mike. I swallow.

"Sara?" Hattie waves at me. Has she been speaking?

"One sec." I clear my throat and turn the phone over. I can't bring myself to look at it. It will be one of two things. Either an excuse about what happened and a reminder of how sorry he is. Or the truth. A truth I don't need to hear from him because deep down I know. I saw the messages. I know.

Oh God. I know.

"Umm. Hattie?" I say, my voice too pitchy. She's looking at my expectantly. "I have a code red."

Hattie's eyes widen and her mouth falls open. "Are you joking?"

The tears begin to spill and my hands start to shake. "No," I manage to force out. "I have to go."

It's actually a little cruel of me to enact a code red on Hattie, today of all days. It was a code we created at university with our housemates for nights out when the creepy dude got a bit too full on, or if a first date was going south. It's a *do not question, get me out of here, save our souls* situation. She knows the drill. And she knows it's going to be near on impossible. But if anyone can do it, it's Hattie.

"*Fuuuuck*." She quickly puts the lipstick down and steps towards me, taking my hands in hers. "How bad? What are we talking? Do I need to get my shovel?"

I sniff. "You don't own a shovel."

"No. But I have a very cute trowel for my indoor plants."

I shake my head, tears dripping onto my dress, lips wobbling. Hattie finds me a tissue and dabs gently at my cheeks, but her act of kindness only makes me feel worse. I'm terrible. I can't believe this is happening. I swore to myself that it wouldn't come to this. But something in my stomach tells me that leaving, escaping this mess, is the best and only option for my future happiness.

"Ok, so no to digging graves." She nods, eyeing me carefully. "What *is* happening Sara?"

"I need to just…" I take a deep breath. "I need to get out of here. I don't want to see anyone."

"Not even Mike?"

"*Especially* not Mike."

"Wow. Ok. Yeah." She looks around searching for inspiration. Then as if she gets the lightbulb moment needed, she turns back to me with a determined smile. "I know what to do. Stay here."

She leaves me on my own for five minutes. My heart races as I do frantic laps of the room, shaking my hands out like it will rid me of some of my fears. What if she runs into Mike? What if he insists on speaking to me?

I hear footsteps in the hallway and then the door swings open.

Hattie's forehead shimmers from running around.

"There's a taxi," she says, breathing heavy. "At the front of the hotel. I cleared the way, but you'll have to go alone because I need to stay by the back doors to the bar, so nobody comes this way."

I practically launch myself at her, holding her close. "Thank you," I whisper.

"How many times have you gotten me out of a code-red situation?" She laughs, but there's a nervous tremor there. We both know I'll owe her an explanation, but right now, she's not going to question me. "You should go. I don't know how long I can hold this together. And once you're out of here, it's all going to kick off."

I step back, releasing her. The guilt almost floors me. "Shit. You're right. I can't let you deal with that alone... I'll—"

"Sara," Hattie says, sternly, placing her hands on my shoulders so I have to no choice but to look her in the eye. "You would do the same for me in a heartbeat. And besides, I have backup. They don't *know* they're backup yet, but they'll help me out." I know she's talking about our close friend Sam and his older brother, Freddie, who's now her boyfriend.

I nod. I do trust them to have her back, and mine.

"Ok," I say.

"Ok, let's go."

I experience a sharp pinch of adrenaline as I follow her down the stairs and out into the hotel's courtyard, the long train of my wedding dress rustling along the cobbled path. Large neatly pruned hedgerows block the view of the event space where the wedding party are waiting for me to arrive.

Hattie gives me a final, brief hug. "Go quickly," she says, nodding towards the street. "I've got this."

I kiss her cheek before striding quickly to the front of the hotel, spotting the black taxi waiting for me up ahead. I dive into the back and sigh so dramatically it comes out like more of a sob.

"Bad day?" the driver asks.

"You could say that," I manage to squeak out.

He watches me in the rearview mirror, as if he's waiting for me to have a total meltdown, but within seconds we're pulling away from the hotel. I look back and wonder what Hattie has in store.

I'm most worried about Dad. The guilt intensifies when I imagine the look on his face. The disappointment. The concern.

As we join the motorway in the direction of home, I finally allow my breathing to return to normal, turn off my phone and look ahead.

Two

Two months later

"**H**ey, wake up," Millie's voice stirs me.

"What the fuuuuck…" I hiss, half-delirious.

"Wake up. I have coffee."

This gets my attention. I sit bolt upright in my bed and stare at my bright-eyed youngest sister who is smiling far too eagerly for this time of day. What time is it anyway?

What day is it?

I glare at her like she's lost her last marble and check the time on my phone. Except I don't, because my phone isn't where I left it.

"Millie, what the *fuck*? I thought I was being murdered."

She regards me, quirking her head in confusion. "Why?"

"Oh, I don't know. Probably because there's an intruder sat at the end of my bed."

"What, *me*? What kind of intruder brings coffee? And, besides, it's ten a.m. on a Saturday. I don't think that's prime intruder time."

I raise an eyebrow. "How would you know?" She doesn't answer and it's just as well because I'm too busy searching for my phone. It can't have gone far…

"You looking for this?" she asks, waving the cube that runs my life in my face. "It was vibrating on your bedside table when I arrived. Everyone was worried about you, so here I am."

I blink, trying to orient myself. Millie snaps her fingers in my face.

"Stop it," I grumble.

"Earth to Sara! You've been virtually MIA since the wedding. Dad's on the verge of a stroke. I mean, technically, that's not your fault. He has terrible blood pressure." My phone buzzes again. "You need a new phone. This one is so old. Are you packed yet?"

"What?" My brain is absolutely not prepared for this kind of interrogation.

Simple fact about me: I've trained my body to only function after at least three cups of coffee and this must be topped up throughout the day, or else I will crash. It's my only flaw.

That and my newest trait: infamous runaway bride.

Millie fidgets, frowning from the end of my bed. "Have you hit your head? Your *flight*! Are you checked in for your flight? It leaves in six hours."

"What are you *talking* about?" I snatch my phone from her to find a string of notifications. I scroll through the most recent ones, all updates about my upcoming trip.

Oh, yeah – *that*.

The honeymoon.

It's been lingering in the back of my mind like a small puddle of grief ever since I ran. I dip my toes in from time to time and let myself cry about it. Not helped by the fact that it was planned for two months after our non-wedding because I couldn't take the additional time off in May. So, the sorrow has lingered. Obviously, I can't go on my honeymoon. That would be... I allow myself to consider it again and almost sputter out a laugh.

What would I even say?

Oh hi, it's actually just the one of us now. Merry old me, all alone. The bride who did a runner and is now taking the non-refundable, all-inclusive honeymoon cruise of a lifetime. Alone. Betrayed and heartbroken. Pfft. As if.

"So you *did* hit your head," Millie scoffs. "Your flight to Venice, obviously!"

"Why are you going through my phone?" I snap.

She makes a face and shrugs. "I'm your sister. Besides, you were unconscious. Also Abby made a note of your holiday in her diary. She thought you'd bail. Not sure why it's me who has to do the flyby visit to check in. Just because I'm the youngest and live in the same street doesn't mean I'm not also important and busy. I have a boutique shoe shop to run."

"Millie, honestly..."

"I brought you a coffee," she points out again to distract me, handing me a reusable cup that I recognise from the café across the road. It's good stuff at least.

I eye her suspiciously as I take a long sip, feeling the warm kick working its way through my blood stream. "What do you want?"

She pouts and quirks her head. "Other than for you to have a shower?"

I narrow my eyes.

"Look, you weren't answering your phone, so Dad and Abby sent me round to check on you. Check you're packed.

Taxi booked, et cetera. You've been so distant and moody recently."

"As always, Mills, you're a treat to hang out with."

She grins with mirth. "*Thanks.*" I give her a look, silence stretching between us.

There's a part of me that wants to reveal all. Especially to my sisters. I feel like they'd at least listen, if only to soak up the drama, but then I think about how to explain it and the words get jammed in my throat. Besides, I don't want to burden them with my problems, knowing they've all got plenty of their own stuff going on.

Sure, people, colleagues, friends, they've been curious. Hattie, for example, knows me well enough to step around the hard parts and squeeze out smaller truths first. Which is why I've done a stellar job of avoiding her.

I'm ashamed to admit that I'm embarrassed about how he betrayed me. It feels like I did something wrong too. I wasn't paying enough attention. Besides, what's the point of talking about it now? I've left him. It's over. Move on.

"Look, do you want me to help you pack or not? Judging by the state you're in, you'll need all the help you can get."

"Ugh, no. I'm not going."

"*What?* Why not?"

"Because I'm not going," I repeat slowly. "You know, on my honeymoon, seeing as I'm not *actually* married."

"*So?!*"

I scoff, staring at her in disbelief. "*So,* that would be insane. You know, since I don't have a *husband.*" I run a hand through my hair. Ah hell, that's greasy.

As if she can read my mind, Millie cringes, mirroring my expression. "I don't understand," she says.

"Tell me what's stumping you and I'll try to walk you through it."

"You're telling me you're not going on the trip of your dreams because you don't have a husband?"

"Hmm, now that you put it like that. Yes. That is correct."

"What? *No.* What?"

"Millie, I'm half awake. Please can I at least drink my coffee in peace and have a shower?" She's no longer smiling. It's more of a confused grimace. I scowl back at her as I climb out from under the covers and hobble to the ensuite.

When I return, she's no longer in my room. I wrap a towel round my head, pull on some clean pyjamas and find her in the kitchen. I bought my converted warehouse flat near the lanes in Brighton four years ago. It cost me a lifetime mortgage and every penny I had, but it was mine and mine alone. Mike was cagey about being mortgage-bound; his credit was iffy. So, I bought it for me, and for *us*. Whenever I stand in my kitchen like this, I'm so thankful I was sensible enough to do it myself. It made moving him out exceptionally easy because there was no doubt about who owned the place.

I hold a finger up when she starts to speak. "Wait. More coffee."

"Oh, come on," Millie groans.

"My flat, my rules," I warn. I turn the coffee machine on and lean against the counter, taking my sweet time, knowing the waiting will be driving her crazy. I finally take a seat opposite hers, cradling a steaming cup in my palms.

"Can I talk now?" she asks.

"One sec," I say, taking a slow, scalding sip. "Go on."

"We've discussed it in the group chat and we've made an executive decision."

"*We?*"

"Yes, your sisters."

I take a moment to check my phone. My messages blew up for the first week after the wedding – so much so, I actually muted several people and even blocked some of Mike's family who were horribly misinformed. Because why would he tell them the truth? He couldn't even spare it for me.

But it's fairly quiet now, just a few messages from close friends. I search for the family chat. Nothing there. Must be the sister chat. But hang on…

"There are no new messages in our group chat."

Millie bites her bottom lip. "*Oh*. We must've used the other one."

I nearly do a spit take. "I'm sorry, you have a group chat I'm not *in?*"

"We made it for the wedding," she says, waving a hand dismissively.

"Liar."

"It's not really relevant right now."

"To hell, it isn't. I want a full transcript sent to me within the hour. What are you brats saying about me?"

"Not everything's about you, Sara," she says, rolling her eyes. "Look, you spent obscene amounts of money on that cruise. I know because when you sent the link to us, Abby gave you a three-page essay about backpacking across Europe to save money and you didn't reply."

"She wasted her energy. I wasn't going to backpack on my honeymoon."

"Yes. Agreed. Can you imagine? There's no way you would travel that way. You're far too..." She pauses and I don't need her to fill in the blank. I give her a sardonic look which she pretends to ignore. "You *have* to go on this cruise. You booked it. Did you even go halves?"

"Well," I say, my gut flipping over on itself at the thought of my lost savings. I had to pay for him too because he didn't see the value in going on a honeymoon. *Yikes. How didn't I see it?* "No, but—"

"There you go! Problem solved. Great. Let's pack."

I take a deep breath, swallowing down a jolt of panic. "*Millie*. No. I don't..." I wrap my arms around myself.

It occurs to me that she hasn't even offered me a hug or asked if I'm ok. Most people would be offended, but it's a coping mechanism we adopted as a family after mum passed. Why ask if somebody is ok when you know they probably aren't? What good will a hug do when your world is falling apart around you?

She groans, but I swear I see a flicker of pity in her eyes. "You don't have much time to make this decision."

"I really appreciate you checking in on me. Honestly, I do." *Even if it's been jarring and has given me a headache.* "But right now, what I need is to be alone."

"Yes, exactly. Alone in the Mediterranean. On a luxury yacht."

"No. Alone *here*. Not in forced proximity with a bunch of strangers."

"But you've been alone this whole time."

"I just don't feel like going anymore. It's tainted now."

Millie's shoulders visibly sag. "Fine. But I'm sad for you. I can't remember the last time you had a proper holiday, can you?" She stands up, shrugging. "I don't usually say this, because frankly I'm the only one who deserves a holiday most of the time, but you really *need* this. You work insane hours. You've been even more stressed recently. I just think you need an adventure. When was the last time you did something *just* for you? And not for someone else? Not for Mike, for me, Abby or Gemma? Dad! Even Hattie!" The question tugs at my heartstrings. It is a rare sight indeed to see Millie looking beyond her own nose.

Dare I say, it's cute. *And persuasive.*

"It's not that simple," I say, shrugging it off.

"Why not? It should be that simple. You've booked a holiday. You've not cancelled your annual leave, have you? I can't think of anything you need more right now than to just get away from it all."

"It will just remind me of…" I can't finish my sentence in the way I want to. "Of how it ended."

"Bullshit!" she exclaims. "I don't know what went down between you and Mike because you tell us nothing. But I know you. And you don't make mistakes. Something happened. Something serious and I know you wouldn't have run if he didn't deserve it. If you're looking for permission to go, you have it from me."

I can't fight a smile. "Thank you, Millie."

"Yay! So what bikinis do you want to pack?" she asks, spinning towards my room.

"I'm still not going," I call after her. "I'm sorry, but it really just doesn't feel right."

"Fine," she says. There's a frustrated pause as she frowns across the room at me. Then she sighs. "I guess I'll just head out then. Give you that much needed space, and all. Besides, I've checked on you, you're alive, everyone can relax."

I mumble a quiet thanks and within seconds my flat is quiet again. Outside, I catch the exhales of buses climbing the Brighton hills and the constant chatter of seagulls soaring along coastal gusts. I know I shouldn't lash out at Millie, but can she really blame me? The last thing I need right now is to be antagonised.

My phone vibrates again.

"Ah, what now?!" I groan. I expect to see a message from Abby, Gemma or Dad, but instead, it's from the cruise. I dare myself to open it, stare at that picture that lured me in all those months ago.

I never thought I'd be a cruise kind of girl, but this isn't just any old cruise. This is an intimate, luxury cruise on a ship that looks more like a giant superyacht. It's all black, sleek, sharp edges. I booked a stylish cabin and it's ready for me now, docked in Venice harbour. The photo they use in their emails features their main restaurant, all cream table clothes and shiny, spotless furniture. Keep scrolling and you'll find pristine ocean views, and beyond that? Mountains and the exquisite backdrop of the Croatian coastline.

That grief pooling in my mind deepens, making my heartbeat faster.

Maybe I *could* go.

Maybe I *could* do it.

Maybe, and this is a *big* maybe, Millie is right. Maybe this is what I need, and I shouldn't feel guilty about it.

Fifteen days of luxury and sightseeing around the Mediterranean. All-inclusive fine dining. Round the clock pampering. The schedule teases me: the cruise starts in Venice; heads down the coast of Croatia, stopping at Rovinj, Split and Dubrovnik; goes into Kotor, Montenegro; heads around the bottom of Italy and back up the coast, docking at Taormina, Rome, Portofino; sails towards Monte Carlo, Monaco; takes you to Toulon; and finishes in Spain at Palamos and Barcelona.

It really *does* sound like the trip of a lifetime. I look around my empty flat.

Would I make it in time if I left now?

I never did cancel my annual leave. I had planned to spend the fortnight moping around and feeling sorry for myself. But… I might as well do that in the sun, right?

Adrenaline hits me like a bus. I'm on my feet and dancing through my bedroom, tugging my suitcase out and throwing it on my bed. I practically beat my clothes and shoes in, packing enough underwear so I'm prepared if I shit myself thirty times on the trip, before finally dressing in loose jeans and a vest. Then I rummage through my paperwork drawer in search of my passport.

In a matter of minutes, I'm out the door and striding up the street towards Brighton station, booking a ticket to Gatwick Airport on my phone. I text the group chat.

Congrats. You brats win. I'm going. Tell Dad. See you soon. I can't believe you set up a group chat without me. Not forgiven!

Three

Venice is exactly how I imagined it.

Narrow streets with colourful, ancient, angular buildings, all crammed on top of one another in a majestic, medieval kind of way. I can't help the smile that works its way onto my lips as I finally come across the Piazza. Pigeons cluster around tourists dropping breadcrumbs as they pose for selfies. I decide to take one myself and send it to the girls.

Soon after I landed last night, my checked bag was collected from the airport by the cruise, who, apparently, even do some of the unpacking for you. A detail I'd managed to forget in the chaos of throwing everything I own into my suitcase. I'm yet to board the boat and be reunited with my belongings, but I'm sure whoever is looking after it will wonder what in the actual fuck is wrong with me. But hey ho, at least I made it. And I only have to carry my hand luggage around, which I smartly packed with spare clothes and toiletries.

I spent the night in a quaint hotel overlooking the Ponte di Rialto, and in my post-breakup, pre-holiday mania, I treated myself to a bottle of wine and room service and set myself up by the window, soaking it all in. I spent the early hours of the morning spiralling over the past five years, my relationship with Mike, how I'd consistently focused on everyone else around me rather than myself. Then, I thought about how he changed for the worse and I can't help wondering if I did something to make him that way.

Was it me? Was I too focused on my career? Did I not give him enough attention?

I wish I knew how to feel.

The next morning, with only a handful of hours to soak up the sights before I board, I shake off my hangover by strolling along the canals in the sunshine, don my dark sunglasses and pretty white sundress, and even talk myself into handing over silly money to ride in a gondola, only to feel supremely awkward the whole time and nearly topple into the canal as I climb out.

And sure, I'm surrounded by couples on their romantic getaways, and yes, I don't see any other solo travellers, but I don't let it bother me.

I'm in Venice! I've never been to Venice!

I've never been anywhere on my own for leisure, and, although I know this should empower me, in this particular moment, it's completely destabilising. Betrayal has made itself part of my DNA, and I hate it. I want to cast it away, but it won't leave. Some part of me feels like it was my fault. And with that comes intense guilt. As if, had I found out sooner by being more vigilant, there would've been less pain.

Bad runaway bride.

Despite knowing deep down I did the right thing, it doesn't dispel the thoughts that I should've handled it differently.

I stop in front of Saint Mark's Basilica and admire the detailed architecture, forcing the thought from my mind. I need to be in the moment. I'm in one of the most beautiful, ancient cities in Europe, and the sun is shining. If I can't force myself to enjoy this, how am I going to get through the next fourteen days in the Mediterranean?

I snap a picture and take a deep breath. *I've got this.*

An hour before I'm due to board the cruise, I pop into a stylish bar with views of the busy port and order myself a spritz, since I've been told Venice is famous for them. I step outside, hoping to find a seat at one of the tables when a massive oaf crashes into me. The sheer force takes my breath away. My spritz explodes from its glass, spilling orange liquid all down the front of my pristine white dress.

Fuck! Are you kidding me!?

"Jeez. Watch where you're going!" the oaf says.

Fight. I'm going to start a fight. I can feel my blood roiling. "Are you serious?! You crashed into *me*!"

"You stepped into my path." He takes a step back, assessing the damage.

"Do you know how much this cocktail cost?" I spit. I can feel Aperol dripping down my cleavage.

"Look, I'm sorry but I'm in a hurry," he says, his voice only partly apologetic. The rest of him seems weirdly anxious, like he's running from someone.

He takes another anxious glance behind him before reaching into his pocket. "Here, buy yourself another one on me."

"I don't want your money!" I hiss, but it's too late. He thrusts the cash into my hands and dashes off. "Prick!" I call after him, drawing the attention of several passers-by.

Perfect.

Now not only are the cruise staff going to think I'm a lunatic, thanks to my unhinged packing, but they're going to take one look at my dress and think I'm an absolute liability. There's no way I can remedy this in such a short space of time.

I avoid pitiful looks from a few women sipping their drinks canal-side before stepping back into the bar. I assess the full damage in the bathroom mirror. It's almost comical. Maybe this is a sign. Maybe I should cut and run, right now, before it's too late.

No! I can't let the oaf ruin my day. I splash some water on my face (no point in trying to sort the dress), wipe off the sticky Aperol from my chest and arms, and take a deep breath.

I've got this. Nothing is going to derail this trip.

Nothing.

I saved ruthlessly after Mike proposed, going above and beyond at work, securing new clients and working my arse off to hit targets to pay for this. Despite where I'm at emotionally, I'm now able to remember why. With five floors above deck, the superyacht is luxury on water. Even the gangway is carpeted. Next to other cruise ships, the *Adriatic Angel* is a beauty, exactly how it looked in the pictures: sleek, majestic and expensive. Because it is. I'm immediately greeted with champagne, a map of the ship detailing all the facilities and a detailed itinerary that includes the entertainment, restaurant times and port dockings.

I'm then escorted by an immaculate attendant to my stateroom. It's not even close to the nicest room on the yacht and yet it's beautiful. Varnished mahogany walls, spotless finishings, a large white bed with red petals sprinkled over it (I'll deal with them and the heart-shaped towels later), watertight glass doors that let in an immense amount of light from the private balcony, and current views of the gorgeous harbour.

I immediately head outside and stare out at the busy port, listening to the seabirds and chop of waves against the steely sides. Occasionally there's the blare of a ship's horn.

I take out my phone and snap a picture for Dad.

He immediately replies with a thumbs up emoji which makes me laugh. I could tell him I won the lottery and he would reply the same way. He called me that night after I'd absconded and I'd put on a brave face to apologise. It's not even that he'd spent much on the wedding, Mike and I paid for most of it ourselves, but I felt guilty nonetheless.

He'd been so excited to walk me down the aisle.

That night he'd said, "Don't you be worrying about me, darling. I'd much rather you ran and caused a bit of a ruckus than stayed and made yourself miserable." I wasn't ready to tell him what happened and I'm not sure I ever will. It's not who we are. I used to think our family relationship was surface level but more recently, I think we're so entrenched in each other's feelings that we don't need to talk about them at all.

I could stand here, leaning against the railings for hours.

Although, I don't, since a fancy all-inclusive bar awaits me.

Stepping out of my ruined sundress, I make myself presentable, in a smart jumpsuit and heels, before heading upstairs.

I realise the error in my ways the second I step out of the lift. *Ah crap.* Two waiters, dressed in tailored uniforms with smart red waistcoats, hold out trays with flutes of champagne on them. "Welcome to the Adriatic Angel, Mrs Locke," the taller one says.

Married-name jump scare!

"Oh no. I'm not..." And will never be... Mrs Locke. "*Sara* will be fine. Thanks."

His cheeks redden and I realise he's done very well to recognise my face. Even if he is wrong. I guess I could've changed the name on the booking. It irks me that when I booked this originally, almost a year ago, I honestly thought I would be Sara Locke by now.

"My apologies, ma'am. The Welcome Mingle is just through there."

I force a smile and nod despite my heart sinking in my chest. Even though I *am* single, I am *not* ready to mingle. In fact, I do not "mingle" unless paid to at networking events. I am decidedly too unsociable for this. Of course, I've managed to surround myself with extroverts in my friendship group – but alone? Not for me.

"Kill me now," I mutter, as I step cautiously into the main area with warm lighting and a spotless, glimmering bar one full side of the room.

I just wanted a quiet drink on my own.

I wonder if there is a way out the opposite direction. Or maybe I can buy a drink then vanish outside. I glance around only to see a sign that says no glass on the deck.

If I want a drink, I'm stuck. I can hardly stay in my room on the first night of the cruise, what a sorry tale that would be. My sisters would never let me live it down.

I'm having fun. This is fun. I need to relax.

I take a barstool and make myself small. It's clear this cruise is mostly older couples who I would guess to be in their late fifties, early sixties. And, from the way they're interacting, I assume a few of them know each other too.

It's like I'm in some kind of fancy country club.

I suddenly feel quite isolated. I down the flute of champagne before one of the waitstaff spots me and brings me a glass of wine he recommends from my preferred tastes. He's good. It's delicious, fruity and fresh.

Another guest comes to the bar, a stool scraping across the marble floors a few feet to my right. The barman is quick to greet them, quicker than he was with me.

"Just a beer please, bud," he says. I recognise the accent, the gentle twang. He must be from Bristol or the Southwest of England. A relatively normal accent compared to the poshies chatting behind me.

I allow myself a quick glance and find a tall, handsome man with swept-back, light brown curls. He's in a light blue shirt and loose denim shorts. He catches me looking and smiles politely. I half-expect a pretty woman to be flanking his side, maybe she's still getting ready.

His smile lingers.

Wait.

What the fuck?!

It's the guy from earlier. The oaf! "*You!*" I hiss. He raises his left brow. I don't think he recognises me – yet. Of course he doesn't, because that's *so* on brand for a rude knob who spills a lady's drink and ruins her dress. He's about to say something but I'm not interested, I'm on holiday, I'm not getting into something with some random idiot in this gorgeous, peaceful bar, so I shake my head and look away, feigning interest in the cocktail menu.

"Excuse me?" A soft hand touches my shoulder. I spin to find a tiny old lady who must be in her eighties glancing up at me with polite curiosity. She's dressed in a lilac skirt and long-sleeved white blouse. I open my mouth to say hello but she's already talking again, "Are you and your husband planning on joining us? You're very welcome to."

"My...?" I nearly spit my drink out. I have to cover my mouth to right myself.

"Your husband!" she says, pointing to the rude, unsuspecting man beside me.

Annoyingly, he seems to find this amusing. "How kind," he says in return. There's something about his voice now I come to think about it, something rich, like he's used to using it. "What a lovely offer," he adds. Instead of, "This isn't my wife."

What the hell?!

It takes a second for my brain to catch up. "I'm sorry, we're not..." I signal between us. Surely he recognises me too? I did have my hair up earlier, with sunglasses on and a different outfit – but still.

There's a twinkle in his eyes that tells me he finds this whole situation highly amusing, or that I'm missing something. Or worse: I'm embarrassing myself. And, well, maybe I am. But right now, I need to set things straight. "I'm here alone."

Oh well. Cat's out the bag, I guess. Unfortunately, saying it out loud sounds even worse than it does in my head. The man watches me, an intrigued look on his face. He's trying to read me. I see this look all the time at work. He's intrigued, compelled to work out what my motivations are.

Well, tough shit, sir. All I'm giving off right now is nervous and jittery.

I need more wine.

"Are you single?" the lady asks, her excited pitch sending shivers down my spine. I have never been subjected to elderly matchmaking schemes and I would like it to remain that way. I can see where this is going, it's like watching a car crash happen in slow motion.

I cringe. "Mmhmm," I offer half-heartedly.

"And you?" she asks the man.

He's still looking at me; I can see him in my peripheral vision. Heat warms my cheeks. Millie was wrong. I should've stayed home. I am *not* enjoying myself!

I think the man nods but I'm trying not to give him any attention and I don't want him to think I'm interested.

"*Excellent*. What luck! You look the same age too. You'll be able to spend so much time together on this cruise. Come, come. Join our group," she demands. "Roger over there, the man in the green shirt with the birthmark on his neck, is a pilot. He used to fly Concorde back in the day." Then in a quieter voice she mumbles, "He married a trolley dolly."

"*Oh…*" Is that bad? "Thanks *so* much," I say, carefully removing my hand from hers. "How incredibly interesting but you know, I was actually just…" I point towards the doors to the deck. "Fresh air."

She nods. "Next time," she says, giving my arm a gentle squeeze.

Time to run again, I guess. I'm not ready to talk to strangers. In fact, I'm not ready for this cruise.

Hot panic lurches through my limbs making me unsteady as I finish off my glass of wine, and head out to the top deck. It's quieter out here, the wind and the sea air calming. What are the chances that *that* guy is on *this* cruise? I don't allow myself to consider this to be yet another sign from the universe and its endless vendetta against me.

I switch to aggressively sweet, but strong cocktails before dinner, soaking in the gorgeous sunset before heading to my table, properly tipsy. I'm relieved when I peek around the room and can't see the curly-haired oaf. But the elderly woman from earlier offers me an enthusiastic wave. I raise my now empty cocktail glass in her general direction.

"Good evening, Mrs Locke." A cheerful waitress hands me the night's menu. "Is Mr Locke joining you this evening?" I look up to meet her warm smile.

"Just me," I sing. She doesn't catch my tone. "Can I trouble you for another drink?"

Four

It doesn't really start to hit me until after my main course. Something heavy lingers in the pit of my stomach, and it's not the food. My vision grows spotty, my hands feel clammy. Is it *insanely* hot in here?! I'm starting to hyperventilate when a gorgeous dessert is placed in front of me, the kind you pour hot chocolate sauce onto to melt the sugar dome. All I can think about is how there's no air in here, and I need to escape.

Breathe, breathe, breathe.

I practically launch myself from the restaurant onto the front deck, where a warm breeze tangles in my hair, and stride straight up to the bow of the ship. I grab hold of the railing and lean against it, dropping my head. A seamless line of moonlight stretches out before me.

Breathe. Come on, breathe.

It's really over. All of it. Not just the good parts, the bad parts too. It's a cocktail of regret, sadness, relief and freedom. And I don't know how to handle it.

Mike is the only long-term partner I've ever had and now it's done it feels like a huge chunk of me, the person I became in the time we were together, has fallen away.

Fuck's sake. Just breathe.

Who am I without him? I've made myself so busy at work since that fateful day that I haven't allowed myself to stop and let it sink in.

Now it feels like I'm actually sinking.

Ugh. God, I can't breathe.

I run one hand over my chest to see if I can somehow swipe this pressure away and find that my playsuit is damp. The sea is calm tonight so it can't be sea spray.

It's me.

I'm crying.

Hysterically.

What a fucking embarrassment!

I wipe at my cheeks, cursing myself.

Breathe. Just breathe. Why can't I breathe?

I lean even further over the railing, listening to the hum of the engines, the chop of the waves. Blood rushes to my head. I try to control my racing heart, but I swear with each breath it gets harder and harder to find any air.

"Uh, excuse me, miss?" a voice comes from behind me.

I can't even turn at this point – too afraid it will steal the last bit of oxygen from my lungs. Blood is rushing in my ears, making every sound gargled.

Just stop crying, you imbecile. You have an audience!

"You know," he continues, "you really don't want to do that."

"Wha-at?" I practically choke out.

"That water is much colder than you think." I don't know why he's telling me this. Does he think I'm going to jump? I attempt to take a deep breath but I'm officially out of air.

I'm going to die.

"Er, can I help you to the bench?" he asks. I don't respond, but a moment later, I feel a large gentle hand on my shoulder. "It's ok," he says. "I'm just going to help you take a seat, alright?" I allow him to pivot my body away from the railing, leaning into his touch. I find myself nodding, clutching my chest. I can barely see through the tears.

I allow him to guide me towards a bench, where I manage to collapse, panting, sobbing, utterly beside myself.

"Hey, I need you to focus on what I'm about to say, ok?" he says, crouching down in front of me. "We're going to explore your senses. Ground you again. If you can, tell me what you can hear."

I gasp for air. "My heart… beat," I manage to get out. The blurry shape in front of me places two soft hands on my shoulders. The gesture is weirdly stabilising.

"Good. What else?"

"Your voice."

"More. Close your eyes if it helps. I'm not going anywhere unless you want me to."

I do as I'm told, finding solace in this man's voice.

"The hum of the yacht. Waves. People in the restaurant."

"Good. You're getting it. What can you feel?"

"My playsuit. My hair on my shoulders. The bench."

"And now think about your feet. What are they attached to?"

"My ankles?"

"Really?"

"I…"

"Just kidding," he laughs gently, dropping his hands. "What are your ankles attached to?"

"My shins?"

"You're maybe being slightly too specific now," he says, a smile in his voice. "Let's go from legs. What are your legs attached to?"

"My torso?"

"And then?"

"My neck. Then my head…"

"Correct. Open your eyes," he says as if I've passed a test.

I blink them open slowly. My limbs and fingers feel like they've been filled with lead but my breathing is noticeably calmer.

"What can you see?" he asks. I blink rapidly, wiping the tears from my eyes and allowing my vision to clear. I'm met with a pair of warm light brown eyes, a sturdy straight nose and a defined, neatly shaven jawline. But his most noticeable feature is the wild, dark-gold curls that tumble down over his forehead.

Oh, holy fuck.

"*You*," I say.

"Good. What else?"

"No, I mean, it's you! *Again!*" I'm too mortified to do anything other than cover my face with my hands. "You can leave now, thank you."

He's quiet for a second. "Ok…? I feel like I'm missing something here."

"I've got this," I say, looking up at him through bleary eyes and attempting to dismiss him with my hand. I can barely raise it.

I very much haven't got this.

And it's clear by his concerned frown that we both know I'm lying.

He tilts his head almost sympathetically. It only sets me off again. I quickly wipe at my eyes with the balls of my hands. "Hey, come on. It's alright," he says, rising to his feet and shoving his hands into his pockets, giving me ample space to escape if that's want I want. "Can I at least help you to your room, or something? I can't just leave you here. It wouldn't sit well with my conscience. Or I can find a female attendant if you'd prefer?"

I press my face into my hands again, curling forward. I muffle, "No. That's even more embarrassing. I just want to hide."

"Ok, sure. Where?"

I let out a ragged breath. "My room would be good." I look up at him and he nods, offering me his arm.

"Great, then let's get you to your room."

It takes me a minute to steady my wobbling knees, but when I finally do, he gives me a reassuring smile.

He's steady. He's also very tall. I'm five foot nine, five eleven in heels, and he's still a few inches taller than me. I peek at his face discreetly – he's handsome.

I clasp his bare forearm, a splatter of light hair and tanned skin under my fingers. He leads me towards the cabin lift and asks for my room number.

I hesitate. "You're not some cruise ship murderer, right?"

"If I was, would I tell you?"

I nod. "Fair point. Room twenty-three."

I'm trying to find the words to explain myself, or rather, the state I'm in, when he stops abruptly and I realise we're already at my door.

"Here you are," he says, gently releasing me. "Do you have your key?"

I tuck my hand into my bra and fish it out. Holding it out for his inspection.

He fights the urge to smile, the corner of his lips twitching. "You ladies always have the best storage solutions." Then as I let myself in, he says, "Will you be ok? I can ask them to send a female attendant to your room?"

Embarrassment burns my cheeks. I'm tempted to deflect, confront him about his oafness in Venice. But maybe now isn't the time. This has already been mortifying enough. "Oh. No. Thank you, but no. I'll be ok. I'm just… tipsy."

He raises his eyebrows but doesn't say anything else, running his hand through his hair and stepping backwards as if he's waiting for me to close my door. I test my theory, checking in the peephole once it's closed. He finally turns, strolling towards the main staircase, tucking his hands in his pockets.

Five

Waking the next morning, I am greeted by an almighty headache which I fully deserve. Have I not learnt anything since my university days? I lean over my bed and grab my phone. It's already nine. Shit. Breakfast finishes at ten and the tour I've booked today in Rovinj leaves at eleven-thirty. This means there's no time to feel sorry for myself.

Pity.

I groan horribly, tossing off the duvet and forcing myself to sit upright. I instantly feel that familiar hangover ache throughout my body. Even so, I manage to shower, get dressed and make myself semi-presentable in record speed, arriving at the clubrooms on the upper deck where I'm shown to a table and offered coffee.

See. This isn't so bad!

I nab a croissant and some fresh fruit from the buffet, opting out of a hot breakfast today, and nurse my hangover with an unhealthy dose of sugar and caffeine. I'm just starting to relax, the dull ache at the base of my skull subsiding, when I spot him.

Bollocks.

He's heading this way.

Fuck!

Not again! No, no, no!

Dread overwhelms me as the memory of last night's emotional breakdown comes flooding back. He probably thinks I'm a rude, insane woman who was practically hanging off the bow of the ship, howling her head off. I dip in my seat, angling my face towards the view of the distant coastline as he strides past. Doesn't matter if he was nice once. His character is still up for scrutiny. I steal a glance in his direction.

I don't think he's spotted me.

What a relief!

When I'm sure he's gone, I rise from my seat, pastries and coffee in hand, acutely aware of my surroundings and make a beeline for the deck, stopping dead in my tracks when I spot in him at the bar. He's fresh faced and wearing a loose fitted dark top. He looks like he smells good – fresh and oaky. A few of the younger guests (there are maybe five people under the age of sixty, including me and that man, on this ship) are talking and laughing with him. I can't help but wonder what their dynamic is. They don't appear overly familiar, but there's a strange intimacy.

Are they hitting on him?

Then one of the girls hands him her cap, which he takes and signs with a sharpie.

Is he famous?

Shit!

Is he famous?!

I knew he looked familiar, I just couldn't place him. I still can't. But then again, I've never been hot on celebrities.

Who is he?!

Imagine if he's a low-key royal or an Olympic athlete, here on holiday and on the first night he had to escort an insensibly drunk, hysterical woman back to her room.

Oh, the horrors.

I force myself to keep walking, moving closer to the door, but just as I'm about to reach for the handle, he lifts his chin to meet my gaze.

Ahh!

His eyes lock with mine for the briefest of seconds and because I'm wholly embarrassed it does something mean to my insides.

I turn on my heel and launch myself out onto the deck, keeping my head down until I know I'm out of view. We'll be arriving at the port soon, and I won't have to worry about seeing him again.

Well, until later. Ugh!

The tour of Rovinj is slow and (honestly?) tedious. Some of the historical facts are fun but the guide delivers them so slowly and without flair, possibly because he's said the exact same thing five million times already, and because I am still, despite appearances, deeply hungover. I keep finding myself drifting, heading instead towards things that interest me.

I've been to a few European cities before and what I love most is their quirky features: alleyways narrow enough you can reach out and touch both walls; rooms that seem to have been added at random, jutting out into the street with wonky windows and colourful shutters.

I wonder about the people who live here, strolling past amber coloured churches with their terracotta roofs, a few small markets and hundreds of cafes and restaurants. Not a high-street chain in sight.

By the end of the tour, I've finally managed to relax. We part ways with the guide at a small market near the port, allowing everyone some time to browse the stalls at their own pace. I'm hyperaware of not missing the departure time – they've made it clear they wait for no one. Even if you're rich and famous. Speaking of, I'm relieved our very own celebrity didn't join the tour. Just the thought of being in close proximity is initiating my fight-or-flight response.

Unfortunately, I do spot him as we're heading back along the dock towards the ship. He's sitting on a bench, his sandy curls bursting from under the black cap he's wedged onto his head. A large camera hangs around his neck and he looks like he's studying the contents.

While his head is down, I pull out my phone. There's no way my sisters won't know who he is if he is indeed famous. It's possible, of course, that he's the captain or something and cruise fanatics get their captains to sign things – but I doubt it. I might be oblivious but I'm not entirely daft.

I find my camera app and hold it up towards him, snapping a quick photo. *Click.*

Shitting fuck.

When did I turn it off silent? It's so loud the people in front turn on me with a scowl.

"So sorry," I say. "I was taking a selfie." They're clearly very sophisticated so I can't decide if they're more offended by the selfie part or my phone making noise part.

Does the embarrassment never end?!

I sneak a look back to Mr Celebrity only to find him smiling. He lifts his camera and points it at me, before clicking several times. I'm pretty sure my face is beet red. When he lowers the camera, he laughs, then winks in my direction.

Well, I deserved that, didn't I?

Back in my room, I send the photo to my sisters for their (mostly harmless) stalking abilities.

Is this man famous?

Six

Cruise Location – Rovinj

Next Port – Split

Time of Departure – 17:00 (GMT+1)

Millie: I assume you're joking????

Abby: This is rage bait for sure

Gemma: are you sure we're related?!

Millie: And she wonders why we have a secret group chat

Sara: I KNEW IT

Millie: Joking obviously!

Sara: So he is famous then???

Abby: I refuse to believe you're not joking actually

Millie: Shall we just disown her?

Gemma: i say we don't tell her

Abby: @Sara is he on your cruise?

Sara: Yes!

Millie: Wild

Gemma: this is so unfair!! the way I would let him ruin me

Millie: I prefer Jax

Gemma: yes because you're attracted to toxic men

Abby: Coming from you Gem?

Millie: J4S are too young for her taste

Sara: Please just tell me who he is.

Millie: The fact that you even asked means you don't deserve to know and I stand by that

Gemma: i think that's a fair comment

Abby: It's Gus Kenwood from Just4Summer

Sara: So he's an actor?

Millie: SEE ABBY. SEE WHAT YOU'VE DONE!

Gemma: sara, i am ashamed to be your sister.

Abby: Wow. Ok. Just4Summer is a massive British boyband. 10 hit singles. 6 albums. 14 years of fame. There's no way you haven't heard their music.

Sara: You're all so dramatic. Fine, I'll google him.

Millie: YOU'RE SO OUT OF TOUCH. I HOPE YOU'RE HAVING THE TIME OF YOUR LIFE!

Gemma: those are both songs btw lol

Sara: What are?

Millie: SARA I SWEAR!

I'm ashamed to say I spend the better part of the night googling him. I even decide to request room service, eating dinner on my balcony, diving deeper and deeper into Augustus Marcus Kenwood's digital footprint.

What I discover is a whole world of fandom, from fanfic to two-hour YouTube compilations of the band hanging out and chatting with fans. They've performed internationally and just come off a world tour earlier this year promoting their sixth album so social media is practically burning up from all the new buzzy content.

Each band member seems to have procured themselves a character. From what I've been able to deduce, my eyes starting to get heavy, a sure sign I've overcooked this unassigned research project: Jax is the bad boy, Callum is the looker, Will is the mother hen of the group and Gus is apparently the joker.

There are a million pictures of him pratting about on stage.

The next morning, I'm still waist-deep in internet gossip when I call Abby to explain everything.

"Hello," she says, brightly. "I need every detail, but first, turn your camera on. I want to see where you are."

I give her a quick tour of my room followed by a view of the sea.

"Tell me about this boyband then," I say, plonking down on the bed. "How have I gone so long without hearing of them?"

"Because you're not very cool."

"I'm cool!"

"Sure," she laughs. "You must've heard their recent hit single, 'Come Again'."

"Maybe?" I shrug. Abby rolls her eyes before singing the chorus. It's the sort of hit single that plays on all the major radios. Very pop rock. And I have heard it before, she's not wrong.

"Ok, fine, I've heard it."

"That's his part actually," Abby says. "But it was his bandmate, Will, who wrote it. And Callum is on the track too."

"Right. So, there are four of them, and they play instruments too."

"There *were* four. But yup. Gus and Will play guitar, Callum's on piano. And Jax, he had this whole saxophone bit at concerts but that was mostly for a laugh." I scroll through pictures of them while Abby talks. I could tell her I've been stalking them for hours and now know pretty much all the headlines, but I humour her instead.

There's no doubt they are all attractive. Jax is the tall, dark and handsome sort. Will has dark hair and light eyes with broad shoulders – he clearly spends a lot of time in the gym. Callum is insanely pretty. But Gus, the curly-haired oaf, well, he's got that boy-next-door vibe to him. And hands down, he has the best smile of the group. I remember the glint in his eye when he winked at me yesterday on the dock. I chew on my thumb as a wash of heat brushes through me. I should confront him about the spritz incident – maybe he'd apologise. Because right now, the two versions of him don't add up.

"Why are you so interested anyway?" Abby asks.

"Oh. You know – not every day you meet a popstar."

"You *met* him?"

"I… I mean. No. Yes, but it's a small cruise so… I've seen him around. But I haven't *met* him, met him." Why am I lying? I *have* met him. Why do I shield my sisters from so much? It's as if admitting I've met him would mean I have to tell her about the first night and me hanging over the ship, sobbing uncontrollably. And I don't want her to worry.

"Uh huh," she says, grinning. "He's my favourite one, you know. I always thought he looked the most fun."

"Really?" I say, trying to keep my face impassive. I remind myself that I don't actually know this person. He's nobody to me. I spoke to him for all of ten minutes. And now I'll be doing my best to avoid him for the remainder of the cruise.

Abby prattles on and I listen, thinking about how this stranger has seen me at possibly my most vulnerable, but my own sister hasn't. Not because I've never felt vulnerable around her, but because I've never wanted the girls to see that side of me. When Mum passed away, the grief was so life altering I'm sure it changed me physically. But I couldn't just focus on my own pain, I had three younger sisters to keep upright too. It was easier to push those big feelings down when I was around them.

I wonder if, over the years, they've come to the conclusion that I don't feel at all.

"Right, it's almost time to disembark," I say.

"What's on the agenda for today?"

"Split."

"Are you going on a tour?"

I scrunch my face. "I'm not sure yet. I went on one yesterday and it dragged on a bit. I might go wandering on my own and see the city properly, you know?"

"Sure, but just be safe," she says.

"Abby, I'm always safe," I say.

"Yes, that's true," she confirms too easily. I guess maybe too safe. Maybe being a little reckless wouldn't do me any harm?

So, when we arrive in Split, I decide to be spontaneous and go it alone. No tour, no schedule, just me and my comfy sandals, my favourite white summer dress and a small handbag for essentials. I'm mindful that the cruise is departing earlier than yesterday, partly because our stopover in Dubrovnik tomorrow is considered a main attraction. The cruise packs it in. There are no overnight stays in the cities since it stops at almost one a day. It's one of the reasons I picked this cruise – I loved the idea of spending every night in open water.

I explore an endless maze of narrow windy lanes, wandering past ancient churches and market stalls. I stop off to pick up some souvenirs for the girls: beaded bracelets for all three and a small, bejewelled jewellery box for Abby. Trinket like things that will take up hardly any space in my luggage.

The hours fly by too quickly. I'm not even sure how long I've been wandering when I stumble upon a charming café serving pastries and artisan cakes with fresh fruit and a shiny glaze on top. I pick one, pay, then take a seat out front along the wall, tucked beneath the awning.

I take my phone out to snap some photos but the screen is dark. *Shit.* I click on it a few times, then twist in my seat to hide it from the sun some more. When I still can't make it brighter, I take my sunglasses off and squint.

Fuck.

I somehow have 5 per cent battery.

How?

Did my video call with Abby earlier totally drain my battery? I could have sworn it was fully charged. I try not to panic, but of course, I panic. A few notifications come in all at once, and in a rush to read one that's come from the ship, the phone crashes out.

And then it's dead.

No, no, no…

I stand up, looking around at the neighbouring businesses. Would any of these quaint shops or stalls have phone chargers? They must do, surely. But all I do is freak out. I haven't been mindful of the time. I was waiting for the one-hour reminder to return to the ship. Clearly, that came through ages ago!

Double fuck!

I launch out of my seat and back into the café.

"Excuse me? *Sati? Molim vas.*" It means, "Time? Please."

At least I bloody hope it does. I only learnt a handful of phrases before flying out and most were in Italian.

The man gives me a pitying smile as if he can tell I'm a very uncultured British woman – which, alas, I am. It is a deserved reaction.

Thankfully, he replies in perfect English. "It's a quarter to three."

My eyes go round. "Did you say *three*?"

He nods before busying himself with something else.

Bugger.

RUN.

I bolt out of the café, my hat blowing off in the wind as I go. I grab it off the cobbled street and grasp it in the same hand clutching onto my bag and run as fast as my sandals will allow me – which is very inefficient and quite slow, in all honesty.

It doesn't help that I also appear to be lost! And hot. It's too hot to be running anywhere. The sun is relentless.

How have I managed to completely lose track of time? I'm never so careless! This is my punishment for having too much fun. No wonder my phone's dead, the number of photos I've taken was enough to kill the battery alone. *How am I* that *tourist?!* What an idiot. This is why smart, uptight Sara exists. This is why I should have gone on a tour.

Now look at me!

They'll wait for me, I tell myself, as I bolt down a dead-end alleyway and have to double back on myself. I practically throw myself at a passer-by.

"Excuse me?" I gasp. "Do you know the way to the port? Ships? Erm… You know, boats?" The tiny elderly woman gives me dagger eyes.

She says something that sounds like a swear word and waves me away with her hand.

Good.

"Have a great day!" I call after her.

Just perfect!

Surely, I can find the main square or at the very least an English-speaking tourist?! I can't be so lost I can't even find my way out of the city. That's mental. Am I so used to having map apps at my disposal that I have become blind to direction?

Answer: yes.

I am screwed.

I ask three more people. One smiles and nods at me like he understands, and hope fills my blood like a drug. Turns out he is British but just as much of a tourist as me and doesn't have service.

Just bloody wonderful!

Another woman refuses to help me. But the final person speaks English and sort of knows the way. His directions are unhelpfully detailed, but I take a shot at it, flying through the alleys and the long, cobbled steps, until finally there's an opening which leads to the port. I break into a sprint.

The port is in sight!

The port where my ship is!

The very ship that is already sailing back out to sea.

Motherf—!

Seven

I'm ok. This is fine. What's the worst that can happen? I'm simply abandoned in a foreign city with little more than some random stuff in my bag, a dead phone, lip balm and a pair of sunglasses.

Shit.

I run my fingers through my hair as I pace towards the port office. I'm hoping they'll be able to slingshot me back onto the boat. Or maybe they have one of those human Iron Man suits I could borrow to fly myself back over there. Hell, I'd hang on tight to a drone. I've seen crazier things.

I take a deep, controlled breath before stepping into the building. There's a large man behind the desk, frowning at his computer screen.

"Hi, erm, sorry," I say, hoping to get his attention. He doesn't acknowledge me, so I wait like the naughty, abandoned passenger I am. After a good minute or so of me awkwardly pretending this isn't awkward, he finally looks up.

"Ah, you missed the ship."

Heat spreads through my face. I swallow. "I did."

"You are Sara?"

"That's me… How did you…?"

The man opens a passport to the picture page before handing it over. "The crew left your passport when you did not sign back in. You must go to next port," he says. "They leave Dubrovnik at four p.m. tomorrow. You must not ignore messages."

"My phone died," I explain, trying to defend myself. "I wasn't *ignoring* my messages."

He levels me with a sharp stare. "Do not let that happen."

"Well, obviously," I say, rolling my eyes. He shakes his head, the sarcasm clearly lost in translation. "It wasn't intentional," I add, for clarification, fiddling with my hands.

He scrunches his face. "You said that was what you did."

"Yes. But not on *purpose*."

"You charge phone better."

This is getting painfully patronising. "Yes. Ok." He nods as if the conversation is over. "Well, can you help me get there?"

"No."

"*No?* I'm on my own then?!"

He shrugs. "You buy insurance?"

"Yes but—"

"Good. Call them."

"I… All the details are on my phone. My phone is dead."

He exhales sharply, like I'm inconveniencing him in ways I'll never appreciate, "How do the young say it? This is a *you* problem?"

The thing I've learned about negotiations, during my career as a commercial manager, is that you can't let the aggressor know you're affected. Unless they like that and eventually bend to empathy. This man doesn't give me that impression. In fact, I'd say he's sick of having to deal with disorganised holidaymakers who miss their cruise.

I want to tell him I'm not actually like them.

But clearly, I very much am.

"Ok… Thanks, I guess."

I step out of the office back into the mid-afternoon sun and stare longingly out at the ship, its sleek shape shrinking as it travels further and further from the port. I huff, placing my floppy hat back on my head to protect my forehead.

"Bollocks," I mutter. Again. "Just great."

But it's ok. I am a strong, independent woman who can absolutely make this work. So what if I miss one night on the cruise?

It's fine. I'm good.

First things first: find a phone charger so I can call my insurance company.

I push my hand into my bag to see what I have at my disposal. There is about a hundred euros in there. I left my wallet with my debit and credit cards in the room because I have contactless set up on my phone anyway and I didn't want to risk losing them abroad. Also in my bag, I have suncream (useful), the trinkets I foraged in the market (less useful), a packet of mint gum (eh?) and a few plasters that have been in this bag since I bought a new pair of heels about two years ago. I haven't needed them yet, but who knows when a crisis might strike?

There surely must be a phone shop in the more modern parts of the city. As soon as I have my phone back on, I'll be able to sort everything else. I turn back towards the town and feel my tummy fizz. I blink a few times to check my vision is correct because…

Popstar is standing where the cruise is meant to be docked, camera hanging around his neck, a confused notch between his brows.

There's nowhere to hide. Not a tree, not a building, not even a Goddamn person.

His gaze slowly turns to me, eyes sweeping up my (probably sweaty at this point) body, before fixing on my face.

I would run away if I could, but the only other direction I can go in leads to the sea. And I can't swim to Dubrovnik. So, I'm stuck. This interaction is unavoidable.

"Hey, you," he says, clearing some of the metres between us. There's a hint of playfulness in his tone. "Did they move the ship or something?" He's wearing a white T-shirt and a black backwards cap. Curls spill out from either side, despite his clear effort to conceal them. His skin is already sun-kissed, the tip of his nose a little red, and his shirt is fitted enough I can make out the shape of his toned physique underneath. I'd be lying if I said I didn't find him mildly attractive, but that's ridiculous. Obviously, I'm attracted to a celebrity. The issue is, so is everyone else. He could have any woman he wanted.

What am I even talking about? Obviously, that is irrelevant!

I shake myself out of it and use words like a grownup. "Yeah. You could say that."

"Where've they moved it to?"

"To Dubrovnik…" I say, letting the moment linger.

He blinks a few times and shoves his hands into his pockets. "Oh, like it's gone?"

"Yeah." I frown. Where else would they have moved it to?

His lips fall apart and he stares out into the distance. "Shit. Is that it?" he asks, pointing at the sleek beauty disappearing across the horizon.

I nod. "The very one."

He runs a hand down his face and kicks a loose stone. "*Crap*. This is…" He doesn't finish his sentence but laughs instead. "What a fucking moron," he mutters under his breath.

"Excuse me?"

"Me. I'm the moron," he adds, without looking my way.

"Oh." I mean, clearly, I am too. So, how could I judge.

Finally, he turns to me. "What will you do?"

I shrug. Honestly? My brain is still calibrating, trying to figure out how any of this is real. Because, right now, I'm stood next to a world-famous popstar I've been cyber-stalking for the last forty-eight hours and my luxury cruise, that was meant to be repairing my mental health, is but a dot in the distance.

Did I pass out? Did I slip and hit my head as I ran through the cobbled streets?

"I'm sorry," I finally manage to choke out. "I'm trying to…" I just wave my hands at the general situation, hoping he'll catch on.

He smiles. "I understand. This…" He waves his hands the same way as I did. "…is super inconvenient."

"Yes." And embarrassing. Probably expensive too.

"I'm Gus by the way," he says, holding out his hand to me.

I give him a look. "Yeah. I know who you are." It feels like a confession.

He tilts his head, curiously. "Hmm. I didn't think you did."

"Oh." I blink rapidly. "Well, I didn't before… when…" Oh, this is mortifying again. How wonderful. He grins, a sparkle in his eye that tells me he now knows I've researched him. *Walked right into that one, Sara!* "What I mean is…"

Ugh. I can't talk myself out of this one.

Thankfully he rescues me. "I only introduced myself because I was hoping you'd give me your name."

I click my fingers. That makes sense. Hopefully it won't take long for me to revert to being a normal person with mature communication skills, instead of this sweaty, socially inept, horridly embarrassed and fumbling version of me.

"You mean you don't know who *I am?*" I say, pretending to be mock offended.

He laughs. "Should I?"

"Wow." I shake my head. "Rude."

He waits for me to answer his original question, brow raised. I blow out a breath, brush down my dress and reset.

I hold my hand out like he did. He takes it in his large, warm hand, squeezing firmly as I say, "Hello, Gus. My name is Sara. Nice to meet you. Even if it is, once again, in unfortunate circumstances."

He schools his face to play along. "Nice to meet you too, Sara. Like myself, I see you are lost in a foreign city."

"Ah, I can see why you would think that. But I'm actually not lost at all. I am, in fact, stranded."

"Quite right. Me too. Tell me, Sara, what do you plan on doing to correct this situation? Because I myself," he says, pointing at his chest, "am probably going to walk to the next city."

I laugh, shaking my head and planting my hands on my hips. "Why are we talking like this?"

"I have no idea. You started it."

I probably did. I'm being supremely awkward. "Good point. But sorry, did you just say you're planning on *walking* to Dubrovnik?"

"I did say that."

I nod as if that's a very sensible thing to say but end up frowning in confusion. "Why, exactly?"

He raises his hands like it's obvious. "I love an adventure. And I have no money."

"So, you are *not* a wealthy popstar?"

"No. I mean, yes. But I have no money *on* me."

"Why on earth not?" I sputter.

He winces. "Because I only took a handful of notes with me this morning and I spent it all on lunch. I didn't want to carry a massive wad of cash around with me. You know, for security reasons."

I take a slow breath. But surely he has everything set up on his apps. "Well, do you have your phone on you?"

He cringes, running a hand through his curls. "This is really embarrassing. I'd like to point out that, normally, I'm much more organised than this."

"Ok?"

"I have a phone," he says, slipping it out of his pocket and glaring at it. "But it isn't my normal phone. I don't have anything set up on here."

"But why?"

"Ah, it's a long story."

"Well, can you not call someone? Get us helicoptered back onto the cruise or something? You don't have any contacts? A private chauffeur to Dubrovnik? Charter a yacht to chase down our yacht?" I realise as soon as I've said it that it's highly presumptuous of me to say 'us' but, other than the spritz incident, he's been fairly sweet so far so he might include me.

He grimaces and rubs the back of his neck. "The thing is, I'm trying to prove I don't need them."

"Who?"

"My team."

"Ok," I say, considering this revelation. "Well, I'd suggest you maybe do. You know, need them. Because you're stranded."

"We're stranded," he points out.

"Yes. *We're stranded*. Is there really nothing you can do?"

He sighs, his shoulders sagging. "I mean, I could call my team. If it was absolute worst-case scenario."

I feel like this qualifies. "Great! Do that!"

"But I don't want to," he says, cringing.

"Why not?"

"Because I spent so much time convincing them I could do this alone. And I can do this alone."

"I'd argue…"

"Hey," he interrupts, laughing when he notices my incredulous expression. "I know this looks bad. I do. But if I call them, they'll send people out here. I'll lose my anonymity and be forced to do this with people shadowing me the whole time. All in the guise of them being worried about me when in actual fact they just want to keep tabs on me. In fact, I'm pretty sure they've tapped my other phone and can track me."

"What?" I say, genuinely concerned for him.

He squeezes his chin. "Yeah, I don't want them to know I'm onto them but there have been some unexplained scenarios. I need the space. I need to just be a nobody for a couple of weeks so I can live my life the way I want to."

I blow out a breath. "Right. I see."

He nods. "So, like I said, I'd walk to Dubrovnik to catch the cruise, if it meant not having to call them."

"Right." I really do not understand his plight.

"But we could walk together?" he suggests with the innocence of someone who thinks that is a sensible suggestion.

"Do I look like the kind of woman who would be up for walking God only knows how far, in this blistering heat, to another city?"

I realise as soon as I've said it, that it invites him to study me. His gaze starts at my sandals (see also: inappropriate walking footwear) and carry on up until he meets my eyes again with a grin. "I suppose not."

"So, I won't be doing that."

"What *will* you be doing?"

I make another wild gesture with my hands. "I don't know! I was kind of hoping I'd just bumped into my solution. But you're not being very forthcoming."

"I am. I offered to be your walking companion," he jokes.

"Point. Made."

He cringes. "I'm sorry. Do you have a phone? Any money?"

"Yes. I have some cash and a phone."

"Great!"

"But it's dead. I need to find a charger."

He nods. "Then let's do that."

I glance behind him at the city and have this sudden anxious thought that we're still chatting and I haven't researched how long it will take to get to the next stop yet. What if it's a whole night of travelling and here we are, wasting time?

I purse my lips. This still feels a little too surreal for me. "Let me just clarify. *You* want to help *me* find a phone charger?"

He shrugs like it's obvious. "I'll help you. You can help me."

"And how would I help you?"

"By letting me join you to the next stop," he says. "I don't actually want to walk to Dubrovnik. I realise that would be insane. Besides, going it alone feels far riskier than in company. Especially for me. Please?"

I can hardly say no. My eldest sister complex would never abandon someone who needed my help. And besides, he was sweet enough to help me when I was in a bad way. I'm sure some men would've run in the opposite direction or even taken advantage of the situation. It's only one night, right? I'll find a charger and once my phone is working again, I'll call the cruise and insurance company and I'm sure all the pieces of this puzzle will start falling into place. Tomorrow, we'll reboard the cruise and carry on with our holidays. Simple.

I laugh. "I can't believe this is happening."

"Tell me about," he agrees.

"Ok then," I say. "You can tag along with me. But on one condition."

"What's that?"

"I'm in charge."

For some reason this seems to tickle him. When he realises I'm not joking, he swallows his laughter, clears his throat and nods. "Ok. That is fine with me," he says, almost too easily. *Hmm.*

"Oh!" I suddenly remember. "You should check the port office first. They had my passport."

He presses his lips together and nods. "Yeah, I best not leave that here. I'll be right back."

Once he returns, passport in hand, I jump to action, striding back into the city in search of the shops.

Eight

Gus is on my heels as I tear through Split in search of a phone charger.

"Hey, wait up," he calls from behind me. I ignore him, eyes peeled on the storefronts. "Where are you going? What's the plan? Christ, you're a quick walker."

"I need a phone charger, remember?"

"Yep. Want me to search for phone shops in the area?"

I stop mid-stride, planning to turn and face him when he ploughs into my side. I nearly fall onto the pavement, but his hand quickly finds my waist, pulling me to him so that I'm saved from further embarrassment.

I ignore the dizziness it elicits and press one hand to his chest, balancing myself and pushing him away in the process.

"Yes. *Please* do that. Search for a phone shop."

He's put on a dark pair of sunglasses and my startled expression stares back at me in their reflection. I can't tell what *his* eyes are doing, but we stand in place for a moment longer before he nods and opens his burner phone. I step back, creating a bit of distance.

It saddens me to think that once upon a time, people travelled unknown cities with paper maps and a pocket full of whimsy and here I am, awash with anxiety because my phone has died.

"Right, there's one down here. But wait," he says as I head in the direction he pointed in. "Can we just... I don't know. Talk about this? Make a plan? I feel like I'm blindly following you like a lost child."

"I'd say you *are* like a lost child."

That fucking grin. Does he like being picked on? Is that his thing? *Gross.* "All I'm saying, is we could have some direction here."

"I need my phone so I can—"

"I get it. And we will make that step one of the plan. But what next? Can I be planning while you're racing ahead of me?"

I scrunch my forehead, then release it immediately thinking about those pesky scowl lines. "What do you suggest?" I ask, softening my tone.

"I, for one, was planning on getting a drink then having a shower once I was back on the cruise. If I am not going to get that now, then I'd like to find it here."

"No," I say. That sounds like a terrible plan.

"What do you mean *no*?"

"You can get a drink from a corner shop en route. Then we're... *I'm*... finding a coach to Dubrovnik. If you also want to do that, that's just grand."

He nods, pressing his lips together. "Sorry, I forgot for a moment there that you're in charge. It won't happen again."

I groan. "Just tell me where the phone shop is."

"Follow me. That way I don't have to crank my heart rate just to keep up with you."

I resign myself to letting Gus lead, hoping his phone is going to be able to help us. The further we stroll, the more modern the city becomes. We emerge onto a street lined with shops, and Gus points at one with a bright red awning.

"Thank you," I say.

He grins. "My pleasure."

It doesn't take us long to find the charger I need. The issue is the lack of a plug.

"Can I make a suggestion?" Gus asks, as I meet him back outside.

"Sure," I say, busily tucking the charger into my bag to avoid glancing at him. Not out of disrespect, although maybe it seems that way, but to avoid the way my stomach flips every time he catches my eyes with that warm, amber gaze of his. It's not every day you're wandering a European city with a famous popstar. Even if it's purely circumstantial (see also: bad luck) and completely non-romantic. But also, Gus has seen me at my lowest, and I don't fancy allowing him to do that again. And I certainly don't want him to ask me about it.

"Why don't we find a place to stay here for the night?"

"Well, until my phone is charged, all I have is a hundred euros in cash."

"I'm sure we can brag our way into a BnB with that."

"Not a nice one!"

He shrugs. "Does it matter? It's just I'd really like to stop tempting my luck. If somebody happens to recognise me and shares it on socials with any kind of time stamp, my team will get wind of me not being on the cruise, and they won't be able to reach me. It'll create a domino effect."

It's late afternoon. Even if I did find a coach to Dubrovnik tonight, I'd still need to find somewhere to sleep. I lift my shoulders up until they touch my ears.

Gus smirks. "What are you doing?"

I drop my shoulders. "What? It's how I think when I'm stressed."

"Hear me out." He waits for me to look at him, so I finally allow myself to. *Whoops, there goes my stomach.* "We'll find a place to stay tonight and make a plan. You'll be able to charge your phone so we have money and ways to get to Dubrovnik, and then we can sleep, eat, and rest so we're in the right frame of mind to sort ourselves out tomorrow."

I blink. "That was a weirdly sensible solution."

"Thank you?"

"Fine. How do we find somewhere with two rooms to spare on short notice in peak season?"

"You're once again forgetting I have access to the internet."

I follow him to a bench by a small park, where he sits and types into his phone. I do not enjoy being at the mercy of an unknown man. It's like allowing a child to pick out your outfit for an important meeting.

Ok, so he's an adult. Yeah, yeah. But he's also a popstar and it sounds like he's not used to running his own life.

After five minutes of people watching of what I can only assume is rush hour in Croatia, he clears his throat. "Ok, there's a place in the Old Town which could work."

"Won't that be really expensive?"

"Apparently not. It only accepts cash. It doesn't have a website. It's just recommended on this travel blogger site for cash-strapped backpackers."

"That sounds dodgy."

"It's a family run BnB apparently. This guy says he uses it whenever he's in Split and they rely on word of mouth."

I sigh, closing my eyes. "This feels so surreal. I don't even know you."

"Ah, but you know *of* me."

"Right. But I don't know *you*. And I really only knew *of* you a few days ago," I remind him. "What if you're a total creep?"

He scoffs. "You can google me if you want," he says, offering me his device. I don't take it. I've already done my research. "The only stories you'll find about me being 'creepy' are fanfiction. And in all of those," he says, grinning proudly, "they actively encourage it."

I make an unimpressed face. As a teenager, *Twilight* fanfiction filled an Edward-Cullen shaped void for many years in between film releases and rereads of my battered, overread books. So, I can't exactly judge him – but... "Hold on, you read fanfiction about *yourself*?"

He shrugs. "Some of it is really good."

"But it's about *you*!"

"Yeah. And it's funny. And kind of hot."

"*What?*" I bark out a laugh.

"I'm not saying I... er, you know..."

I do know, but I'm not going to make this easy for him. Making men squirm is one of my favourite hobbies. I tilt my head thoughtfully. "No? Do explain."

His lips do that thing again, like he's trying not to smile

but they're betraying him. "What I'm saying, is I liked reading about myself through fiction. It's a weirdly good escape. They make me someone I'm not. Usually better. Sometimes worse. Nearly always less boring. And sometimes I send my sister screenshots to wind her up."

His eyes catch on mine, and I look away just as fast. "You have a sister?" I actually did learn this in my research, but I don't want him to know that. Besides, I'd like to hear his side of things.

"You're not very online, are you?"

"I'm usually working. I don't have time for apps. I'm barely on Instagram."

"Yeah. Figures. You'd have heard of my sister if you were." We fall into silence, and I readjust my legs before forcing myself to look at him. He's staring at me, expectantly.

"Well, shall we?" I say.

"Ladies first," he gestures playfully.

"You have the map, Popstar."

Less than twenty minutes later, on tired, sore feet, we find ourselves strolling down the quiet, shady back streets of Old Town. Gus points to a sign. "This is it."

"What is this?"

"It's the BnB."

I look up the stone facade and its crooked windows with green wooden shutters either side. We're essentially in an alleyway. It's clean and tidy, something I've generally noticed in Croatia, but there's a problem. "There's no door."

"I guess it must be here somewhere."

"Well, why would they put a sign here? If there's not a door, how are we supposed to get in?"

At this exact moment, a middle-aged, dark-haired woman pops her head out of the window above us and talks rapidly. We both stare at her, mouths agape.

"I can't tell if we're upsetting her or she's being friendly," Gus remarks.

"I take it you don't speak Croatian?"

"Nope. You?"

I sigh. "Also, no."

The woman stops talking and waves her hands. A second later she pops back out but with an older man. "You are English?"

Gus nods. He's still got his cap on backwards as his tips his head, there's a lovely triangle shape formed in his throat. He has a straight nose and ears that look like they've been attached too low. And yet, he's handsome because he has the kind of face made to smile. I bite my lip and look up too.

"Is this the bed and breakfast?" he asks.

"Yes. You must come round the front. We show you to rooms."

"How do we get there?"

The couple share a look like we're two dim-witted Brits. I mean... if the shoe fits, right? "Round the front."

"Yes, which is... which way?" Gus makes a point of checking both directions.

"That way," the man says, pointing down the street. "Take two rights. You find red door."

"Right. Ok. Thank you. *Havala*."

Without really thinking about it, Gus's hand finds my

lower back, guiding me towards the narrow alley.

The couple are already stood waiting by the red door when we round the corner. The woman is saying something with bags of energy, clapping her hands with excitement, her smile infectious. But when she grabs both our hands and squeezes, I realise she's gotten the wrong end of the stick. *Not again!*

"Oh no—"

"My wife says you are a very beautiful couple."

Before I can say anything, Gus laughs. "Thanks so much."

"*Gus—*"

"We show you to room," the man says, ushering me along. The woman is talking again, pointing out things in the courtyard. They must be half our size and don't duck at all to access the red oval arched door leading into the house. Gus squats and I lean forward.

It's all very quaint and pretty inside, marble floors sparkling, bursting with character. The only exception is the porcelain doll perched on one of the windowsills that I swear gives us a look as we step past.

We're shown to a room at the top of three flights of spiral stairs, with one small double bed and a single, narrow window looking out onto the street below.

"The bathroom is on the ground floor," the old man says. "It is shared. Please knock as there is no lock on the door."

One night. One night. One night.

"I'm sorry," I say. "You didn't say how much the room is?"

"Eighty euro," he answers.

"And what about a second room?" I ask, as he's trying to close the door behind him.

He frowns back at me, confused. "No other rooms available. Good evening." And then the door is closed with a click.

Oh my God.

Nine

"Why did you *thank* the woman for saying we looked like a nice couple?" I ask, frowning at Gus. "No wonder they've put us in a shared room. There's only one bed for fuck sakes!"

"It's for fuck's *sake*."

"*And?* It literally doesn't matter. What matters is the fact we only have one room."

"I'll sleep in the hall if you'd prefer."

"Fine," I say, nodding. That is an acceptable solution.

He scoffs, but his eyes are alight with humour. "You'd totally let me sleep out in the hall, wouldn't you? What if that doll in the window murders me?"

"Then I'd say you shouldn't have missed your cruise."

"You're incredibly mean."

I roll my eyes. "*Please.* I'm realistic. Besides, I'm a single woman travelling alone. You can't just impose yourself on me. What's to say you didn't hold back on purpose?"

Gus bites his bottom lip as he places his sunglasses on a side table with a tile decoration on top. "I'm pretty sure you trust me already. If you didn't, you wouldn't have agreed to let me join you."

I twist my lips, because for some reason they're attempting a smile. I would hate for him to think I'm relaxed in his presence. It would ruin my whole argument and I'm not ready to admit defeat yet. "Why did you miss the cruise anyway?"

"I kept checking this phone because I thought it automatically updated. But unfortunately, it's a piece of shit that's stuck on London time. So, I was an hour behind schedule."

"Why didn't you use the clocks in the city?"

"I thought I was being clever."

"Wow."

"Yes. I see now that I was being the opposite of that."

I sigh, raising my arms. "Well, I decided to forego the tour and wander alone, lost track of time and didn't realise my phone was practically bleeding to death in my bag. So, I didn't get the cruise updates."

"I probably did. But those messages went to the phone hidden under my pillow."

"Aren't your team going to grow suspicious if your phone never moves?"

Gus shrugs. "Probably. But for all they know, I'm leaving it in my room on purpose. And technically, it *is* moving."

"You really care about doing this alone, don't you?" His expression sobers before he clears his throat. He looks away, running his thumb and forefinger down his nose. I've seen him do that before – maybe it's his giveaway.

"I've felt very hemmed in for the past twelve years. We formed the band when we were still kids and although we aged with it, the team still had a way of handling us like children. They don't literally lock us in our hotel rooms anymore, but they still treat us like prized assets. I just want to pretend for a moment that I'm a normal twenty-eight-year-old man."

"And not a giant baby?"

His smile bounces back. "Exactly."

I take a moment to examine the room. It's… cosy. But it's clean and there's a plug in the wall by my bed. I practically launch myself at it, taking the charger out of the packaging and plugging my phone in.

"You know, we're lucky this charger only cost me ten euros, otherwise we might not have even had enough for this room."

"So, what you're saying is you have ten euros left to buy food?"

"No, I didn't say that. We need to keep every penny we have just in case. And although I'll have my phone to pay soon. I haven't tried it abroad yet. What if it doesn't work?"

"Right," he says, rubbing the back of his neck. He looks around like he's trying to find a place to set up. He settles on a part of the tiled floor closest to the window, where a slight breeze blows in. As he sits, I hear a grumbling sound. He rolls his head back, pinching his eyes closed.

There's no doubt that was his stomach but the fact he isn't saying so and is deliberately choosing to suffer in silence, only betrayed by his own anatomy, layers me in a whole new level of guilt.

Dammit. I tap my phone screen but it's still dead. It dawns on me that I'm also starving, and waiting for the phone to charge might take a while.

"What would ten euros even get you around here anyway?"

Gus opens his eyes, his expression cautious. "Probably pizza."

As I take the first bite of cheap, cheesy pizza, I'm grateful that we had ten euros left over. It only afforded us two large slices each but it's enough to sustain. The mozzarella stretches and falls down my chin. I moan in satisfaction as the rich, tangy tomato sauce overwhelms my tastebuds. Gus is back in his spot, camped out on the floor below the window, his curls ruffling in the breeze.

"Good?" he asks, grinning at me with his mouth full.

"So good. Damn."

"How's your phone?" he asks.

"She's coming back to life."

"Good."

"Actually, I booked two tickets on a coach to Dubrovnik that leaves in the morning."

Gus manages to drag all the cheese off his next slice and takes a minute to right himself. "Fuck. That's hot. Sorry. What did you say?"

"I booked us a coach." Thankfully I could book it online using my payment app. Although, upon checking my account, with my savings pillaged, I barely have five hundred quid left before payday, which is still a fortnight away and my credit cards are virtually maxed out thanks to my non-existent wedding.

"Wow. You've booked for me too?"

I shrug, choosing not to make it a big deal. "I felt sorry for you."

He laughs, short and sharp. "I am but a pauper's son."

"I mean, I assume you'll pay me back at some point?"

"Absolutely. I thought that was a given. Of course, I'll pay you back, plus interest."

I scoff. "That's completely unnecessary. I just need you to pay for you, that's all."

"At least 50 per cent interest on top – *minimum*," he mumbles.

"No," I say, taking another bite full of pizza.

"Fine. One hundred per cent."

"That's literally not how you negotiate."

"No, really?" he asks, but I can tell he's messing with me. "Let's say two hundred per cent and call it quits."

I sit taller, frowning. I'm so onto him. I hate the thought of owing people. I don't want his money. It's why I've always worked myself to the bone. It's this innate need to be able to stand on my own two feet and support my family if I need to. The thought of this man paying for me once he has access to his money again and more, lots more, doesn't sit well with me at all.

"What's in it for you?" I ask, narrowing my eyes at him.

He makes a semi-outraged face like the answer is obvious. "You're saving me from being outed to my team? You're paying for me to travel with you out of your own bank account? You're being *sort* of nice to me?"

"I'm *not* being nice to you," I say, but saying it out loud seems so silly I have to muffle a laugh.

He grins. "I stand corrected."

I swallow thickly, a ball of anxiety settling in my stomach. "I don't need your money. I don't want it. I just want you to fund your part."

He chews on his bottom lip, watching me curiously. "I feel like what I'm asking you to do is actually quite a big ask. I'd like to pay you more than you're spending."

"Why's it a big ask?"

"Because I'm…" He sighs, glancing away. "I'm going to sound like Ron from *Anchorman*."

"You're kind of a big deal?"

He laughs. "Well, yeah."

"Ok, well, sorry to sound like a broken record, but I'd hardly heard of you until a few days ago and I'm sure most of Croatia are in the same boat."

"What a metaphor to apply to this situation."

"Can you be serious?"

"Not really, no."

"Oh my God," I squeal, before realising I sound like I'm flirting. *Am I flirting?* Absolutely not. Don't be ridiculous. I clear my throat. "You're quite annoying."

"Hey, I got us pizza! Surely that's worth some brownie points?"

"With *my* money."

"Which I'm going to pay you back at two hundred and fifty per cent interest."

"No, you're not!"

He laughs while trying to chew on another bite. "All I'm saying is there is a risk you're seen with me, and my fans make you an unhealthy obsession. It's why I don't usually date normies. Easier if they already know exactly who the person is. Worst case, they get some PR out of it. Best case, it raises their profile."

"*Normies.*" The word sounds so derogative.

He scrunches his face. "Sorry, I didn't mean it like that.

I just mean, it's easier for people who are already in the spotlight. You know?"

"Why, what would they do to me?"

"Well," he takes a second to chew before continuing, "they'd probably just find out who you are, where you're from, who your family is, what your hobbies are, national insurance number… That sort of thing."

I don't know why I find this funny but I do. "You're *joking*."

"I wish I was."

I sigh. "Well then. Enjoy travelling to Dubrovnik alone. Count me out."

His eyes widen. "I'm not selling it very well. You also get great company?"

"Is someone else joining us?" He doesn't even fight his smile this time, instead he stomps his feet and bursts out laughing.

"Buuuuuurn. Oh, you're so mean. Stop it, or I might fall in love with you."

"*Shut. Up.* Right, you can *definitely* sleep in the hall."

"No. I'm sorry. I take it back," he says, straight-faced, swallowing another laugh. "I'm going to be good now, I promise. Shall we talk about something more sensible?"

"Maybe we could be silent?"

He takes another bite of pizza and chews quietly for about five seconds before saying, "Nah. I'm not adept at silence. Tell me why you're cruising the Med all alone. That's ballsy."

I stare at the ceiling as a seed of betrayal grows more branches and punches me in the heart. "I just wanted to travel in style. I don't get much time off work. Even when

I'm off, I'm not really. This time though, it was different. I logged out and told my boss I wouldn't be checking in. Probably the first time since I started there that I've actually switched off."

He eyes me. "What's different this time?" *Nope*. Not answering that. I don't need to get into personal details with this man. I change the conversation.

"What about you? You could probably afford to cruise anywhere, right? Why here? And why not your very own private yacht?" He pauses for a second and I wonder if he's going to call me up on changing the conversation away from me.

"I've been to most places. I'm well-travelled but rarely for fun. I'm hoping this will be the first of many solo travelling experiences. I like seeing places in detail. The smaller moments, you know? The life of a place. Fascinates me how different cultures span cities, towns, even streets. I love all that. Hence why I have my camera. So, I can capture it.

"Plus, I didn't grow up with money. I can't bear the thought of taking a yacht all by myself, it's too pompous. Boring too. I like being around people, I enjoy soaking in the buzz." He smiles at me. "You know, you missed out the other night. Edith, that elderly lady, she was a hoot. Those experiences are exactly what I signed up for. Two weeks of being treated like a normal person, enjoying things as they come."

I blanch – this conversation is leading to *that* evening. "Yeah, that makes sense." I look down at my hands. "You know, about the other night... I was feeling..." I don't know how to finish that sentence.

"You don't have to explain yourself. I get it. Trust me."

He quickly steers us back to the original question. I chew on my lips, trying to brush the moment away. "Anyway, the Med seemed like the easiest location to persuade them I could do this alone. It's easy to come get me when I inevitably fuck up and need rescuing."

"I don't know why they didn't trust you?" I mock.

He fights that grin. "Considering I'm so responsible and time-conscious?"

"And you'd never put your safety into the hands of strangers."

He smirks. "Would I ever? You know what? I don't care. I feel alive for the first time in a long time. And I'm settling in for a painfully uncomfortable night on a tiled floor."

"I gave you a blanket," I point out.

"Yep. Because you're so kind and generous."

I shrug. "It's character building," I say. And because I can't help seeing him trying so hard not to smile, I add, "Which you clearly need."

"*Clearly*, and on that note," he says. "I probably should know more about you. Any characteristics I ought to know about? Any criminal records?"

I look away, licking my lips.

Gus nearly chokes on the pizza he's chewing. "Oh my God," he mumbles, eyes wide. "What did you do? Am I in danger?"

"No. It was just a D and D."

"Dungeons and Dragons?"

I make a face. *What is wrong with this guy?* "No… what? Drunk and disorderly. I don't like to talk about it."

Something about this news delights him. "What did you do?"

"Not telling you. All I'll say is it involved a Subway and a seagull."

I can see him calculating the possibilities. "I have so many questions."

"Keep them to yourself. I grew up in Brighton. Seagulls feature in nearly all my stories."

"I like Brighton. You still live there?"

"I do."

"Do you like it?"

"I enjoy the energy of the city. It's been my home since I was a kid. I don't know if I could see myself anywhere else. What about you? Where are you based?"

He twists his lips. "I'm from the Cotswolds. But I don't feel like I have a home anymore. I've been here there and everywhere for so long now. More recently I was staying in the townhouse in London that my band and I bought years ago as a base for when we were in the studio. It was kind of lonely to be honest."

"The band weren't there?"

He frowns. "No."

He goes back to picking at his slice after this, so I seize the moment to phone the cruise company. I give up after the sixth ring when they don't answer and try the insurance company instead. After sitting on hold, listening to the elevator music for twenty minutes, they pick up, only to quickly inform me that I didn't pay the additional surcharge to cover abandonments.

Excellent.

We're truly on our own.

We talk until Gus decides an evening walk will do us good. We amble the streets of Split with full bellies and a relaxed feeling in our bones, knowing we're going to make it to the port in time to catch the cruise again tomorrow. If anything, it's a moment of clarity that I wouldn't have seen the city like this at all if I'd made it back to the ship in time. I'm completely at ease as we walk the cobbled alleyways, listening to the bustling, busy restaurants, with tables lining the walls outside. I allow myself to soak it in.

Gus takes a few pictures, and I pretend not to notice when he snaps a few of me.

On the way back to the BnB, I pop into a small store to stock up on things we need, such as toothbrushes, toothpaste, a pack of clean underwear, deodorant and a hairbrush. I'm thrilled to discover my phone wallet app works here. The shop also sells cheap T-shirts, and I gasp dramatically when I find a black one with Just4Summer branding on the front. Four young faces grin enthusiastically, like all their wildest dreams have come true before they're even old enough to leave school.

I hold it up against me, spinning to show Gus. "It's five euros. What a rip off!"

"Hey, now. I feel like we're pushing our luck if you wear that. Especially with my face on the front."

I snort, grabbing an XL so I can wear it like a nightie. "You barely even look like this now. When was this taken? In nursery? Surely, that will make us *less* suspect. Who walks around in a T-shirt with the face of their companion on it? That's insane."

"You're actually buying it?"

"I'm going to wear it to bed," I say, thinking nothing of it.

But after I've paid at the till and turned back, he's stood outside the shop again with a cautious look on his face. I pause. "Oh shit. Was that insensitive?"

"Was what insensitive?"

"Me. Buying that T-shirt."

"No, Sara. That's…" He licks his lips and forces a smile. "You're fine."

Ten

When we return to the BnB, the owners offer us red wine and practically beg us to sit with them in the courtyard. The old man feeds us with the history of the building and how it's been in his family for hundreds of years. Always run the same way.

Later on, once the sky has turned a dark navy, littered with stars, we manage to persuade them to give us more bedding, making up a story about being chilly sleepers, despite the nightly temperature here at this time of year being lows of thirty degrees, and Gus sets up on the cold floor as I tuck myself in for the night. I do feel a bit sorry. But then again, I don't want to share a bed with a stranger. No matter how famous he might be.

We leave the window open, the shutters squeaking when the warm wind whistles through the alleyways.

A mosquito taunts me, brushing close to my ear and then away again. I end up sleeping with the white sheets right over my head, hoping to deter the bastard. The next thing I know, there's light peeling through the closed shutters and I can hear footsteps on the stairs outside the room.

I sit up in bed, looking for my roommate. He isn't on the floor. In fact, he isn't in the room.

There's a light rap on the door. "Sara, you decent?"

"Yeah?" I croak.

He carefully creaks it open and steps in glancing at me with a bright-eyed expression. "Good morning, sunshine. It's a lovely day outside."

What? Why should I care? What time is it anyway?

I don't need to say any of this, I can feel it being wonderfully portrayed by my face.

Gus carefully places a coffee cup on the side table next to me and steps away. "There were some pennies left after the pizza so thought I'd treat you to a coffee."

"With my money?"

"That I'm going to pay you back with five hundred per cent interest," he points out.

Which… "You said two hundred yesterday."

"Did I?"

"Ugh." Is all I can manage, flopping back down on the bed and pulling the covers over my face. "What time is it anyway?"

"It's nine."

I sit up so fast I swallow air, gasping. "WHAT?"

He flinches. "It's nine?"

"The coach leaves at ten! It's a twenty-minute walk from here!"

Gus frowns. "So, what you're saying is we have twenty minutes to drink our coffees and time for a leisurely stroll to the coach?"

I do the math. "That's forty minutes."

He nods, checking his phone. "Well, yeah, more specifically, it's a quarter past nine."

"Fuuuuck," I groan, throwing my legs out of the bed and stomping through the room to the door. I slam it behind me before realising I forgot the dress that I need to wear again today, without my clothes which are hung beautifully in the closet in my cabin out at sea. I storm in again, grab it and head out.

Gus laughs under his breath. "Not a morning person, I see."

We make the coach with five minutes to spare. There are tons of backpackers milling around, locals who probably work between the cities and a couple of elderly people waiting at the bus station. Gus gently takes my elbow and squeezes it, pulling me closer. I frown at him over my shoulder.

"It's really busy," he says. "I'm going to have to hide my face."

I wiggle out of his grasp. "Then put your sunglasses on. Put your cap on frontways and, well, if you really cared about being noticed, surely you should've shaved your hair off? It's pretty recognisable."

"How dare you," he says, deadpan.

"I'm just saying."

"I forgive you."

"There's nothing to forgive. I'm purely stating sensible facts. *Oh!* You should wear the T-shirt I bought last night. Nobody would expect you to be wearing your own band merchandise."

Gus gives me a look. "There's no way you don't know that was fake merch."

"Is that why you got all offended? Because you won't get your tiny cut in the sale?"

He makes a tutting sound. "*Please*. Big of you to assume I get anything from merchandise with my face on it."

I wait for him to put his rubbish, flimsy disguise on before we board the coach. By the looks of it, it's mostly full of hungover backpackers and tired travellers. I doubt they're going to have any interest in Gus.

I allow him the window seat to tuck himself away out of sight from the other passengers and must have ended up falling asleep because the next thing I know he's nudging me awake with his elbow.

"Hey, sunshine," he whispers. "You're snoring and attracting attention."

I sit bolt upright, glancing around to see one girl, a bit younger than me, quickly turn away. A fresh panic rushes through me. If I'm snoring, then I'm probably dreaming, which means… I shake myself out of it.

"I don't snore," I tell him.

"Ok. Sure. Then you bark in your sleep."

"I do not," I whisper back at him.

"I wouldn't have woken you, except I'm trying to keep a low profile here and you're rattling the coach chassis."

I frown. "*This* is why I don't share rooms."

"Because you snore?"

I stare at him for a moment, scrutinising his expression. When I don't look away, he raises an eyebrow.

I sigh. "Not *just* because I snore, but a little bit that, yes."

"I see. Was it because of the sleep talking?" I tense all over, clenching my hands into fists. Gus's eyes drop to my hands, and he takes a deep breath. "I'm just messing with you, Sara. It's all good. I woke you before people started to notice."

I breathe the tension out of my body slowly and blink back the pressure behind my eyes. I'm good at pushing emotions back, I've had plenty of practice. It's just there's nothing attractive about a twenty-nine-year-old woman who cries out for her mum in her sleep.

"Don't let me sleep again, please."

We share a moment of prolonged eye contact, his light brown irises almost golden in daylight. I feel a rush of energy sprint down my spine. "I'm sorry," he says even quieter. "I didn't mean to embarrass you."

"No, it's… Thank you for waking me. Please don't let me snore again."

He presses his lips together, a notch forming between his brows. He doesn't say anymore but gives me one solid nod instead.

The journey moves slowly. I half expected to be on a wild coach trip like that one time Hattie and I went clubbing in Malia and nearly died twice on the shuttle from the airport to our hotel, the driver running stop signs and letting its back wheels hang over the edge of sheer drops. At least that driver would get us to Dubrovnik with plenty of time to spare. It's bad enough, I've resigned myself to seeing very little of the city, now I must be on the most sluggish coach journey of my life just to rub it in.

About two hours into the drive, the coach pulls into the one and only stop between the cities. A small town on the main road along the coast of Croatia. The driver hops out of the coach and stands there for a few moments smoking a cigarette.

Fine. We all need breaks, I suppose.

But then, a taxi shows up and he gets in. I watch it leave, flying back the way we came.

Oh, so now he can go fast!

Are we being stranded here? I let out a strangled laughed.

The main door to the coach has been left wide open and some of the passengers have gotten out to stretch their legs, far too relaxed about this. I leave Gus and head outside. He doesn't ask after me, but once I'm on the tarmac, I peek back to see him watching me curiously through the darkened window.

"Hi," I say to a young blonde woman wearing a baggy white Nike T-shirt, her hair pulled into a long, high ponytail. "Do you speak English?"

She gives me a look. "I am English, babe."

Great. "Did you see the driver leave us?"

"Yeah. Happens all the time here. He'd finished his shift probably. A new driver will be along at some point."

"Ok… Like soon?"

She shrugs. "Sometimes. Sometimes not."

I gawp at her. "You're so chilled."

"Yeah. Not in a rush, am I?"

"Right. Ok. Thanks then," I say, climbing back onto the coach.

I check the time again only to feel a splash of rage when I see my phone, which I've barely touched today, is already on 25 per cent battery. It was fully charged a matter of hours ago. Why do they do this? One minute they're fine and thriving, the next minute they're on a rapid descent into decay.

"What's the situation?" Gus asks.

"My phone's dying."

"Again? You need a new phone."

"*No. Really?*"

He runs his tongue over his top teeth to bypass a grin. "That wasn't the situation I was asking about."

"Oh, the driver has just left us here. I guess he only drives it so far. That girl I spoke to seems to think they'll be another driver along soon."

"It's going to get hot in here without the air-con on."

I roll my head back and close my eyes to think a minute, my shoulders creeping higher with tension. It's twelve fifteen. The bus left Split five minutes late at five past ten. The journey said it would take just under three hours which gave us an arrival time in Dubrovnik of twelve fifty-three. But the coach was going so slowly, I find it hard to believe we're less than an hour away.

The cruise leaves the port at four on the dot. The gangway goes up approximately fifteen minutes before.

We *should've* had plenty of time.

I open my eyes again. My phone confirms it's gone midday already. I attempt to use my maps app to see if there's a quicker option but not only does using the app's basic function drop my battery by 5 per cent, I also have absolutely no signal whatsoever.

Ahh!

We wait another forty-five minutes, and I turn my phone off to save the final ounce of life it contains, when a taxi finally rolls up and without so much as a 'how do you do' a new driver climbs in and turns the engine on.

We've essentially been sat in a metal sweatbox for an hour so now the air-con is blasting again, cooling the thin layer of moisture on my skin, shivers racing up and down my limbs. For the next hour, I can't believe I'm considering the chance of me going into a hypothermic reaction. In Croatia. In July. What the hell? I pull the T-shirt I bought last night out of my bag and drag it over my head.

"I feel like you're trolling me," Gus mutters, glancing my way.

"I'm just cold," I say, shivering, not for effect, but the timing is undeniably helpful. Gus puts his hand out towards me.

"Want me to warm your fingers up?"

I glare. "No."

He chuckles, taking his hand back. "We could swap? You'll be out of the fans a bit more if you tuck in behind the chairs."

"I'm fine," I say.

"No, you're not. You just put a five-euro, extra-large black T-shirt with my face on it over a lovely summer dress because you're shivering your butt off."

"I just said, I'm fine. We've got maybe twenty minutes left of this journey," I say. "I'll survive."

But unfortunately, the universe hears me.

Five minutes later, as we're staggering up a hill at the pace of an old man inspecting a snail, the coach makes a choking, spluttering sound which has the driver grunting and cursing as he pulls over onto the gravelly side of the road.

"Oh, get fucked," I say. "There's no way! No. I don't believe it."

Gus sits taller, risking being seen, a notch between his brows, to get a better look too. The driver pulls the handbrake and climbs out. There's a collective discussion between parties on the coach. For some reason, nobody follows him out there to see what's going on, we all simply wait to hear our fate.

When he returns, he shrugs and starts talking really fast in Croatian.

Gus nudges me. "What's he saying?"

"I don't bloody know, do I?"

"Ask someone."

"Who?"

"People are getting off the coach."

"Yes. Thank you. I *also* have eyes."

"Should we get off too?" he asks, ignoring my jabs.

"I don't know!" I say, waving my hands with frustration. "I know as much as you!"

"I say we follow them. They must know something." Gus nods for me to climb out ahead of him, my black T-shirt hanging down over my butt, the white maxi dress underneath it. I look ridiculous. Like an obsessed fan with rubbish style. Gus puts his dark sunglasses on before we're even outside.

We stroll behind the coach so we're out of sight. I see the girl with the Nike T-shirt again and practically pounce on her. It feels akin to relationships formed in club toilets at two a.m. I don't know her name, don't know a single thing about her, but she might be my best friend in the whole world in this exact second. "Oh hey. You didn't happen to catch what he said, did you?"

"Nah. But I asked that man over there to translate," she says, turning away and lighting a cigarette. She has an aversion to providing detail. I feel my hackles rising.

"And what did he say?" I ask, reminding myself to use my polite *talking-to-strangers* voice.

She frowns up at me. Why is she frowning? She's the one missing out key details. "He said the man is waiting for a mechanic to arrive." She may as well have added "duh". Then she adds, "Could take a while."

"What's a while?"

"I don't bloody well know, do I?"

I feel like I'm speaking to my sisters. I just need a full answer. Why couldn't she have given me all the details she had right away, and I wouldn't have needed to ask her all these follow up questions she clearly finds so irritating. Gah!

Back to my other problem.

Popstar sits on a boulder at the side of the road, staring into the far distance.

The sea sparkles from here, amber-coloured islands in the distance, the sky a dazzling blue, not a cloud in sight. He's looking at his surroundings like he wants to get his camera out of the Konzum carrier bag he's been using to lug his stuff around in and take a few photos. But he doesn't and I think it's partly because he's trying not to draw attention to himself.

"Right," I say, approaching him and explaining the situation I've gathered off my new bestie, Nike Girl. "What's the time?"

Gus takes his phone out and shows it to me. "Nearly two."

I shake my head. "*No*. That can't be right," I say, snatching it from his hands. "There's no way we've been travelling for four hours!"

"We haven't. We were parked up for over an hour waiting for a new driver to arrive."

"Shit," I breathe out.

"It'll be fine," he says, waving a dismissive hand. I can't quite describe the feeling I experience, but the closest I can get to it is – I imagine this is how a wasp feels seconds before it uses its stinger. "*Don't* say that."

"Say what?"

"*That*! Don't be so dismissive of this situation. We need to get on that cruise! In *two* hours! It leaves in two hours." I look away, running a hand through my hair and dropping my bag at my feet. "We're so screwed."

I plonk myself down beside Gus and press my face into my hands with a groan. I'm tired, sweaty and aching from sitting on that coach for nearly four gruelling hours and now I'm almost certainly going to miss my dream cruise again.

"We could walk," Gus suggests.

I laugh at his joke because it's either that or cry.

"No. Really. It says it's an hour and thirty minutes' walk from here to the port of Dubrovnik."

I look up, squinting at him. His gaze is focused on his screen, so he doesn't catch me taking in his side profile, loose curls falling over his forehead, that strong manly nose, full lips and prominent triangle in his throat. It happens to be one of my minute attractions in a man. A really good Adam's apple.

Clearly, I'm having a moment because staring and lusting after a popstar who is used to models and beautiful actresses as his dates when I'm but a lowly randomer is definitely not a helpful use of my time. Albeit a decent distraction.

He turns just in time to stare at me as I realise what I'm doing, and heat rushes up my neck and into my cheeks.

Honestly. What am I? A schoolgirl? A rampant Just4Summer fan? Absolutely not.

"Sara?" he asks, blinking.

"Hmm."

"Did you hear what I said?"

"I did. We could walk."

He nods. "An hour and a half. It's two now. When did you say the cut off is?"

I look away, my breathing a bit heavy. I swipe a bug off my clammy skin and clear my throat. "Four."

"Then this could work. We'll have thirty minutes to spare." He jumps to his feet, holding out a hand for me to take. "Let's go. God knows how long it'll take to sort the coach. There's no time to spare. Let's get you back on that luxury cruise."

I let him pull me up but don't immediately race off. Well, because… "I'm in a dress and strappy sandals. You're hardly dressed much better. And, well, I don't know. It feels risky."

He twists his lips, considering. "If you'd rather wait, then we'll wait."

But I long for the luxury cabin with the air conditioning and large walk-in shower. I'm desperate to change into new clothes and wash my hair properly. I have a face mask waiting for me on my dressing table. And I can't do another night sharing a room with Popstar, especially as I'm already embarrassing myself.

I bite my bottom lip and groan. "Ugh. No. You're right. I'll suck up the blisters. Come on."

Ten minutes later we realise this was a terrible idea. The road along the coastline is not designed for walking. Cars rush by, beeping their horns, drivers throwing their hands up at us out of the window because they had to suspend a few seconds of their brain capacity to overtake us without running us over. Poor souls. As they pass, the wind blows dust and sand everywhere. Thankfully, we have sunglasses on to protect our eyes, but my sweaty skin is now layered with dust too and my mouth tastes like I've been chewing dried mud.

Good. Fine. Whatever.

Gus pulls out his phone now and again, especially when we reach a layby or a safer section of the road, to look for better routes. But there's nothing. It's an hour on this road, then we're near enough to the city for footpaths all the way up to the port.

"I've already got a blister," Gus informs me up ahead.

"You beat me."

"I don't think getting a blister first is a prize I wanted to win."

"You think we made a bad choice?" I ask.

"Nah. We need to get you back, so, we'll get you back."

"Oh. I have plasters if you want one?" I bloody knew they'd come in handy!

"No. Let's just keep going."

We navigate the busy road, trying not to become roadkill and taking occasional breaks for foot resting. I can already feel my ankles swelling. Sometimes they do this in the heat, so adding intense walking into the mix, almost definitely won't help. There's a reason I don't run anywhere.

We're about thirty-five minutes into our gruelling hike when a louder horn blares for us to move out the way. Before I know what's going on, I find myself pinned against Gus, as he uses his own large torso as a human shield, pressing me against the cliff edge, wrapping around the road. I can feel my heartbeat pulsing in my neck. I can't tell if it's from the adrenaline of nearly being hit by a massive vehicle or because he's holding me like some kind of furious alpha cowboy from one of Hattie's smutty romance novels.

It whooshes past us, the skirt of my dress rustling around Gus's legs.

He softens his hold once it's passed and looks me over, his face so close to mine I have to swallow to right myself. "Are you ok?"

"Fine," I squeak, which… *Sara, you need to get a grip.* I clear my throat and step fully out of his hold. "I'm fine. That was a totally unnecessary reaction. I was fine. I had loads of room. And… *oh no.*" I stare wide eyed at the road ahead of us.

"What?" is his breathless reply, hands on his hips.

I point. "Is that our bloody coach?!"

Gus stares in that direction now too, his lips falling apart in disbelief. "You're *joking.*" He takes off sprinting, waving his arms like they might see him and stop for us. He looks incredibly gallant chasing after the bus, it's actually kind of sexy. Again, I think about Hattie's fictional cowboy boyfriends she frequently updates me on.

I need an ice-cold drink and a fan. Maybe a dip in the sea.

I blame the heat. Yeah. Must be that.

"Gus!" I yell at his retreating figure. "They're not coming back. It's no use."

Ok and now I'm starting to sound like a damsel in distress. It's the corner for me as soon as I'm back on that damn boat. Time out for at least a solid twenty minutes until I sound like myself again.

He evidently agrees as he stops, dropping his arms at his sides. "Fuck!"

I take this pause to pull the T-shirt off and stuff it back in my bag, adding a plaster to my heels and offering Gus one too, who once again refuses.

Eleven

"All we can do is keep walking," I say once I've caught him up, panting. It's an obvious statement, of course, but it feels required. "And quickly." The ache in the balls of my feet are burning, the blisters on the back of my heels are raw and my ankles have weakened to the point it feels like my legs and feet are connected by some of kind of spongy material.

But we have no other options.

Neither of us have signal yet to call for a taxi or any kind of help.

In hindsight, I'm smarter than this.

This was a rash decision. I'm blaming it on Popstar.

And so, we walk, walk, walk until the city skyline starts to come into view, boats and ships appear on the horizon out on the peacefully, choppy sea. The sky is spotless, the sun so bright it turns my vision golden and speckled whenever I look up.

"You know, I'm sort of gutted I won't get to see Dubrovnik. It was one of my highlights for this trip," I tell Gus, head down, trying not to trip on one of the loose, fallen rocks at the side of the road.

He hums in agreement. "Yeah. Me too," he says. "If I tell you I'm a *Star Wars* fanatic, will you be mean to me?"

"No," I say. "I reserve judgement for people with a lack of interests."

Something about this statement makes him laugh. "*Star Wars* was pretty much the only thing my dad and I had in common growing up. And more recently too. Trying to get back into his life was easier with the lure of *Star Wars* Premiere tickets. Perks of being famous, I guess."

"What, like, the actual red-carpet events?"

"Yeah. Dad always went right in, and I'd do a circuit in exchange for tickets. But nobody really cared that I was there because I wasn't in it."

"So, you mostly did it to see your dad?"

"Yeah. He can be tricky. He's a countryman. Likes his garden and walks through fields but I rarely get home these days, so I wasn't seeing much of him. He doesn't really understand the whole music thing. He's never even been to one of my concerts."

"*Really?*"

"Yeah. It's not his scene. Too busy. Too loud. He prefers the sound of birds." Gus laughs like it's not an issue. I expect him to expand on it but instead he pivots back to Dubrovnik, saying, "Some of *The Last Jedi* was filmed in Old Town apparently. I'd like to see the comparison."

But now he has me intrigued. "You don't see your family much then?" I ask. "You know, with you being a jet-setting popstar and all."

"No, honestly, I see them maybe twice a year if I'm lucky. Christmas is the big one. I've done well at getting home for Christmas Day most years since my career blew up. My sister pops up a lot more, but that's because she dabbles in the celebrity lifestyle and enjoys using my fame to get herself into parties and events."

"You make her sound like a diva."

Gus snorts. "Well, she's not *not* a diva."

I ponder what it would be like to be the younger sister of a famous popstar and can barely fathom it. "How old was she when Just4Summer really took off?"

He cringes. "Twelve. Maybe thirteen. I was sixteen when we were picked up by the label. It wasn't until a year later when we guest starred on a McBusted tour that our lives really took off."

"So, she would've been young. That's a lot for a girl to deal with. You know, alongside puberty, periods, boys and all the drama that surrounds you at that time."

"You seem to know a lot about it."

I laugh. "Well, despite the rumours, I was once a teenager. Plus, I practically raised my three younger sisters."

"I see. I bet they were lucky having had you to watch out for them."

My lips tip downwards before I can stop them, so I'm glad Gus can't see my face. "Oh, I'm not sure they think so. I'm told I was rather mean."

"*You? Mean?* I refuse to believe it."

"*Ha. Ha.* I'll have you know, raising them brats is the reason I'll likely die thirty years before they do, purely from the stress of it all. I swear some of their meltdowns altered my chemical makeup. The least they deserved was a little *mean*." This has Gus cracking up.

"Tell me about them," he says.

"What do you want to know?"

"What are they like?"

I sniff, unsure where to start. "Bitchy. Clever. Awful. Funny. Irritating. Beautiful. Intense. Ambitious." I laugh. "They're a lot. Millie is the youngest – she's the most intense and would probably scream for a solid five minutes if she ever found out I actually hung out with you. I will tell her one day. I'll save it for her hen do or something.

"Abby is the second youngest. She's very sweet but sometimes to her own detriment. If I want to talk to one that will use an ounce of empathy towards me, I tend to call her.

"And Gemma is only a year and a bit younger than me. She's suffering from some kind of daddy issues; I can't work out where they've stemmed from since it was our mum we lost when we were teens."

It slips out of my mouth before I realise I've said it. It's a weird one; I don't love bringing up Mum's death because it makes people uncomfortable and they don't usually know what to say and then I feel guilty that they feel weird.

"Sorry, too much info."

Gus stops in his tracks and turns to face me. "How is that too much info? I feel like we've barely scraped the surface of Sara." I stop a few steps in front of him, glancing up at his scrunched forehead and soft eyes. "I'm sorry to hear about your mum. Must've been tricky to lose her at that age and have felt so responsible for your sisters."

"Dad was around. He worked long hours as a fireman, but he *was* around. It wasn't *just* me."

"But still," he says. "That sounds hard."

Ugh. Kill me. A rising panic grows in my lungs. I don't like pity. Pity makes my skin crawl. I am fine. I am strong.

I am not a victim. And I especially don't want a man to see me as any type of weak, so I change the conversation.

"How we doing for time?"

I know he almost asks a follow up question. He looks like he isn't done with his Sara scrutiny but then his eyes are drawn to his watch. "Slightly ahead of schedule. Just gone half three."

"Come on then," I say, nodding ahead. "No time to spare."

Another fifteen minutes later and we're strolling along proper paved paths towards a modern port with several huge cruise ships. It was something I considered – going on a bigger cruise. I would've certainly saved money, but they just didn't feel like *me*. I like my peace too much and besides it didn't give the quaint honeymoon vibe I was after.

Hence, the smaller more expensive option.

It should be near by now. We keep strolling, searching for that sleek, modern design. I turn my phone on to see if there are any messages coming through about where they're docked but it only gives me departure times.

"This is weird," I say. "In the messages, it says the departure times from the port are every fifteen minutes. I don't understand. That doesn't make any sense. Surely there's just one time?"

Gus frowns at me, bewildered. "Let me see?"

I twist the phone to show him as the battery percentage jumps lower again.

"Huh. Where is it then?"

"I have no idea. But it's not *here*."

After a few more minutes of hoping it might magically appear and losing hope, we find ourselves in another port office. This time a friendly middle-aged lady helps us gladly, unlike the grumpy giant in Split.

"Which cruise are you on please?" she asks. I reel the details off to her as she types on her computer, her face getting increasingly confused. "Are you sure you are departing from Dubrovnik?"

"Yes. Absolutely." I show her the messages.

As if she gets a lightbulb moment, she smiles broadly. "Ah yes. I can see here that they've made arrangements to taxi guests in from the ship to the port of Old Town on smaller boats. You'll need to go there instead."

"*Oh*. And how far is that?"

She takes a map out of her drawer and places it on the desk, marking where we are now and where we need to go. Of course, it's the absolute opposite end of the city.

Gah!

I school my voice. "And how long will that take?"

"About a thirty-minute walk or ten minutes by taxi."

I glance at Gus. Gus glances at me. With a hasty thank you, we use every last spark of energy in our bones, fighting the sunburn and blisters, to race towards the road in hopes of finding a taxi.

Twelve

Luckily there's a huddle of taxis in front of the port. We dive into the backseat of the next available car and Gus tells the driver where we're headed. "We need to get there fast, if at all possible, please. We're very late." He's so polite. I don't know why that surprises me about him. I guess I thought a famous popstar might be brattier than this.

The driver twists in his seat, his slick, silver hair combed back.

Huh. Why do taxi drivers always smell so good? It's a heady mix of mint and tobacco. Or maybe it's because I smell terrible. "I can only get you to entrance of Old Town. You go rest of way on foot."

"Perfect. Thanks, mate," Gus says.

We're barely strapped in before he drives keenly through the city streets towards our destination. His radio is playing loud Europop I haven't heard before. Gus whips his sunglasses and hat off, rearranging his curls and running a hand down his dust-covered face.

It doesn't matter that that's exactly what a furious alpha cowboy would do because I'm not thinking about that.

The taxi driver keeps checking his rearview mirror. Initially, I suspect it's due to the busy city traffic, but as it continues, I notice his gaze intensifying on Gus with wider and wider eyes.

Oops. Should have kept that disguise on, Popstar.

He presses some buttons on his phone, set up with hands free in the centre consol, and Gus stiffens at the opening beats of a new song playing over the speakers.

It's a more defined sound than the Europop we were just listening to.

"This is your song, no?" the taxi man asks, absolutely buzzing with glee.

Good. This is fine. No need to panic.

Why didn't we have a briefing session on what to do in this situation? I stare at Gus, wide-eyed. But he laughs, sitting back.

"Oh, I see. You think I'm that guy from the band."

"You are!"

He shakes his head, amused. "Nah. Sorry mate, I just look like him. I get this all the bloody time. It's so funny. I'm actually here with my wife. We're exploring Croatia."

Not the wife thing again. Nobody is going to buy this. And besides, I'm the worst actress on Earth.

I let my face do the talking. Gus holds his hand out to me, a questioning grin on his face. I want to shake my head, but then again, I also don't want him to get noticed. If he gets swarmed by fans, then there's not a chance we'll make it to the boat in time.

I drop my hand into his gently. His fingers wind with mine, twisting so that I'm nudged even closer towards him.

"My daughter is in love with this man," the taxi driver says, pointing at his phone where the album cover is displayed.

There's a glint in Gus's eye. "Ah really? I think the guy singing now is the one who looks like me actually."

I take too much interest in the song. There's a scratchy sort of depth to it that's kind of sexy.

Ok, fine. So, I *can* understand why girls go crazy for it.

Once we arrive outside Old Town, the driver pulls into the taxi drop-off and I open my phone to access my wallet app so I can pay. Except I can't. Because once again my phone is dead.

Bollocks.

"Shit," I say. "Did we have any of that cash left?"

Gus blinks at me. "No, we used it on the coffee this morning. Why?"

"My phone is dead. Do you have any way of paying?"

"No, I…"

"You can't pay?" the driver asks, twisting in his seat.

"I'm *so* sorry. My phone has died. It's been *the* worst day." I regret to admit I consider using one of my old university tricks for a free ride and flash a tit, but luckily, he comes up with a solution before the words find my tongue.

"You are, Gus. You are," he says, pointing at the subject. "You sign this T-shirt, and I let you go."

"I'm really not…" Gus starts but one glance at me and whatever my face is portraying (horrified exasperation), has him nodding. "Alright. Yeah. You got me." He laughs. "I *am* Gus from Just4Summer."

"My daughter has poster of you all over house. You are him. I am not dumb."

"I'm sorry. I'm trying to stay undercover. Alright, you've got a deal. You have a pen?"

The man fishes around in his glove box and produces a red biro. He then proceeds to pull his T-shirt off, leaving us with the view of his hairy bare chest. So at least one of us got our tits out.

"Write it to Adriana. Say you love her," he says, pointing at Gus – almost intimidatingly. Although he gives me a smile, gesturing with his hands. "Obviously his love is only for you. But you'll spare him this one time. Yes?"

I shrug. "Oh, sure. Love to share."

The corners of Gus's lips fidget again as he gets to work signing the shit out of that sweaty white polo top.

Once he's done, the man shakes his hand and we're flying back out the doors and through the main streets of Old Town. Gus puts his hat and sunglasses back on as we push through tour groups and busy queues that clog the pathways. It's busy, hot and extraordinarily beautiful. A slice of me, as I pant desperately towards our destination, weeps at missing the chance to see it properly. Maybe I can come back one day.

Neatly-kept limestone buildings with pretty, shuttered windows surround us as we charge down the main street towards the bell tower. The paved road is uneven and so spotless it's almost slippery in these sandals. When I glance to the sides, distracted by its beauty, I see fascinating side streets practically brimming with history and quaint little businesses. My heart snaps – I want to explore this city almost more than getting back on the cruise.

We come to a dead end outside a cathedral. There's a wedding going on, people cheering outside, throwing confetti at the bride. I find myself staring as Gus witters on about where to go next. It's not that I'm jealous... Well, ok, maybe I am. They look happy and deliriously in love as the groom dips his bride and the guests cheer and clap. I don't think that scene would've happened at my wedding.

And the fact that I'm admitting that to myself now, at this inconvenient time for reflection, makes me both envious and horrified. How close was I to securing a future that I didn't even really want? What happened to me?

"Sara!" Gus barks, waving a hand in front of my face. "Where did you go? Are you listening?"

I blink several times, then nod. "Yeah."

He laughs. "No, you weren't."

"I am now." I shake myself out of it. "What next?"

He proceeds to show me the leaflet we were handed at the port office. According to the map, the port is meant to be through an arch, under a bell tower, at this end of Old Town. We glance around, trying to find said arch.

Once we've worked out where to go, we bolt in the right direction.

As we're navigating twists and turns, the bell chimes from the tower.

A tourist walking in the other direction shouts, "RING THE BELL!" This is followed by a round of laughs from passers-by. I don't have time to work out what it means.

"What time is it?" I ask Gus, panting as we push through the crowds. It's so damn busy here. I think late afternoon is peak tourist hours, despite it being sweltering. Surely, this place is so much nicer in the evenings or early hours when it's cooler.

"I don't want to tell you," Gus says – a far too ominous a response for the situation at hand.

But it's for good reason.

At the port there's no sign of our ship.

No staff in the familiar uniform.

Only fancy smaller yachts with expensive looking owners.

There's no way our cruise, despite looking like a yacht, could squeeze into this harbour. I walk a little further along towards the end of the dock. The cruise is there, but it's a speck in the distance, as big as the end of my thumb and appears to be moving away.

I exhale slowly, and as I do, a devastating feeling washes through me from head to toe. I feel a warm tear run down my cheek. Pressure starts to build in my chest again, so I take a seat on a stone bench and press my face into my hands.

Someone takes the spot next to me, and I can tell by his soft breathing that it's Gus.

"This is karma," I whimper. "I deserve this."

He makes a tutting sound. "I find that very hard to believe," he says.

I sit tall again, giving him a miserable glance. "I ran away."

I knew coming on my honeymoon was a bad idea. I knew it was too soon. I don't believe in fate and myths and luck like my friends do. I'm too much of a realist for that. But I do believe this is the universe's way of telling me that I've royally fucked up.

"I was meant to be getting married two months ago," I say, sniffing. "And now I'm here on my own."

"Shit. Ok, what happened?"

"I couldn't go through with it. I left before the ceremony."

His eyes widen. "So, you're like a runaway bride?"

I make a half-laughing, half-sobbing sound that ricochets off the huge stone wall behind us before dropping my head again and whispering, "Yes."

Gus blows out a breath. "That's... I mean, are you ok? What happened?"

"Ugh. It's so complicated."

"Try me."

"I think he was cheating on me."

He makes a face. "You only think?"

"That's the thing," I say, splaying my hands. "That's exactly it. A few days before the wedding, I stumbled across some overly emotional, flirty messages to one of his female colleagues. He told her he loved her and said some less than flattering things about me but then brushed it all off as a joke. He made her out to be the one who was acting weirdly. I still don't know what was going on beyond that. I had a feeling but no evidence and he swore it was nothing. And... Well, we were meant to be so excited for our wedding... I didn't know what to do. I went numb."

"Oh Sara," Gus says, sighing. "He sounds like a prick!"

"The thing is, I feel like I should be more distraught."

Gus turns his whole body towards me so that his knees graze mine. "You mean like the other night? That seemed pretty distraught to me."

I knew he'd bring this up again. I mean, how could he not? But the casual way in which he says it has me squirming. "That was... No. I was just really drunk."

He raises his eyebrows. "Right. So, you feel like this whole thing is karma because you don't feel sad enough about not marrying the man who was probably cheating on you?"

"Yes," I say but shake my head. "No. I mean, it's not that. It's that I can't shake this guilty feeling. It's like I did something wrong or made a bad decision that led to this, even though I know I didn't."

"I don't know you well, but I suspect you make good decisions."

"And how did you come to that conclusion?"

"You don't seem like the type to make random, mad-dash choices. Current situation notwithstanding." He grins, trying to shift the mood but blows out a breath when my lips wobble. "So what? What's the guilt really about?"

I've been thinking about this exact thought for weeks. Trying to claw together the reason that my stomach swoops every time I think about the wedding. It's as though I'm in trouble, as if I've done something wrong. I know I haven't. I know it was all him. And yet I can't shrug this horrible feeling that maybe I should've waited until I had more evidence, that I shouldn't have trusted my gut feeling alone.

I don't know how to explain this to the man I barely know so I take a different angle.

"Well... This is also *our* honeymoon. Even if it was all my idea and I've virtually bankrupted myself to make it happen."

"Ok so let me get this straight. You're feeling guilty because you're on a holiday you planned and paid for yourself, and you feel like you shouldn't be here... for yourself?"

I pause while his words sink in. "Well, when you say it like that it sounds insane."

"Right." He nods, expression telling.

I shake my head. "No. You don't get to do that. Men aren't allowed to diagnose insanity in women. You lot used up your quota with all those witch trials. It's not allowed anymore."

"I'm not calling *you* insane. I'm calling your guilt insane."

"Well, you're not allowed."

"Ok," he says, raising his hands. "I stand corrected. I am a bad man. I am infected with the patriarchy."

"Yes. Yes, you are. You need cleansing."

"How do you do that?" he asks, genuinely curious.

I shrug, drying my tears on the back of my hand. "I'll throw some vodka at you later and it burns right out."

"Delicious."

"*Ugh*. What do we even do now?" I ask, feeling depleted and pathetic.

I never usually allow myself a moment of self-pity like this, especially in front of other people. I'm unsure what it is about Gus that makes me feel like he's immune, it's probably because he's a stranger who I'm likely never going to see again. And yet, something tells me I, maybe, dangerously, and inadvisably started trusting him.

A celebrity, no less.

Gus crosses his arms, then spreads his thighs as he leans back on the bench with a sigh. Exactly, what a FAC would do. "I say we find somewhere to stay for the night. Explore the city. Figure out our next move." He pauses to see if I'm going to protest. When I don't, he continues. "We can eat copious amounts of carbohydrates, fish and garlic, then share a bottle of wine."

"No," I say, shaking my head. "I want my own bottle."

He laughs. "Deal. Have we got enough money?"

"For wine?"

"For a place to stay."

"I have *some* money. It should get us through the night. Only issue is I *only* have access to my money through my phone, which is dead *again*, so we'll need to find somewhere to charge it."

Gus nods, hopping up from the bench and holding his hand out to me to help me up.

"I'll call my sister. I'm sure she won't mind throwing some money our way. I'll keep the reasons vague. She too likes to charge me interest," he says, with a spark in his eye.

"I don't want your bloody interest," I say, giving him a stern look.

He only grins, passing me his phone. "Type your bank details in. I'll ask her to send it to you since I have no access to my bank right now."

"Oh, sure." I take his phone, sniff back the last of my tears and give him a look. "But won't she find that suspicious?"

He shrugs. "I doubt it. I've been in weirder, vaguer situations."

"You're not an elaborate scam artist, are you?"

"There's only one way to find out."

I shake my head, fighting a smile. Once I've sorted the details and passed his phone back to him, I say, "Right, shall we go on a hunt for an internet café then?"

He nods. "It's possible that the taxi guy has already outed me to the press but let's give it a go, shall we?"

"Nah. Adriana would never disrespect her favourite popstar like that."

"True." He holds a hand to his chest, dropping his chin. "She is my one true love."

I faux gag. "Please tell me you didn't write that."

He snorts. "Nah. We're trained not to do that. It encourages unhinged behaviour from fans."

"What's the most unhinged fan experience you've had?"

He cringes. "Can't talk about it."

"That bad?"

"No. I legally *can't* talk about it."

Despite myself, I actually laugh. "Are you serious?"

He nods. "The second most unhinged thing was finding a fan hiding in my closet after a concert, wearing the exact same outfit as my then girlfriend was that evening. Same hair, same clothes, even the same make-up."

"No! She was going to trick you?"

"I mean… She was a least a foot shorter and didn't speak English… I know I'm a bit of a fool, but you have to try harder than that."

"Amazing," I shake my head. "I applaud her dedication."

"She moved on to Callum anyway. And now there are *two* restraining orders against her."

"Solid effort."

He grins across at me. "I'm starting to think you're the type to root for the villain."

"I just like seeing women kicking arse. That's all."

He clicks his finger at me. "Great point. I have no comeback. Charge phone and then wine?"

I nod. "Yes. Like a bucket of wine."

Thirteen

Cruise Location – At Sea
Next Port – Kotor
Time of Arrival – 12:00 (GMT+1)

A few hours later, we stroll through the old town in a daze, heading in no particular direction. I don't know about Gus, but my feet are burning. I'm parched, burnt and exhausted. We were fortunate enough to find a café where I could charge my phone, swapping with Gus once I hit 50 per cent.

We're hoping to find somewhere tucked away so Gus can maintain his cover while we eat and drink and beg whoever owns the place to let me charge my phone some more. Luckily, we find a wine bar off the main street and manage to grab a table in the back.

Gus orders half the menu before cringing and glancing at me. "I keep forgetting I'm spending your money. I'll chase my sister. She hasn't replied yet."

"It's all good, I've already told you!"

"Yeah, yeah, but soon as I'm back on the ship I'll transfer you what I owe plus the seven hundred per cent interest."

I groan. "No interest."

"Fine, Sara," he says, smirking. "You drive a hard bargain. I'll pay you—"

"Stoooop!"

"—one thousand per cent."

"You're really annoying. Has anyone ever told you that?"

He adds two bottles of red wine to the order before glancing back at me, swallowing. "Yeah. I've heard that before," he says lightly, but it doesn't diminish the shadow of something deeper in his words.

I almost press him on it but then our drinks arrive and he raises a glass.

"To freedom," he says coyly.

I roll my eyes. "To getting back to our ship," I counter. "Ok, so," I start, pulling up the map and zooming out. "We need to get to Kotor tomorrow by midday. According to the itinerary, the ship is only in the harbour for a few hours. It's the only stop where the ship actively recommends you join a tour."

"It's like they don't trust their guests not to miss the cruise."

"Can you imagine why?"

"Not a clue."

"We could drive tonight?" I suggest. "At least then we'd get there in time. I'm sure there's a car hire nearby."

"Oh good, just what this trip is missing, reckless endangerment."

I eye him. *Fair point.* "Fine. Also I'd hate to waste those bottles of wine you just ordered." He nods, agreeing as I check the travel time between Dubrovnik and Kotor and sigh. It's only a couple of hours but there are border crossings which cause delays. "We'll need to leave early in the morning to be safe, I'm not taking any chances."

"How early?"

"First thing," I say, giving the bottles of wine a weary glance.

He laughs at me. "Going by this morning, I fear waking you up early and getting you out the door before dawn might be a challenge in itself."

I don't even look at him for fear of giving him the satisfaction of being correct. "You've known me for twenty-four hours, Popstar. You don't get to pretend you know me."

He just smiles as if to say – *but am I wrong?* Which is not the point. Not the point at all. Is there some truth to it? Maybe. Does he get to be the one to point it out? No. He does not.

"Hiring a car seems like a lot of work. Why don't we book a coach—"

"No," I interrupt him. "No. I am not doing another coach."

"Ok, ok," he throws his hands up in surrender. "We can hire a car. Assuming you drive?"

I shake my head. "I do but…" my voice trails off. *Damn.* "I don't have my driving licence on me."

"Huh, too bad," he says, shrugging.

"Wait. Do *you* not drive?"

He twists his lips. "Of course I drive! I did my test years ago – passed first time, by the way – I just haven't actually used it in a while. And I also don't have my licence."

"Ooh. You're defensive. Ha! *Did wittle popstar always have a driver?*"

He points a finger at me. "Stop it. I'm trying to grow here. Can't you tell? Be kind to me. I'm a novice at all this. Just because you've been an adult since you were born."

I have to laugh at this. Despite everything, I hear myself

properly cackle. I hold onto the table for balance.

"You have no idea how on the money you are. My dad has always said that about me. Says I was parenting him before I was three."

Crinkles form at the corners of his eyes as he fights a full-blown grin. "See. I told you. I have a good grasp of who you are, Sara. It's one of my superpowers."

"You have more than one?"

He shrugs. "I do but," he leans across the table towards me and whispers, "the other one is top secret."

"Hmm, sure." I've dealt with my fair share of men like him. In my experience a witty man, the type that can laugh your knickers right off, often comes with trauma and commitment issues.

I would delve deeper, but at that moment, the waitress returns with bowls of Croatian-style tapas. I immediately grab my fork, stab some patatas bravas and close my eyes as the first delicious, garlicky bite oozes over my tongue. "*Ohmyfuckinggawd.*"

He smiles, a spark in his eyes like I've just done something very funny.

Again.

"So, what do I have to do to get security clearance and find out your top-secret superpower?"

He's mid bite. "Nope. That's also classified." He takes another sip of wine and changes the subject. "Let's plan. So, we're not getting a coach. We can't get our own car. What do you suggest?"

"Well," I say, "Search results suggest either a ferry from Dubrovnik to Kotor, which takes two hours and leaves at six a.m., or a taxi."

"Six a.m. ferry sounds torturous. Let's take a taxi. Can we get one?"

I have several suggestions on my phone, but I opt to ask our waitress for help instead. She's more than happy to, and within ten minutes she's managed to arrange a taxi for the morning, picking us up outside Old Town and taking us straight to the dock in Kotor. I can actually feel myself starting to relax.

To keep things simple, I browse places on Airbnb nearby that we can book instantly. Fortunately, there's a quaint loft a few blocks away, and without thinking, I book it.

It's only after the confirmation email comes through that it occurs to me that we're sharing again. And there is only one bed.

Fourteen

As the sun drops below the horizon, the ancient city is swallowed up by shadows that consume the narrow alleyways. We take turns popping into shops to source a fresh change of clothes, and after that we enjoy an evening walk exploring the city. We stop off for cocktails at this little bar tucked into the old walls, watching the waves shimmer under the amber sky.

"So, your honeymoon, huh?"

I groan but it's half-hearted now I'm suitably tipsy. It's not the same as the other night. I'm not panicking as he brings up this conversation. I'm not drowning in the betrayal. I'm looser now, almost relaxed about it. That horrible sinking feeling but a whisper in my gut.

"Yeah. The most romantic trip of my life," I say sarcastically.

"I think it's great that you came anyway."

"I nearly didn't."

"And that would've been a tragedy. You wouldn't have seen this view, sipping a delicious cocktail in excellent company," he points out, nodding at our absolutely divine surroundings.

"Again, is somebody else here that I don't know about?"

He smirks, taking a sip, his eyes never leaving mine.

I sigh. "I just can't believe I didn't clue on, you know?" Because that's the real crux of the issue. Two months on, the heartbreak, embarrassment and betrayal is subsiding. But in its wake I'm left with this sense of having let myself down for missing it, for not reacting the way I wanted to in the moment, for allowing him to hurt me. "I'm so fucking angry with myself."

Gus shakes his head, putting his glass down. "How could you have known?"

I shrug. "Maybe I worked too hard. Maybe I wasn't around enough. Maybe I just didn't open my eyes and see what was happening right in front of me?"

He nods like it adds up. "I know how you feel," he says. "I've been in the same position."

"You have?" I don't know why this surprises me. I guess I thought nobody would cheat on a celebrity. Clearly, I'm very wrong.

He makes a dismissive face like it's nothing to him anymore. "My skin grew tough pretty quickly in this industry but I learnt one important thing."

I lean forward, resting my chin in my hands. "And what's that?"

"You can only control what you do. How you react. The things you say. The way you treat others. It's the only part you own. I used to think people did things because of the way I acted. I'd be let down and immediately place that blame on myself." He twists his lips. "I changed how I acted and they still let me down. Because it didn't matter what I did. It was never about me, it was about them."

"So you're saying I shouldn't blame myself?"

"I'm saying, if you'd done everything differently, it might've still ended the same way. I know it's easier said than done, trust me I do, but assigning his actions to him and making him accountable in your own mind will help you."

I swallow. "I'm plenty angry with him. I realised on the wedding day that even if it was only messages between him and his colleague; it was already betrayal. Especially with all the things he said about me, acting like I was ruining his life by being an *uptight workaholic* who never had time for him. That I was impossible to be around. He never said any of this to my face. I felt blindsided. In the end, it didn't matter if it had gone further than that. He'd already lost me. So, I never asked."

Gus nods like he's impressed.

"What?"

"I'm just impressed by you, that's all."

The room we've booked is up a narrow alleyway which is essentially a quarter of a mile of steps. My whole body wilts before I remember this is nothing compared to the challenges I've faced in my life and pull myself together. By the time we reach the building we're both out of breath. Me more so. And my ankle feels like it's made of sugar paper.

Obviously, I don't voice any of this. I don't want him to think I'm complaining.

Gus types the code into the box that releases the key,

then we climb more steps. Four flights to be exact. He opens the door, and we find ourselves in a clean, cosy loft room that might be nice if it wasn't the same temperature as the fiery pits of hell.

"Ah," Gus says. "I just worked out why this was available at such short notice."

"Is it because it rivals Dante's *Inferno*?"

"More like the fiery pits of Mount Doom." Gus strides across the room, ducking to avoid banging his head on the low beamed ceilings. "Ooh there's a fan." He clicks it on, and we both stand there, dripping in sweat as it burps and hiccups to life.

"Turn it off, Popstar. The engine in that thing will make this room even hotter cause that isn't doing sod all."

"Give it a second. It might warm up."

"Exactly. That's what I'm afraid of."

He concedes, switching it off at the wall.

Once we've plonked our bags down and gotten used to the cramped space, we take turns in the bathroom. It's just as tight in here – I have to sidestep into the shower. Once I turn the water on, I can't seem to make it cold enough. It's tepid at best. I dry off then dress into some clean knickers and pull the J4S black T-shirt back on, as it's practically a nightie anyway, before running a brush through my wet hair and pulling it over one shoulder.

Back in the room Gus is frowning at his phone in deep thought.

"Everything alright?" I ask. My brain skips straight to the part where he's been found out, his team are on the way to get him, and I'll be stranded alone again. I should be fine with that, but something squeezes somewhere. Something crazy, like I'd miss him. Or miss the company, at least.

He glances up quickly like he forgot I was there. His eyes snag on my bare legs for half a second before he finds my eyes and smiles. "Fine," he says. But it feels so forced, I can't be sure. He takes his turn to shower and when he comes back out any trace of upset is gone. It's slightly cooler now that the sun has set and the windows are open, but not by much. I settle on the lumpy bed, eyelids heavy, mumble good night and kill the lights.

It's then that I hear Gus's broken breathing as he fidgets on his carefully laid-out blanket and pillows.

"Are you ok?" I whisper in the darkness.

"Mmm. Fine," he says, utterly unconvincingly.

"Are you hurt?"

"Nope."

"*Gus*," I warn. "I'm a big sister. I have a sixth sense for this stuff. I can tell something is wrong with you."

"I'm ok, Sara," he says but his voice is so schooled I can tell he's lying.

I sit up and glare down at his long silhouette on the ground. I close my eyes for a second as I feel my brain trip over itself with compassion. I could be so powerful if I just stopped caring. *Think of the things I could do.* "Gus. Would you like to swap?"

He laughs, a strained sound. "Sara, I could be dying and I would still insist you had the bed."

"Why?"

"Because..."

"I'm a woman?"

"I didn't say that."

"Were you going to? Is it because you're infected with the

patriarchy?” I tease, attempting to get a rise out of him. I know he isn’t. All the same, it’s fun watching him squirm. “I forgot to throw a shot of vodka at you earlier. Is it because you think women are the weaker sex? Is it chivalry?”

“Holy shit. *Sara.* I didn’t mean…” He breathes out heavily, barely disguising the hiss of pain as he rolls onto his back. “Look, I’m fine. I’d say the same thing to anyone, man or woman. Please go to sleep. It’s not a big deal.”

“Nope. I won’t be able to now, knowing you’re suffering on the floor.”

I swing my legs out of the bed and pull the top sheet off, scanning the floor for a good place to throw my pillow.

“What are you doing?” Gus grunts as he sits up. “I’m not suffering. It’s a light backache from all the walking.”

That does it. “Swap. Now.”

“No. I’m not swapping.”

“Then I’m going to match your stubbornness and sleep down here too.”

Gus groans before resorting to more exasperated laughter. “Sleep on the bed. *Please.*”

“No.”

“Ugh. What if we both sleep on the bed then? But top and tails?”

“I do *not* want your blistered, clumpy feet anywhere near my face.”

“I washed them?” he offers, as if that might be my issue here.

I make a face. He can’t see it in the darkness, but I make it, nonetheless. “Washing them doesn’t make them any less clumpy. My statement stands. You take the bed. It’s only fair.”

"What if we build a pillow fort between us?"

"I'm not the one who's worried about sharing a bed."

He's standing now, a tall, dark figure with the navy sky outlining his head from the window behind him. "Well, *I'm* not bothered."

A forbidden thrill runs through my body. "Fine. Let's share the bed. If you think it will help you recover?"

"I already said this isn't for me. I'm just hoping you'll stop harassing me and let me sleep in peace."

"Right. Sure."

He helps me up from the floor, then places his pillow down on his side as I do the same on mine. He then proceeds to roll the knitted throw up long ways and lies it down through the middle of the bed. "There you go."

I sniff a laugh. "Practically twin beds."

I can't see his face properly, but I swear I see that cheeky glint sparkle in his eye as he climbs onto the mattress. He's only wearing boxer shorts, which is the same as the night before, except he had a sheet wrapped around him all night, so it wasn't even an issue. Now, it feels quite a bit more intimate.

He's certainly not shy. That's for sure.

"Did you check your bank account by the way?" he asks.

"Yes. Your sister sent a grand. I won't need it all, so if you send me your details, I'll transfer the rest back."

"Sure," he says, sarcastically. "I'll do that."

"Gus…"

"I'll sort my sister out. You don't need to worry about her, she has plenty of money. She won't even miss it."

I consider fighting it but instead, I roll over, throwing

my legs out of the bed and say, "I'm just going to nip to the loo."

There's a small wooden staircase between the main bedroom and the cramped hall that leads to the bathroom. I'm not sure if it's the wine, or the cocktails, or the stupid, misplaced adrenaline rushing through my limbs that does it, maybe it's simply that my body is tired from all the walking in shitty, unsupportive shoes, but either way, my body and brain don't collaborate, and I mess up my footing on the stairs.

My ankle feels like it snaps in half.

"Argh!" I yip. My hands save my face from smacking against the tiled floor but pain lurches like fire through my lower leg.

His shadow is over me in seconds, his hand on my upper arm.

"What happened?"

"I fucking tripped. What an idiot."

"You're not an idiot. It's dark and you don't know the place."

"Still…" I whimper. Pathetic. "I don't have time for this. *We* don't."

Gus breathes out slowly as he tells me to close my eyes and pops the light on. I slowly peek through shuttered lids at him kneeling by my legs. He stares at my already swelling ankle, mystified.

"Not much for first aid?" I ask.

He cringes. "Can't say I've ever had to do it."

I roll my eyes. "Just help me up, Popstar. I'll need some ice."

"With water?"

"No. In a towel," I say. He simply frowns. "To put on the swelling. It helps."

"Right. Yes. Ok," he says, running a hand through his hair. "This stuff doesn't come naturally to me."

I twist, flinching at the way the pain intensifies at the slightest movement, and sit up to take a proper look at it. It's definitely swollen, but then again, so is my other one. Hopefully, it's nothing.

"How come they're so swollen?"

I sigh. "I have poor circulation. It always happens to me. My friends dragged me on a walking holiday one time, and my ankles got so big they had to cut me out of my jeans."

He tries not to smile. "Well, thankfully, you aren't in jeans."

No. I'm in just a very oversized T-shirt which is bunched up at the top of my thighs. As if he's drawn attention to the fact he awkwardly wets his lips and glances back towards the bed. "Can I pick you up?" he asks.

"Really?"

"Unless you'd rather crawl to the bed?"

"No," I say, feeling my lips draw down. "I'm sorry about this but I do still need the loo though."

He nods, his eyes softening. "Ok. So, I'll lift you onto the loo."

"You can't do that!"

"Why not?" he asks.

"Because…" I use my hands to gesture wildly at invisible truths in the air. "You're not a nurse."

"We can pretend." He says it so casually it could be taken innocently, and yet, there's a tone there. I tilt my head to let him know I'm onto him. He laughs. "*What?*"

"I am not role-playing doctors and nurses with you."

"Hey, where did that come from? I'm simply offering to help you to the loo then back to bed where we will share a double mattress with zero romantic tension. I don't like your insinuations."

I sniff. "Hmm. You've had too much media training."

At this he guffaws. "I promise you that is not what my team say. There's no such thing as too much media training." He reaches out, offering me his arm. I already know it's going to be rock solid even before I touch it. My hands grasp onto him as his other arm comes around me, his fingers pressing against the softer part of my lower back.

He also winces as we rise. Which reminds me. "Oh, your back. Don't hurt yourself."

"Hush. I'm fine. I'll help you those last few steps to the loo," he offers, as I place my spare arm around his shoulders for balance. Once I'm close enough, I huff at him which he takes as a cue to leave.

"I'll wait outside."

"Gus," I call a minute later, having hopped painfully across the bathroom to wash and dry my hands. "Ready."

He opens the door. Before I can even think about how best to navigate this, he wraps one arm under my legs so that I'm forced to grapple with his shoulders as he swoops me off my feet. I can't fight the squeal that escapes me as he strides up the steps, switching lights off as he goes.

"So the bad news," he mutters, "is that we have no ice."

"Is there good news?"

"I have found a flannel which I can pour some room

temperature water on to wrap around your ankle?"

I whimper again. It's not a good look on me. "I'll be ok."

"I can go out?"

"No, it's fine."

"I'll go out," he says. "I'll ask a restaurant."

"And what if you're spotted?"

"It will be in pursuit of your comfort so…"

"No, Gus. Honestly, I'm fine."

My eyes haven't adjusted to the darkness at all as he softly places me down on the bed. But he doesn't immediately remove his arms from underneath me, his knee pressing into the mattress, dipping from his weight. "You know, you're allowed to be vulnerable, right? You don't have to kick yourself when you're down."

Air fills my lungs a little too quickly, that pesky sharp sensation building behind my eyes. I don't know what it is about his words, or the way he pulls his arms from underneath me away so carefully, like I'm breakable, like I'm something to handle with care, but I feel it remove a weight from off my chest.

I frown. "I don't like being a nuisance. It's not fair on the people around me."

"You're not a nuisance. You had an accident."

I shrug. "Still."

"Sara," he pauses for effect. "You're not a nuisance."

I want to push the words away. To reject them. Because that's not true. I don't get to be broken, or sorry, or clumsy. That's for everyone else. I have to have my shit together all the time in case somebody else collapses.

His footsteps sound as he heads back to his side of the bed and I breathe carefully to force the emotions back.

"Good night, Sara," he says, shuffling beside me. "Thank you for worrying about me."

"Night, Gus." I swallow thickly to control my voice. I don't want him to know how much he's affected me. "Thank you for taking care of me."

Fifteen

I wake to find my mouth watering.

This is most unusual since it's usually as dry as the Sahara Desert in the morning and requires instant hydration via strong coffee. Not this morning though. This morning, I am greeted to the delightful waft of freshly baked pastries.

I slowly peel my eyes open.

Gus is already dressed, hair damp from a shower. He's sitting by the window, staring out at the city view. On the table nearby I spot four cups of coffee and brown, folded paper bags which I pray are filled with warm pastries.

I sit up slowly, frowning. "You got us breakfast?"

He glances at me over his shoulder, smiling. "Good morning, sunshine. We have forty-five minutes until we need to leave. I've been building up the courage to wake you."

I mock scowl at him. "What's that supposed to mean?"

He presses his lips together and shrugs, playfulness lighting his eyes. "Nothing. Nothing at all."

"Hmm," I say. "Pass me the coffee. And whatever is in those bags."

"*Please*," Gus says, dragging out the sound in a way that has my core clenching.

"Please," I say, holding his stare until he laughs and brings it to me anyway.

He passes a coffee straight into my hands and places another cup beside me. "I got you two." He waits for me to thank him, but my brain isn't fully awake yet, so I just end up blinking at him till he grins and walks back to the window.

"I do prefer my own room," I mutter. "Although I could get used to bedside service in the mornings."

He chuckles quietly before tossing a small box on my bed. I get this weird flashback to Mike's proposal and nearly choke on my first sip. It wasn't that Mike tossed the ring at me, it's just he didn't exactly get down on one knee either. But the déjà vu is jarring. I take a moment to regain my composure before looking down at the object. Fortunately, it's much better than a ring. It's painkillers. And then I remember: my ankle. *Oof!* As if my brain has just caught up, a dull ache makes my toes tingle. But it wasn't my first thought upon waking, and I'll take that as a good sign. I hope I can walk on it as who knows what the day ahead might throw at us. I wash two tablets down with more coffee and hope for the best.

Exactly forty-five minutes later, I'm dressed, fed and appropriately caffeinated. We head to Pile Gate, the ancient access point for Old Town and wait for the taxi to arrive with our jumble of bags. Part of me is worried the driver won't show, but all my anxiety dissipates when a modern black Mercedes stops out front.

"Oh, thank God," I say, sighing. After yesterday's sweaty, coach ride, I think we deserve a little luxury.

"This is more like it," he agrees, stepping forward to open the door for me. He offers me his hand.

He's babied me since I first stepped out of bed this morning, my ankle now a lovely shade of blue. Gus isn't much better himself. He hisses every time he has to stand up or bend down. I'm just glad that we've picked a sensible option to get to Kotor. I read on travel blogs last night that taking the coach through the border controls can take hours so I'm hoping it's much quicker than that for us.

The driver takes on the hilly lanes with ease as we zoom out of Dubrovnik. Once we're on the main road, I get a great glimpse of the city below us. The terracotta roofs and blue sea beyond is a delicious contrast, no wonder it's such a desired holiday destination.

I frown at my phone once we're past.

"I haven't had a notification about docking in Kotor yet."

Gus has been busy staring intensely out of the window his side, but he relaxes now, turning his attention to me. "Maybe it's because they're planning on docking in the evening. I'm sure there were two evening stops."

"You're probably right."

"I reckon we get there, have a stroll, grab some lunch, then before we know it, they'll have arrived and we can safely reboard our luxury cruise."

I throw my head back and close my eyes. The last forty-eight hours has been stressful. But also sort of fun? "I might sleep for a whole day."

"You're telling me, you didn't sleep like a baby last night?"

I glance at him nervously. I wonder if I spoke in my sleep again. I wonder what I said if I did. It's been years since I've shared my space at night – other than with Mike, obviously – but he never brought it up because he was such a deep sleeper and he either got used to it or never felt like it needed to be discussed.

I almost want to know if I still say the same things I did as a teenager. The things that made me cry whenever I got home from a sleepover because it was all my friends could talk about the morning after. It didn't take me long to cement myself as the outsider in friendship groups. I have always been too stubbornly independent to lean on them in a way that was required for those deeply intimate relationships – that is until I met Hattie at university, and she forced herself into my life with her chaotic, loveable energy.

"I don't know if I did," I say. "Was I snoring?"

"Not badly."

"*Ugh*. You're lying."

He doesn't deny it but shifts the conversation. "In all seriousness though, Sara, I just wanted to say thank you for bringing me along with you. I really appreciate that you didn't leave me to fend for myself at the port. I would probably be back in the UK by now otherwise. I actually feel like I've been able to enjoy being in another city, for the first time in…" His voice trails off and he shrugs.

I swallow. "Thanks for not being a terrible travelling partner."

He snorts. "Did you think I was going to be?"

"Do you know what you reminded me of? When I first saw you. You know, when you practically smashed my spritz all down my dress?"

"What?" he says, glancing at me in shock. I laugh at his reaction. "That was you?"

"You really didn't recognise me?"

He runs a hand down his face, lips parted in disbelief. "This makes so much sense now."

"What do you mean?"

"You practically balked at the sight of me that night at the bar."

"Ha!"

"I'm so sorry," he says, sincerity glowing warm in his eyes. "I was in hot pursuit. I'd been spotted and needed to get on the ship without being seen. I didn't want anyone to know where I was going or what I was doing."

"It's ok," I tell him. "I get it now."

He watches me for a moment, then nods.

I sniff, taking us back to the conversation before. "Have you seen *Shrek*?"

He makes a face, scrunching his nose. "I don't know if I like where this is going."

I can't help the evil chuckle that rattles out of me. "I thought you were going to be a real diva like Prince Charming."

Gus nods slowly before taking his cap off and flicking his curls back exactly the way Charming does it in the film.

I can't even fight the smile. "*See*. Can you blame me?"

"What I'm hearing is that you think I'm charming?"

"I *thought* you would be annoying and self-serving."

Gus blows out a dramatic breath. "Well, look at you, judging books by their covers."

"I was wrong," I admit, nodding. "You're only annoying."

"Ha!"

"You're not self-serving because you brought me coffees, pastries and painkillers and that is honestly one of the nicest things anyone has done for me in ages."

His smile softens at this statement. He almost looks sad. "Really?"

I feel like I've given something away, something I should have kept to myself, so I shrug. "Yeah, I guess."

"Oh, Sara," he sighs, shaking his head. I turn towards the window, cheeks ablaze.

We arrive in Kotor three hours later.

I sit in awe, taking in the old fortress, the lush mountains surrounding the city and the bay. As the buildings come into view, a thrill runs through me with the promise of another Old Town to explore. There's something about these ancient buildings, that make me feel so grounded and light.

It feels like an honour to be able to explore them.

We tip the driver once we arrive, having asked him to take us as close to the sights as possible. I check my phone for an update, but no word from the cruise yet. We agree to head straight to the docks, but there's no sign of the ship. We're actually ahead of schedule, for once. With time to spare, we decide to make the most of it. Gus dons his uncanny disguise, with those blacked-out sunglasses and backwards black cap and we spend the day wandering. We walk down narrow streets that lead to a beautiful square, filled with little tables and colourful awnings. Gus must take about a million photos. I pretend not to notice when he turns the attention on me.

We grab lunch at a cute café just as the sun dips behind a patch of grey clouds, drinking copious cups of coffee and fancy pastries with delicious fillings.

"You know I think we should go to the port office," I

say, after a few hours of sightseeing. "At least we can check what time the cruise is meant to arrive."

Gus nods. "Ok. Let's pay and head down there now."

I smile, taking a final sip. As we head in the direction of the port, steadily, thanks to my ankle, I ask, "What's with the camera then?"

"What do you mean?"

"Well, do you like photography? Have you always done it?"

"Oh right, yeah. It's what I *wanted* to be," he answers. Which makes no sense because…

"As in you didn't actually want to be a popstar?"

He shrugs. "It's not that. I did. *Obviously*. But whenever someone would ask me what I wanted to be as a kid, I always said a photographer. I used to go through disposable cameras weekly. When other kids asked for sweets or Pokémon cards, I asked for a camera. There was nothing I enjoyed more than picking up that little envelope from the corner shop, full of photos I'd taken, and spend the next few days going through them. Picking my favourites. Working out how to improve them for next time."

"Aww," I say, imagining him as a kid, all hopped up on excitement. "That's actually pretty sweet."

"Recently, I've been doing this thing: playing what ifs. What if the band had never got together? What if we hadn't been at the local fair where we were discovered? What if I'd actually punched Jax that morning for pissing me off and we all fell out and none of this ever happened? What then?"

I stare at him wide eyed. "Why did you nearly punch him?"

"He was texting my girlfriend."

"What?" I say, gobsmacked.

"Yeah."

"But weren't you like sixteen?"

He nods. "Yes. But I was in love with her."

"Oh. Well. That's cute."

He laughs, shaking his head. "Unfortunately, it turns out she was in love with Jax all along. She was just using me to get to him."

"Ouch."

"Yeah. To be fair, I got over it very quickly."

"Always a sign of a deep, endearing love."

He elbows me gently. "My *what if* led me to what I would be doing now, if I hadn't become a popstar."

"And that's photography?"

He shakes his head. "Honestly? I probably would have ended up doing carpentry with my dad and that would have been totally fine with me. But I loved photography, and art, growing up. After all the disposables, my parents bought me this snazzy camera for my thirteenth birthday, and I took it everywhere with me. So, I'm trying it out again. And I'm enjoying it. I have a laptop back on the cruise. I plan on editing what I have so far."

"So you want to explore it professionally?"

Gus sniffs. "I don't think anyone is going to take me seriously. I'm just exploring the person I might've been. Eleven years of my life have been committed to music, entertainment, drama. I'm not sure how much longer I have in me for all of that."

This piques my interest. I haven't really asked him about his career much; I get the impression celebrities get bored of being asked the same questions again and again. But now I know how open he is, I indulge myself. "Was there always drama?"

He groans. "Always. Always, always, always. If it wasn't me, it was one of the boys. If it wasn't them – literally, we could do *nothing* – we'd be dragged into something we weren't even involved with."

"Yeah. I couldn't do that."

"What do you mean?"

"The speculation. The drama. The invasion of privacy. I could never be famous or date someone famous. It would send me wild."

Gus holds onto that for a long moment. I realise what I've said and it's too late to take it back.

Finally, he says, "I have nothing to compare it to, really. Because this all started when I was so young, but relationships are tricky to navigate when you're in the spotlight. In some ways, I'm spoilt for choice. In other ways, I find the people who *want* to date me, want to date me because of *what* I am and not *who* I am."

"That's really tough," I say, scrunching up my face.

"It is. And it sucks for me. They want Gus from Just4Summer. They don't want *me*."

"And those are different people?"

He shrugs. "No, I mean… I'm not faking it when I'm on stage. I'm not a different person. Two sides of the same coin and all that. But I do fear that one day, when that all fades away, and I'm a nobody, there'll be no one left who'll want me for me."

I press my lips together thoughtfully. "Well, at least you'll be rich." Gus throws his head back with laughter. I'm sure he's about to correct me on that matter but we arrive at the port office and wait in the queue.

There're a few couples and a family ahead of us, but once it's our turn, I say, "Good afternoon. Do you have any idea when The Adriatic Angel is docking in Kotor please? We missed it in Dubrovnik."

The woman behind the desk speaks fluent English. I know because I've listened to her converse with the last few people. German and French too. But now she blinks at me, her expression wary.

"You have not heard from the cruise?"

I shake my head. "No. I haven't had any messages today. They usually send updates."

She purses her lips. "I see. Let me just speak to my colleague."

She spins in her chair and starts speaking in another language. I flinch as they get louder, certain they're arguing until they smile at each other, and she spins back.

"I'm sorry but your cruise is not stopping in Kotor."

"Not yet," I correct. "But it is going to. It stops here."

She shakes her head. "No. I'm afraid it has gone straight to the next port." She leans forward to type on her computer. "Ah yes, to Taormina, in Italy."

It takes me a few solid seconds to register her words. "No... That's... I don't understand."

I feel a large, warm hand press against my lower back as Gus interjects.

"Thanks for your help," he says, his voice tactfully smooth. "Can you tell us why they've skipped ahead?"

She gives us a look like we're completely out of touch. "Well, because of the storm."

I share a look with Gus. We glance out the window at

the pristine blue skies. Then turn to her again. She *has* to be messing with us.

"*Sorry, what?!*" we say in tandem.

She points at the TV screen on the wall behind us. Slowly, we step away from the desk and head in that direction. It's a news update… Of course, it's a local news channel so we don't understand a word, but the graphics are decipherable. A massive storm front is heading straight towards the Adriatic Sea.

What the…

Gus stands beside me; his hand still pressed against my lower back. I don't think it's something to read into. He's probably relaxed like this with everyone. He has that kind of personable energy. Even so, I can't deny I'm starting to like it.

It means nothing. Focus Sara!

I have bigger fish to fry.

I run both my hands through my hair and pull at the roots a little.

Fuck.

Sixteen

Cruise Location – At Sea
Next Port – Taormina
Time of Arrival – 10:00 (GMT+1)

We stroll down the portside, past the cruise ships, towards the smaller docks with the fishing boats and private yachts, at a loss. A seafood restaurant beckons us. It's quiet, with small, clothed tables set up outside on a raised front overlooking the bay.

Gus selects a table closest to the view but discreet enough for his face to be obscured from passers-by. He gives me an apologetic look. I'm still trying to come to terms with our situation.

"I can't do another day of this," I say. "It's not that it's been so bad. It's just, well, I want to be the adventurous type, but I'd just like to do it in extreme comfort and surrounded by copious amounts of *free* food and drink."

"Not me," Gus says, smirking. "I'm having the time of my life. This is the closest I've felt to freedom in years."

I roll my eyes, taking a sip of the ice-cold water I ordered.

"What are we going to do? We can't drive to *Sicily*. It's a whole sea away. The cruise will be on their way already, docking tomorrow morning. I don't know how we catch them up now."

Gus sits back, sighing. "We could fly?"

"Through a storm?"

"Well, I'm sure they'd go around it."

I open my phone and growl. The damn battery is flashing again. It's like it's taunting me. "Stupid thing. Why now? Why pick now to start dying on me?"

Gus tries not to laugh and hands me his phone over the table. I google flights but everything that's from an easy airport to reach from Kotor has a switch in either London or Paris. We might as well go home. And besides, I don't fancy dragging Popstar through a busy terminal and queuing for security. He'll almost certainly be recognised, and where would that leave me?

I'm searching for ferries that cross from Kotor to somewhere in Italy when his phone lights up with a call from 'Grace'. I practically throw it at him like it suddenly became a live, slippery fish. Gus catches it and groans when he checks the name. It's probably a girlfriend or a hook-up, surely popstars have a few of those on speed dial? I expect him to hang up and shrug it off as nothing (you know, like a lot of men would) when he answers and pops her on speaker phone.

"What do you want?" he asks, dryly.

"Just checking you're not dead," the woman says.

"Why would I be dead?"

"Your security team is on to you. Apparently, they find it surprising your phone hasn't moved from the ship at all, despite docking several times. They actually asked me if you're just hiding in your room. You know, like a fucking freak."

"And what did you say?"

"I said that's likely. Because Gus is a fucking freak."

He grins. "Good. Glad you cleared that up."

She drops something at the other end of the line and curses. "I didn't tell them I have this number or that you'd decided to abandon the cruise."

"No idea what you mean."

"Oh please! You were seen in Dubrovnik three hours after your cruise left port with a pretty blonde, dickhead."

Gus bites the inside of his cheek and eyes me from under his curls. "Wasn't me."

"Alright, Shaggy."

"Have you handled it?"

She sighs. "I tried. The girl who posted it isn't replying to my DMs. I reckon you'll be ok though because your face is fairly obscured. I think they're more interested in the woman, truthfully. Which, speaking of, who is she? She's not in my social circle. Is she a model? She looks tall. Or an up-and-coming actress? Fair play if she is, that's a great way to get your name out there. Oh, of *course*. That's who I sent money to, isn't it? It better had been for a good cause."

He glances at me again. I'm pretty sure the warmth in my face is giving me away. "It's… actually not like that."

"Shut up," she says. "Don't lie to me."

"I'm not."

"But you like her? Oh my *God*. Was she on the cruise? Is she some *normie*?"

Gus cringes. "Grace," he warns. "She's right here."

There's a moment of silence down the line.

I mouth, "Is this your sister?" at Gus. Who nods slowly, a spark of humour in his eyes.

"She's a whirlwind," he mouths back.

"Erm… Ok, first of all," Grace begins, "I don't appreciate being bombarded like that. Secondly, *hi?* Gus's new… *friend?* I guess?"

"Sara, meet Grace. Grace, meet Sara. Grace, Sara is helping me, well, *collaborating* with me to get back on the cruise. She's been a lifesaver so far since my burner phone doesn't have any banking set up."

"Wow," she says, her tone dripping with sarcasm. "You're such a moron."

"Thank you, as always, for your kind and loving support."

Then she cracks up laughing. "So, *wait*. This cruise you went on to prove you could holiday by yourself for two weeks…" More laughter. "You ended up missing the boat on the second day and now you need some poor stranger to help you?"

"And I did seriously consider not helping him," I point out.

Gus tilts his head at me as if to question whose side I'm on.

Grace is laughing harder, proper big belly laughs. "This is brilliant!"

"Right. Thanks for your useful input, Grace. We need to go since we're currently stuck in Montenegro."

"Sorry, *you're what?*"

"I'm not saying another word. We just need to get to Italy as soon as possible."

The laughter intensifies.

"Sara, please steal my number from his phone and message me if you need someone to bitch to about him," Grace says.

I smile. "Thanks for the offer."

"Any time! Oh, and Gus. Do you want the update or not?"

A shadow passes over his face, the light in his eyes dimming. He lets out a steady breath and says, "No. I think it's best I wait."

"You sure?"

"Yeah. Don't tell me."

"Alright. But be warned, the news might find you."

He nods like it's a given but doesn't expand. "Bye then."

"Love you," she sings.

Gus rolls his eyes. "Yeah. Love you too. Now bugger off." He hangs up and sighs, watching me with an amused look on his face. "Well, that's Grace. Luckily, we have too much shit on each other for her to dob me in."

"At least now you know they're tracking you."

"Oh yeah. That does put my mind at ease," he jokes.

Now that we're off the phone, the waiter comes over to take our food and drink order. "I'm Petar by the way. You are a beautiful couple."

"Thank you," Gus says with a huge smile before I can correct him. "Hey, you don't happen to have any ideas on how we can cross that," he says, pointing at the sea, "and get to Sicily by tomorrow, do you?"

Petar holds a tray in one hand, his other on his hip. He frowns and it makes his forehead scrunch up. "Right now? There is a storm coming, you've not heard?"

"Yeah, we know. But it won't be that bad, will it? It's summer."

We all once again stare at the blemish free skies above us.

"You would be surprised. The storms. They hit hard and fast." He frowns for another second before holding a finger in the air. "Hang on, I may have an idea. I will speak to my cousin," he says, striding back towards the kitchen.

"Gus," I lean forward, "what if he's in the Mafia?" I whisper.

He laughs. "What makes you think he's in the Mafia?"

"I don't know. It's just the way he said cousin. What if this restaurant is just a front for some kind of smuggling."

"Right. And now we're about to be… what? Smuggled across to Italy by the Mafia?"

I screw up my face. "Well, fine. When you say it like that…"

Twenty minutes later, deep in a plate of garlic king prawns, another man comes striding out towards us, closely followed by Petar.

"This is my cousin, Luka," Petar says, "he will help you." He gives him a firm slap on the back before moving off to help another table.

"I'm told you need passage to Italy."

I stare wide eyed at Gus who definitely sees me but pretends not to.

"Yes. We are in need of passage."

"My brother's wife's son's friend is a fisherman. He boats over to Bari in Italy once a week. It just so happens he's going this evening. You will arrive by sunrise. I can put you in touch if you like?"

Gus chances a glance my way, but I have questions.

"What kind of boat does he have?" I say, my voice tight.

"It is red."

What?

"What will it cost?" Gus asks.

The man shrugs. "I can ask him. He usually just enjoys company."

"Isn't there a storm coming?" I say.

"Roko is excellent captain."

"Well of course, he has a red boat," I say, kicking Gus's foot under the table.

"Exactly. Yes. Red boat." Luka smiles with full sincerity.

Gus clears his throat to stop himself from laughing. "Luka, my man. This is incredibly helpful. Can we take minute to think it over?"

Luka nods, giving us thumbs up as he walks backwards towards the bar and doesn't once take his eyes off us.

"I have chills," I say.

"I know, what are the chances?"

"I really hope you're joking," I hiss.

Gus tilts his head, splaying his hands like it's obvious. "We'll be in the right country by tomorrow. It'll be an adventure. Come on! Think of the photos I can get out at sea. The sunrise?"

"Oh yeah. And what about those forty-foot waves? And the fork lightning?"

He looks at the clear, dazzlingly blue sky as if to make his point. In fairness, it's mocking us. "Yeah, I don't know. I think that storm stuff is nonsense. There's barely even a breeze." He blinks, pressing his lips together to prevent a smirk. "And besides, as you said, he *is* a great captain of a red boat."

"What if the red is rust?"

"Then the boat has experience. Even better."

"No," I say, affirmative. "No. It's over. I'm going to go to the airport and get the next flight back to the UK. I think I've tested my karma plenty. It's time."

Gus blows out a breath, sitting back again. "Ok, fine. I'll

come with you, then." His tone is resolved. *Defeated.*

"Oh, no, you don't have to."

"Nah. We're in this together now. I'm not going on without you, it will just feel weird."

I throw my hands up. "Gus. That's very annoying. I'm just going to feel horribly guilty now!"

He smiles, but it doesn't touch his eyes. "Nothing to feel guilty about, you've been very helpful. And," he takes a breath, "exceptionally good company."

Of *course* he's going to be sweet about this!

"Ugh! You're telling me you *really* want to get on some random boat and cross to Italy? You don't think that's insane?"

He shrugs. "I think a little crazy is good for you. Either that, or life is going to be dreadfully boring. Making decisions based on what's sensible can really wear your soul down."

Pfft. I don't think he knows how much his words cut through me. It's a throw away remark, I suppose, if you're a wealthy superstar who can fall back into a bed of cash without harming anyone else on the way down. However, in my experience, whenever I've taken a risk and failed it's hurt other people in addition to myself.

Before I started in my current role, I wanted to work in TV. I had this idea that I'd follow my passion, that I'd do something for me just this once. I took an unpaid internship for the summer instead of stepping straight out of my business economics degree into the well-paid graduate role I'd been offered. The very next week, Dad was injured at work and was on a reduced salary, Millie had driving lessons that needed paying for, Gemma and Abby were both at university and needed a maintenance fund to pay for their accommodation or they'd lose their housing. Just like that, one selfish choice and I was the problem.

Luckily, the graduate position was still open. And, in hindsight, the TV job wouldn't have been for me. But it taught me a valuable lesson: it isn't practical to dream. Not when you have people relying on you.

And yet, there's nobody relying on me right now. If I'm going to do something risky, take a chance, maybe this is the time to do it.

"So?" Gus asks, signalling to Petar for the bill. He raises one eyebrow, a quirk in his lips. "We heading to the airport or the docks?"

I groan, running my hands through my hair. The real-world version of me would never do this. I'm the girl who plays it safe. And there's nothing wrong with safe, right?

Right?!

I'm just fighting this feeling that heading to the airport and calling this adventure off would be something I'll regret. If I'm being honest with myself, which I rarely am, I'm enjoying Gus's company, with his charming humour and cheeky quips. Maybe, just maybe, I'm not quite ready to give that up just yet. Even if it does mean heading out to sea on an unknown vessel in a potentially horrific storm.

Is it reckless? Absolutely. But what if I don't go? Will I just wonder for the rest of my life at what might've been? Somehow that feels worse.

"Fine," I say, resolute, almost surprising myself as much as Gus. "Let's do it. I mean – what's the worst that could happen?"

Gus presses his lips together, thoughtfully. "I'd hate to say. Let's not tempt fate."

"Excellent suggestion. I won't dwell on it."

We share a nervous but excited smile.

"Luka?" he says, "Show us to the red boat!"

Seventeen

The second we arrive at the end of the dock I know we're doomed.

The boat is only a bit rusty but it's a small vessel. I'm used to seeing boats like this in Brighton Marina, the ones hobby fishermen use in calm conditions. It's bigger than a speed boat but it can't be more than twenty feet long. It has a white, sheltered helm at the top where I spot a wooden steering wheel and a random blue bucket by the door. It's been tethered to the dock by a fraying rope; a damp broom leans against one side as if someone has been washing the deck. At least it's clean, I suppose. Below that there are two grubby round windows to the cabin.

An old man who cannot be any younger than seventy waves for us to come aboard.

He points at himself and says, "Roko."

Gus and I copy, offering our names and receive a lovely, toothy smile in return.

He does not speak any English at all which is to be expected. So instead, Gus and I follow him around the rickety boat, for what I can only assume is some kind of demented safety briefing, as he points things out, like the half-inflated flotation device, and a fire extinguisher that has been artfully abandoned on its side at the bow of the ship.

It's fine. I'm being carefree.

We'll just crash out on the floor in the cabin as we cross the Adriatic. By the time I wake up, we'll be in Italy. I can do that.

The wild part of me is *thriving*.

The other part is screaming for me to abandon ship before it's too late.

Finally, he shows us down to the cabin.

I have to say, I've seen some things in my time. I did a cleaning job at one of the nightclubs for a summer down on Brighton seafront and… You know what? I won't recall the details. All I'm saying is, the smell of rotting fish and, well, rotting old man, in here has me regretting those garlic prawns.

Roko kindly clears off the wooden benches that surround the built-in table, dumping the paperwork and boxes that were covering it in the kitchen area which has opened tins strewn across the worktop. He points for us to sit, so we do, and then talks some more. I already know that Gus doesn't speak his language, but he laughs at all the right moments which pleases our captain greatly. Roko leaves us after this. Moments later the engine spits and grumbles to life, and the whole boat vibrates around us.

"I'm scared," I say, wide-eyed, holding onto the table.

Gus is aghast. "What? *Why?* Roko's sound."

"Oh, so you understood that?"

"Well, no, I didn't. But you can tell he's a laugh."

"*Shut up*. No, you can't! For all you know, he was walking you through his plans to poison us and throw us into the sea."

He makes a tsking sound. "Roko couldn't lift my dead body."

"That's not the poi—" I squeal as the boat lurches, and we cruise away from the dock. "If I die, and you survive, please can you tell my sisters that their secret group chat is both petty and unjust?"

"That feels incredibly specific. Not 'I love you'?"

"No. They need the truth."

He laughs. "How do you know they have a group chat without you?"

I shrug, breathing steadily through my nose to exhale the anxiety away. "My youngest sister admitted it. And the worst part is I'm not surprised at all. I guess I deserve it." Now really isn't the time for deep introspection and self-reflection but, seeing as I'll probably die out here, why not? "They all hated me when we were younger."

"I doubt that's true."

"No, it is. I had to get them and myself to school most days and make sure they weren't doing stupid shit. All I did was look after them the way I thought our mum would've wanted me to. Dad was great but he wasn't good at girl stuff." The boat hits a wave and my soul exits my body. "He didn't understand," I continue, voice shaky, "when a relationship was getting toxic. He didn't know what things we needed to fit in. You know, silly things like Jane Norman bags and the latest hairstyles. And the types of shoes that wouldn't get you bullied." Gus nods thoughtfully, though it occurs to me this probably doesn't make much sense to him.

"I think I mothered them too hard, and they couldn't separate me as the bossy, uptight sister. In the end, while I was trying to make them happy and safe, I pushed them away instead. It's the biggest regret of my life." *Is this trauma dumping?!*

Gus leans back, stretching his legs out under the table, his trainer nudging my sandal.

"I think you're giving yourself a very hard time for what sounded like an impossible challenge. I'm definitely not a model big sibling either so I can't impart my advice but what I do know is it sounds like you only ever had their best interests at heart."

I exhale. "I did. I only ever tried my best. And now I just feel like they've pushed me out of their group. It feels like them and me. Not *us*." I sigh, regretting bringing this up at all. *What is it about life-threatening situations that make you overshare?!* "Anyway, let's go back up there. The bay will look gorgeous at this time of day. I'm sure you'll want to get it on camera." I don't wait for him to respond, slapping my hands on the table (to find it's sticky – *ugh!*) and stride up the stairs back onto the deck where Roko spots me and waves from the helm. I hobble towards the front of the ship and lean on the side, staring at the gorgeous scenery of lush green mountains, clear water and terracotta roofs littering the vanishing coastline. I feel the breeze whip through my hair in just the right way and close my eyes.

That's when I hear Roko's mismatched footsteps march hastily towards me. He keeps repeating the same word over and over again. I blink at him trying to figure out if I'm in some kind of horrible danger.

Also – *who the fuck is driving the boat!?*

I look up towards the helm. Nobody. Nobody is steering the boat.

Just great.

"*Delfino!*" he says again.

"No way!" comes Gus's excited response, who bounces up behind me and practically leans over my body, holding onto the side of the boat, pointing. "Look! Dolphin!"

Roko smiles and nods enthusiastically. I turn back at this point, right at the moment a sleek silver beauty leaps out of the water. I bite my lip to contain my excitement. I feel a tap on my back and when I peek over my shoulder, I am horrified to find a dead, slippery fish dangling in my face. Roko motions throwing it into the sea.

"Oh! Sure, ok. Am I allowed? I feel like this probably isn't allowed. But whatever, I guess." I pinch the dead fish between my thumb and forefinger before lobbing it into the water. Seconds later the dolphin launches itself out of the water again.

It's mesmerising.

That's when it hits me, and I have to chew on my wobbling lip to prevent tears escaping. I wouldn't have experienced this if I'd chosen to fly home instead. I feel the smile bloom on my face, the excitement lacing through my veins. *I did it!* I did something risky – something for me – and it's going to be ok.

The dolphin follows us through the bay and out to sea. I see it at least another thirty times.

I must lean there for so long, watching, I don't even notice when the others leave.

Click.

I spin to find Gus down on one knee, his camera in hand

pointed straight at me. I glare at him which only makes his lips curve upwards.

Click. Click. Click.

"Will you stop?"

He drops the camera. "Do you really want me to? I'll delete it if you insist."

"No," I say, before I can stop myself. "Don't delete it. I want evidence of this."

He half-smiles. "Evidence of what?"

"That I took a leap of faith and agreed to get on this boat with a little old man called Roko and a famous popstar. Because I'm almost dead certain that firstly, nobody will believe me, and secondly, I will not believe myself once I'm surrounded by my ordinary, sensible life again." He doesn't laugh at this, his smile dropping off to something more sincere when he nods and lifts his camera again. "Oh, and nobody really knows we're here. So, I guess your photos will make a good documentary one day if we don't survive and they recover the camera."

I'm facing him now, my hair blowing partly across my face.

"Right." Gus is fighting a laugh. "Glad that's the first place your mind goes." He takes a minute to look at the photos he's taken. "Did you hear when my sister called you a pretty blonde?" he asks, changing the conversation.

I did. "Did she?"

"Yeah," he says. "I agree by the way."

I shrug the compliment away. "I'm too uptight for pretty."

"Ah, I see. I must be wrong then."

Click.

"You are."

He stands upright, and shakes his head as he steps towards me, a subtle movement. He carefully props the camera up on one of the blue, upturned barrels before coming over to lean beside me. He stands close, his arm touching mine, and I regard him as he looks ahead.

Click.

"Oh."

I turn to look at the camera. In the corner of my eye, I see him look at me.

Click.

"I'm confused," I say, facing him now. He keeps his eyes locked on mine, that half-smile pressed along his lips.

Click.

"What are you doing?" I say, pretending to be exhausted by his antics.

He shrugs, reaching out and brushing some of my hair back behind my ear as the wind picks up again. I swear my breathing shatters at his touch, a slipstream of sensations racing from where his fingertips graze me all the way down to my core.

I swallow, watching the way his pupils expand, his gaze dropping to my lips.

His curls ruffle now too. I fight the temptation to reach out and tangle my fingers in them.

Click.

I should step away. Stop whatever trance he has me in. I'm not the sort of girl to buckle at a single compliment, but it's the way he's leaning in, slowly taking stock of my face. No one, including Mike, has looked at me like that in *years*.

He steps closer, raises his hand, gently running his fingers down the edge of my jaw, lifting my chin towards him.

There's a buzzing in my ears, like my blood is rushing too fast, my heartbeat in my throat.

Are we...

A horn blares.

It's so loud I slap my hands over my ears and crouch down.

When I look up, Gus is laughing. He points at the culprit. I follow his hand to Roko at the wheel, doing that toothy smile again, clearly very amused. Alright, maybe he is the joker Gus clocked him to be.

"On that note," I say, my face hot with embarrassment. "I'm going to walk away now."

Eighteen

"**I**s this normal?" I ask from the cabin several hours later, gripping hold of the screwed down table like it's my own personal anchor. "This doesn't *feel* normal."

"Let me go check," Gus calls back over the roar of the waves, crashing against the side of the boat. I'm practically green now we've hit open ocean, leaving the more timid waters of the bay behind. I don't generally get motion sickness, but this is another level. The boat is jumping waves. The front, where I'm sat, is being thrust upwards, pausing for half a second, only for it to come slamming back down, my tummy swooping, those prawns climbing ever higher up my throat. I would scramble towards the toilet beside the kitchen but, honestly, I'm afraid of what I'll find.

Through the small window opposite me there's a flash of light. I count slowly to work out how far away we are from the eye of the storm, only to make it to three before a booming clap of thunder crashes overhead.

All I know is that one moment I'm conscious of my movements, aware of my surroundings. The next, all I can process is how tightly I can grip hold of the things within my reach.

The lights in the cabin flicker then shut off completely. There's a long and vicious growl which could be attributed to the engine, more thunder, or something even worse. Either way, I pinch my eyes closed and make silent pleas to the universe that I don't die at the hands of Roko and his rusty fishing boat.

I'm sure there are more flashes of light. At one point, it's so bright my eyelids turn pink. I have no idea how long I'm like this before large, warm hands squeeze my arms. Strong legs link with mine under the table, grounding me further.

"Gus?" I whisper.

"I've got you, Sara. Roko isn't worried. He says we're ok. It's ok."

More thunder. More crashing downwards after riding a wave, the boat completely at the sea's mercy.

I change my grip, releasing the table and finding Gus instead, my head pressing into the warm groove of his shoulder. He continues to hold me, rubbing soothing circles over my back.

"Distract me," I say. "Tell me something."

I can feel Gus's pulse against my cheek. Curls run along my arm wrapped around his neck.

"Did you hear when Grace asked whether I wanted the news?"

I nod against his chest.

He exhales softly, trying to calm his own breathing too. "The band is almost definitely breaking up without me. It's why I had to get away from it all. We finished the world tour back in March and it ended on crap terms. We used to be like brothers, you know? But after all this time, it's like I barely know them anymore." The boat pitches forward before rocking back again, rain clapping against the deck so aggressively it sounds like needles. I tighten my grip on Gus and he lets me. "This whole thing was meant to be just for the summer, twelve years ago. Just four mates messing around with guitars and some cover songs at a summer fair." He readjusts himself, not letting go. He smells *really* good. "You ok, Sara?"

I grumble in response.

"I know it's a cop out but I just… I had to get away."

I'm more intrigued by this distraction than I care to admit. "And why are you breaking up?"

He takes a moment to consider. "I'm told this is the natural order of things. That we had a good run, went on longer than was good for our careers. That, in the end, the others were always going to go on and do different things with their lives."

"Like what?"

Gus shrugs. "Will has his daughter, Olive. Her mother is rarely around, so he's just trying to be the best dad he can be. Callum's uncle died a few months ago and he inherited a farm park that he needs to fix or sell or… I don't know. He stopped talking to me properly ages ago. Same with Will." He pauses as the boat sputters violently. "The two of them had this big fight over their own fucking egos and then I was torn between them."

"What about the other guy?"

"Jax?"

"Yeah."

He tightens his grip. "We don't talk about him."

I swallow. "So, you think it's a given," I say, "but you still don't want to hear it?"

"It just pisses me off. I know that if they make the call, it's over. That they don't need my decision to call it off. It's just how easy it is for them, you know? It's like they broke it, so they don't give a damn about throwing it away."

"It took all four of us to build the band," he adds. "Now they each take turns tearing it apart. And I have to sit here and watch them do it without any say or input. One man doesn't make a pop band. We were barely holding onto it all after…"

"Jax?"

Gus clears his throat. "Mmm."

"And now you're hiding from it all."

"No, I'm not *hiding*. I'm just choosing to be ignorant. That's what the photography is about. It's about doing something I loved before the band. Something that's just… mine."

I nod, my breathing steadier. "I get it."

"It's been twelve years. So much of my life. What I can't wrap my head around is how none of them are mourning it like I am."

"Well, maybe they are. Not everyone let's people see them sad or in pain. Sometimes those emotions are best kept to yourself."

"That may be true," he agrees. "But it was a team effort for so long. We each gave so much of ourselves to this life. All the suffering, sleepless nights, the anxiety. The times when we felt so out of control. It's like it was all for nothing. I feel like a massive chunk of me is missing without it. I don't know how I rebuild, you know? What on earth do I do, Sara, that will measure up to what I've already done? Where do I go from here?"

"I think that has to come from *you*. But maybe you're putting too much pressure on it. Maybe it can be something smaller, something that brings you joy, something completely yours."

Gus sighs, resting his chin on my head. "Man, you must be the best big sister."

"Well, if I am, I'm still doing something wrong."

The main light in the cabin flickers on again for a moment then hisses and buzzes back off. I whimper as the boat crashes down once more, my tummy dropping even faster. Gus hugs me to him.

"Gus?" I whisper.

"Yeah?"

"If I die…"

"You're not going to die," he interrupts, prodding me gently in the back.

"But if I do, can you tell my sisters I died doing something reckless?"

"I don't know about that," he jokes, pretending to consider my request. "What if they blame me?"

"They won't. You're a popstar. They'll thank you for coming by and Millie will probably hit on you. I apologise in advance."

I don't hear him laugh, but I feel the trembles of it.

"And if *I* die—"

"You probably will."

"—tell Grace you did it. She'll thank you and make you an honorary member of the Kenwood household."

"I'd accept."

"But seriously, if I die—"

"Which you will," I interrupt again.

"—can you do me a favour?"

I pause, pretending to consider his request. It's only fair. I sigh dramatically for effect. "It better not be weird."

"Take my camera. Get your arse back on that cruise. And make sure you have the time of your life." He must feel my hesitation because he continues. "You do deserve it, Sara."

I groan. "I'm trying to believe that. But I feel like the universe is telling me otherwise."

"This life-threatening storm is purely coincidence."

I actually laugh and he squeezes me a little tighter. "I hope so. Like I said, I think its mostly disappointment in myself now. I can't believe I didn't throw him out the second I found those messages. It makes me feel sick when I think about how I nearly married him."

"Because you wanted to be wrong. Being right would alter your future, and because running meant letting people down."

I push against him to make space between us, but our legs stay entwined underneath the table. "How do you know that?" I peer up at him.

"I guess that's what the music industry felt like for me. You listen to the people around you and hope they have your best intentions at heart. And if you question them, test their loyalties, you're the one who is difficult. The one they can't work with anymore."

"It's horrible to have someone so close to you betray your trust," I say.

"God, I know. Trust me. It completely destabilises your reality." He blows out a breath. "I fear I never learnt from it though. Because even knowing what I do, I still struggle with it."

I frown. "Why's that?"

"We had a two-year clause which meant we'd have to work with our production company to promote our music, do events, all that sort of stuff. We're six months into it. And suddenly, I'm the only one left."

Being that I negotiate contracts for a living, my ears prick up. "If we survive, I'd be happy to look at that contract with you."

"And I would share it but—"

"But there's a clause that prevents you," I finish for him.

"You got it."

"Well, there must be a loophole," I say.

"My agent says there's not."

"Hmm." I ponder on all the inevitabilities that may prevent someone from exiting a contract early when others have managed to terminate.

"Sara?"

"Mmm."

"I hope you know that you did the right thing."

I sniff, tipping my head back. "I know it in my heart. I lost all love for him the moment I saw those messages. It was like waking up from a long dream. Everything started to fall into place; my reality wasn't what I thought it was."

"Your heart is wise."

"That better not be a line from one of your songs."

He snorts. "See, if you *were* a fan, you'd know. That's all me."

"Oh, so my wisdom is rubbing off on you. How annoying."

"It's the life-threatening situation. There's no other explanation."

I gasp. "So, what you're saying is, you *do* think we're going to die?"

He only laughs, kissing the top of my head as we crash against another wave and the boat groans.

Nineteen

We arrive in Italy early the next morning, feeling somewhat battered and bruised.

Roko is animated when we disembark, insisting we listen to him, pointing at the port with instructions we don't understand. I finally have the rather brilliant idea to employ a translation app. Who knew Roko was speaking Italian? He instructs us to go to the Guardia Costiera, who will apparently have us checked into the country before any onwards travel. Not doing so could have us arrested.

Good old, Roko.

He refuses our attempts to get his bank details so we can pay him, though Gus puts up an admirable fight. Instead, Roko offers rigorous handshakes to express how much he enjoyed our company. I find that hard to believe considering I spent most of the night wrapped around Gus, whimpering like a baby.

Once we're away from the boat I can't help but relish the fresh, salty air. It's hard to work out whether the rotting stench of sardines is ingrained in my nostrils, or if it's actually just coming from our clothing. I step closer to Gus, pulling his dark T-shirt towards my face and sniffing.

He scoffs. "Sara, is this you flirting?"

"Shut up. You *stink*."

"Now *that* is you flirting."

I glare at him for several seconds, but the longer it goes on the wider his smile becomes.

"How are you smiling right now? Are you not in shock? Exhausted?"

He shrugs. "Honestly, I'm just happy to see the light of day and have my feet back on solid ground. There were moments last night when I didn't think that was likely."

"A-ha!" I say, "I *knew* you thought we were going to die."

"Someone had to keep a cool composure."

"Hey. I was fine!"

"I'm pretty sure there are fingerprint-sized bruises all over my neck and shoulders. You know, from where you clung on for dear life."

"I will abandon you," I say, pointing at him.

He only laughs.

I make a face, looking away to take in our surroundings. The water is calm again, the sky a perfect, innocent blue. You'd never know the weather here was capable of such calamity.

"I need a shower," I say, "as do you. And we need *another* set of clean clothes, all before we plan our next steps." I drop my arms, my shoulders sagging. We didn't get any sleep last night as the boat fought its way through the storm. "I'm exhausted."

He nods. "Yeah, but I've stayed awake longer."

"Probably not sober," I guess.

Gus nods, a notch forming between his brows. "*Never* sober. But before we do anything else, let's get some coffee and breakfast."

We claim a table at a quaint café on the edge of the older part of Bari, only a few strides from the port. Gus insists on ordering, keeping his sunglasses on inside, before returning to the table we picked outside with two strong coffees and a kind of brioche bun filled with cream.

"Apparently this is called a Maritozzo," he tells me. "Oh, and you can charge your phone inside. There's a plug behind the counter. I'm pretty sure the server knows who I am."

I roll my eyes. "Paranoid much?"

He rolls his eyes back, but even more dramatically. "You're welcome."

I take a big sip of my coffee, groaning as I feel the delectable caffeine working it's way through my veins. An hour later, and two more coffees down, I take my phone back at 70 per cent charge which will have to do. "The cruise is in Taormina today," I report. "It docks there in a couple of hours and leaves at six p.m. It looks as if it will take anywhere between six and fifteen *hours* to get there from Bari via train, coach *and* ferry, so I think we're just going to have to accept that we're not going to make it for that one."

He nods. "Agreed. There's too many things that could go wrong. I think we've had enough trials for a lifetime."

"So, it makes sense to carry on to Rome, in that case. The cruise is out at sea for two nights after they leave Sicily because of the ball they throw for the guests."

"Ah, I'm sorry," he says, his face etched with disappointment.

I glance at him over my phone. "Why are you sorry?"

"Because you're missing the ball."

"I'm not fucking Cinderella," I say, scoffing. Gus laughs quietly in response as if my reaction confirms the fact. "I don't care about the ball. I mean, the cruise was brimming with old men and wealthy families. It was hardly going to be a rave. And besides, I'm technically heartbroken and it wouldn't be my scene."

"You're *technically* heartbroken? How does that work then?"

"My heart is *meant* to be broken."

"But it isn't?" he asks, genuinely.

"I don't know," I reply truthfully.

"I think you'd know," he says.

He's probably right. I think I know that more happened between Mike and his female colleague than I discovered. I think my heartbreak was overtaken by betrayal. And now, I think there's something new at play that I can't quite put my finger on. But I'm so tired it's not something I'm able to process right now. Instead, I shake my head at Gus and begin searching the best route to Rome.

"Unfortunately, it's quickest and cheapest to travel by coach to Naples. Saves us nearly two hours and means no waiting around at the station where it changes. Then from Naples we head into Rome by train. We should be there in about five hours."

Gus chews on his bottom lip, running a hand through his curls. "That's a long stretch on public transit."

"Yes. But do you have a better idea?"

He swallows. "Not really. Not unless we rent a car and drive, of course."

I shrug. "I *still* don't have my licence on me."

"*Fuck*. I forgot."

"What's the worst that could happen? Are you a big name in Italy?"

He gives me a sardonic look. "We're an international success, Sara."

"Alright, Elvis. I'm just saying—"

"I've been recognised in Vietnam."

"Good for you," I say sardonically. "You're *really* famous, I get it, Popstar. Would you like me to shave all your hair off now, so nobody recognises you?"

He shakes his head slowly, horrified by my suggestion and without saying another word rises from the table and heads in the direction of the clothes stores we passed on the way in. Clearly, I've finally rattled him. Our coach is booked and we're going to gamble with trains being available once we reach Naples.

In the meantime, I find an H&M and decide to play it safe, hoping I don't get kicked out for stinking like rotting seaweed. Gus heads upstairs in search of something for himself too – sunglasses on. I grab a pair of leggings, denim shorts and a nice yellow and white summer dress I can throw on if needed. I add some clean underwear, a T-shirt bra, and am on my way to the checkout when I spot something that makes me cackle so loud the woman behind the till jumps.

I add another item to my purchase.

Gus has somehow already managed to get dressed when I step outside. He's doing that strange thing hot men do sometimes where they lean against a wall, arms folded, with one foot propped up so their knee points out. He's picked a loose-fitting, vintage-style grey T-shirt, black shorts and white trainers too.

He looks impossibly cool. *Such a popstar.* Especially with those curls peeking out of his cap. It doesn't help that those mischievous warm eyes don't leave me as I walk towards him.

Ugh. No.

Cannot be *seriously* crushing on the tall, cute popstar. That would be cataclysmic.

Even so, as I get closer and dig my hand into the bag, I can't stop the smile that stretches across my face.

Gus tilts his head. "What on earth does it take to get you to smile like that?" he asks, his lips curving upwards.

"This," I say, pulling out a new Just4Summer T-shirt, except this time it's only the logo. "Would you believe I found this?"

He blinks several times, rubs his nose. I pride myself on having a good read on people. It's what I do for a living. It's my job to work out who is the snake at a negotiation table, who is the angriest about an offer, whether someone is going to bail on a contract – that sort of thing.

And my joy at finding the T-shirt shifts fast as I watch Gus force a laugh.

I stuff it back in the bag, my smile dropping. "I won't wear it."

"Why not?"

"Because…" I don't want to make you uncomfortable. "It was just a joke. I have other clothes." I fidget on my feet. "Where did you get dressed by the way?"

Gus shows me to the surprisingly clean public loos where

I change into my new denim shorts and T-shirt, switching into new sneakers too before binning all the fishy-smelling clothing.

"Right. Let's find this coach."

Mum is singing along to the Mamma Mia *soundtrack as we drive home from the cinema. I'm rolling my eyes because I hate it when Mum sings even though it makes me smile because I love seeing her happy.*

It's funny because despite knowing this is a dream, it takes me longer and longer to acknowledge the fact.

We reach the roundabout where she always reminds me, and I feel my nose twitch as the pressure builds behind my eyes.

"You know this is where I get off, right? It's always here," she tells me.

My lips quiver and I glance at her. Her darkening blonde hair is tucked behind her ears; her icy blue eyes are the spit of mine as she blinks.

"Don't go, Mum," I whisper.

She does that big smile she does. It reminds me so much of Millie. It's so full of energy and trouble. "It has to be here, darling."

"No. Mum. Just a little longer."

But like always, the second we hit the roundabout a switch occurs. Mum is gone and I'm behind the wheel.

And every single time, I find myself on a roundabout with no exits.

"Sara," a soft voice is nudging me awake.

I sit up fast, taking in my surroundings. It's bright. I wince.

The engine hisses as the coach presses on up a hill. Gus is beside me. In fact, I'm on Gus. Somehow, I've managed to get my head into the crook of his neck, and my legs are in his lap.

When the fuck did I do that?

My own body betrays me.

I don't move right away. Better to give myself a moment to reset. I clench my eyes closed and let the adrenaline wash through my body. I used to imagine all the feelings pouring like liquid out of my fingertips. I try that now.

"Sorry," I whisper.

Gus has one hand on the back of my head, holding me to him, stroking me gently. "Hey. You're ok."

"Was I sleep talking?" I ask, eyes still closed.

I feel him nod, his chin pressing into my forehead.

His voice is low as he says, "I woke you before it got bad."

The fact that he knows it gets bad is horrifying on its own. What has he heard? What has he chosen not to mention? With the panic attack at the start, the sleep talking and now this, he must think I'm insane.

"What did I say?"

"You just kept saying 'Mum'," he murmurs.

I groan, slowly untangling myself from him and rolling my head back. Most other passengers on the coach seem to be either sleeping themselves or have headphones on. It doesn't appear as if anyone cares about my mishap.

Gus rearranges himself too, twisting towards the aisle again. He insisted on me taking the window seat this time. I could've leant that way, used my bag as a pillow, but no. I used the popstar as a human mattress.

Great. Good. Just brilliant.

"Sorry," I say again.

"Stop apologising. It's fine."

"It's embarrassing. I'm nearly thirty," I whisper-hiss.

Gus leans forward, grabbing a bottle of water we bought at the bus station and offers it to me. I take a sip and hand it back.

"What was she like?" he asks.

"Who? My mum?" Nobody ever asks me about her. I don't think I've spoken about her out loud in years, except for with Dad and my sisters. Gus nods.

"She was… fierce. But funny. And outrageously creative. None of us inherited that from her. I haven't got an artistic bone in my body; it's why I like what I do. It's structured and clean and I can tidy all the loose threads up into a contract. Mum was messy and chaotic. A lot like my sisters, I guess."

"You miss her," he says, peeking down at me, his face so close to mine I can feel his breath brushing over my nose.

I nod, swallowing.

"You don't have to tell me if you don't want to but talking about it might help," he says, his voice muffled so that only I can hear. "What is the dream about?"

I close my eyes again and press my face into the top of his arm. I realise, as soon as I've done it, that it's an intimate gesture, especially when he presses his chin to the top of my head, the light bristle there sending shivers from my scalp racing down my spine.

"She leaves me. We're driving towards a roundabout. Then, every time we reach it, she disappears and I'm the one driving."

"Makes sense," he says.

I sit back, frowning. "No, it's doesn't. She leaves me going round and round until I wake up crying. None of that makes sense."

Gus reaches out and tucks some of my messy, loose hair behind my ear. He's so gentle with me, I feel that hardened heart of mine soften, tears building at the back of my eyes. "You took over, Sara. At least from what you've told me. She leaves, you take the wheel, and you keep on going round and round, right?"

I swallow the spiky lump in my throat. I hate how it feels like he's taken a knife to my chest in the most careful and sweet way. It's entirely contradicting. I want to hate him for it, but maybe he's onto something.

"I don't know how to get off."

"Maybe the exit hasn't revealed itself to you yet?" he says. "But it will come."

His eyes are so hooded, I watch as he finally drifts off to sleep himself, head leant back against the chair. Moments later, as the coach turns a tight bend, his body shifts and he ends up leaning his head against my shoulder.

Just as well he's out for the count as it means he can't see me furiously wiping tears from my eyes with my new J4S T-shirt.

Twenty

Two hours later, we arrive in sunny Naples.

The coach drops us off right outside the modern, glass-fronted train station, smack dab in the city centre. It's absolutely heaving with passengers, from rushing commuters in smart suits, to interrailing students, their massive backpacks hitched high on their shoulders. I can sense Gus's tension, and he does his best to keep his head down.

There's a familiar waft of fast food that, in my exhausted state, is more tempting than I'm willing to admit. I wet my lips as I glance around, looking for any sign of a ticket office. I spot it towards the front of the station.

"Come on, Popstar, this way."

As we reach the long queue, Gus carefully takes me by the elbow and spins me to face him. I have no idea what it is about the gesture, but something swoops in my belly. I stare at him bemused. "Can I help you?"

He looks like he's trying to word his question carefully, gnawing on his bottom lip.

"I know we're tired after last night but, now we're here,

I'm really keen to wander Naples for a few hours. We could book onto a later train. I have plenty of charge in my camera." He pauses, raising his brows. "What do you say?"

I blow out a breath. "Well, we *are* missing out on Taormina. And we have two whole nights before the cruise docks in Rome. I guess I'm intrigued… I don't see why not."

And so, on impulse, we spend the following two hours prowling the bustling streets of Napoli. Gus finds a small phone shop in a market that sells portable chargers and I plug my phone in and slide it back in my bag. Ideal.

Gus seems to have a plan and that plan involves a ton of walking, and then some more walking, only pausing intermittently when his artistic eye catches something that he wants to capture on camera. But I don't mind following him around the city, taking in the sights and stopping whenever I see a food stand that speaks to me.

Who knew Sfogliatella, a shell-shaped pastry with a sweet creamy filling, could change a woman's life in a single, delicious bite?

As he told me before, Gus seems to be drawn to the life of a place. The hectic backstreets with balconies positioned at seemingly random levels, bougainvillea and other climbing plants searching the shadows for a whisper of light, wires webbing between buildings. It's as if he's mesmerised by the chaos, the realness of the place. I wonder if that's because he felt so isolated from the normal world most of his adult life.

At one point, a small tabby cat sticks its head out of an overflowing bin behind a restaurant and Gus makes it his muse, the tabby trotting towards me and curling around my shins, its fur a soft scrape against my skin. Gus gets down on his stomach and points the camera at her height.

I stand still, waiting impatiently for him to finish.

As if he clues on, he takes his time, lips curving below the camera lens.

Warmth rushes up my neck and all I can do is tut in response, patting the tabby on the head and striding away so that he has to clamber after me.

Thankfully, my ankle seems to be holding up. Probably due to to the new trainers which are only rubbing slightly against my big toe. It's the sort of pain I can ignore and nurse later in Rome, wherever we end up staying.

"You know, we should go to Pompeii," I say suddenly, spinning to face him, surprised by my own impulsiveness. Because we could. And it's been on my bucket list for years. There weren't any cruises, that I fancied, stopping in Naples so I'd written Pompeii off as an option, but I've long been fascinated with the ancient, ruined city and I'd even gone as far as to research how long it would take to travel there from Rome, knowing that was a planned long dock stay for the cruise.

Gus eyes me with surprise. "Right *now*?"

"Yes! It's only a half hour train away, right?"

"If you say so..." he says, shrugging. "I'm not going to say no to an adventure."

The ancient city is just like all the online blogs said it was, frozen in time. We were too late to join up with a tour, so we wander on our own, weaving through former streets, glimpsing pieces of beautiful mosaics and tiles. We clamber over the uneven cobbled path, Gus and I both in equal awe.

The sun is punching down on us as we stroll along

streets, past crumbling buildings that were once homes and shops and bakeries. Most of the buildings are without ceilings, jagged pillars, which used to hold up roofs over the markets, stand without purpose. The dark mountains behind create a vivid backdrop, a frequent reminder of what happened here. So much life was behind these walls, so much destruction in so little time. It's hard to fathom the fear they must've felt.

When I stroll into the more intact buildings, with fascinating, ancient artwork decorating the walls, I feel as if I'm intruding, like I'm strolling through somebody's house uninvited. Some of the art is so graphic I'm almost blushing as I pass, listening to Gus's soft breathing behind me. He doesn't take photos inside and I wonder if it's because he feels the same as me, as if the spirits of those who lived here never really left.

Once we're back outside, I pause at one doorway, peeking into a cramped space.

Click.

I spin on Gus. "Can't you see I'm having a moment?" I ask, unable to hold back a smile.

He nods, grinning, looking at his camera screen that he shields from the sun to see properly. When he hears a group of young women laughing, his curls fall over his sunglasses as he tenses, checking the nearby area. His shoulders relax when they move on. I wonder if it's always been like this for him, the fear of being seen, being followed. I wonder if he even knows he reacts that way. He swallows and takes a steadying breath as he turns back to me.

"You're so photogenic," he says. "I think you might be my new favourite subject."

I feel his compliment rush through me like the first sip of an ice-cold drink. Obviously, I like it, but that's the problem. It's all becoming a bit *too* flirty and there's absolutely no way a world-famous popstar is a suitable rebound. I need to shut it down.

"*Right*." I step towards him with my hand out. "Give me that."

He frowns. "Why?"

"Because you've got hardly any pictures of *you*."

"Trust me, plenty exist."

"Not of you in Pompeii. Having a moment."

He concedes, pulling the camera strap over his head and passing it to me. "Do you know…"

"Shut up," I interrupt. "I did A-level photography." I only did it for a month before switching to economics because I changed my plans for university, but I don't tell him that.

"Yeah, that's what all photographers say."

Gus steps up towards the building where he just photographed me and instantly moves as if he's some kind of male model posing for *Men's Health*. He looks good but it's not *real*. It's not the man I've come to know these past few days. "You really know how to work your angles, huh?"

He runs a hand down his face, repositioning. "Unfortunately."

"You should shake it up. No, even better. Just walk around. I'll shoot you candidly."

"Don't shoot me," he says, turning back and pointing. "My team will be livid."

"Shut up and walk."

He throws his head back with laughter.

I spend the next hour or so hiding behind walls and

jumping out at him, or waiting for him to actually let his guard down before taking his photo. My favourite one, as I click back through, is of Gus giving me that disbelieving, daring smile, his hat on the ground because I'd jumped forwards and flipped it off, his hand out to snatch the camera back.

I finally give it back to him once we're on the busy train back to Napoli, crammed into a standing corner. It's too hot and noisy for my taste but Gus ends up holding onto a bar beside me for balance, bringing us face to face. A bead of sweat escapes his curls, running down his forehead, along his nose and onto his lips. It's too late when I realise I'm staring, wetting my own lips, his eyes tracing the movement of my tongue, his breathing measured.

I swallow, trying to look away but the train lurches and I'm thrust forward, crashing into him. Gus catches my waist, the feel of his touch burns through my thin T-shirt. Finally, our eyes lock again and for a split second, I think he's going to kiss me, his breath fanning my cheeks but instead he swallows, releases my waist and uses the same hand to brush my ponytail behind my shoulder, throwing me a knowing grin.

Hell, I'm in trouble.

Back in the city centre, we try some of the touristy areas, soaking in the culture and history of the city. We grab pizzas from a bustling pizzeria and sit in a small piazza watching the world roar around us as the sun goes down.

"This place is so chaotic," I say after we watch two men on mopeds yelling Italian curse words at each other, throwing their hands in the air.

Gus nods, his mouth full. "It *is* busy here."

"We should think about heading to Rome soon."

"I have an idea," he says. He finishes chewing. "But you can say no, of course."

A bit of stringy mozzarella escapes my pizza and ends up on my chin. I squeal. Gus laughs and before I know what's happening, he's using his thumb to wipe the sauce off my chin then licks it clean. I don't know what to say. He doesn't acknowledge it. Something in my core is doing somersaults. I swallow it down, eyes wide.

"What do you think?" he asks.

Has he been talking?

I blink. "About what?" My cheeks are hot.

When he glances at me again, he gives me a bemused smile. "Is that pizza so good your ears stopped working?"

"Mmhmm. Yes. That's what happened."

"I asked if you'd be open to staying at a friend's house. Grace has just pinged his number through and warned him I might message."

I shrug. "What like... for free?"

Gus nods. "I know that means you can't make as much interest off me," he teases.

"I don't want your interest!" But something about that statement doesn't ring true, so I change it. "I'm not taking any interest from you. Financially speaking."

I didn't need to clarify.

His lips quirk then flatten. Gosh. Damn. I'm acting like a tit and he's so onto me. "Devaney owes me. The least he can do is put us up for the night."

"But me too? I mean, I can stay in a hotel. It might have to be a hostel as my funds are running low."

Gus tilts his head at me. "Really?"

"*What?*"

"We're in this together now. Look at us. Still alive. In a city we weren't even meant to be in, having the time of our lives."

He's not wrong, because I do not regret visiting Pompeii. I've seen more of Italy in a day than I probably would've on the whole cruise. But... I'd prefer him not to know this. His ego is showing. "I don't know if eating pizza right next to a bin whilst we watch angry Italians throw hands at each other is the time of my life."

"Sara, are you coming with me or not?"

"Ok, yes. But I really hope your friend isn't weird."

"Only if he drinks tequila."

"Oh. We have that in common."

Twenty-One

The train from Naples to Rome is smooth. I try to make Gus take the window seat for extra security, but he insists on giving it to me, wrapping one of his new T-shirts over his head to hide his face. He throws his head back, his breathing softening as he drifts off to sleep, the lights down low in this carriage, then I ceremoniously fall asleep on him too, head pressed against his firm bicep.

Am I tempting fate?

I don't know because I'm too tired to care and he didn't object to me using him as a human pillow before, so why not now?

It only takes an hour and a half on the high-speed train, a fantastic idea on Gus's part but because we left Napoli late, we arrive in Rome near midnight.

Thankfully the city is still alive, the streets brimming with people enjoying themselves in the cooler shadows of the night. Gus managed to reach his friend before the train left, who sent the address to his villa. We catch a taxi from the station and find ourselves at a set of large wooden gates fifteen minutes later. He's on a tidy, ivy-strewn street with expensive security systems and fancy cars.

Gus presses the buzzer, then waves and smiles at the camera pointing down at us from the roof.

A crisp American voice asks, "What do you want?"

"Let me in dickhead," Gus responds, still smiling.

I feel my eyebrows rise. Oh, so they're *friend* friends. The gate hums and Gus opens it, signalling for me to lead the way. The courtyard behind the gates is full of Italian Cypress trees, with a marble water feature of a woman draped in cloth sitting proudly in the centre, trickling peacefully, shutting out some of the city noise beyond. A stone-paved path leads to a set of decorative glass doors.

Gus steps past me, offering me his arm for support. I don't know if I look as beat as I feel, but right now, on my level of exhaustion, and my ankle right on the brink of giving up, this gesture does unseemly things to my core. I quietly link my arm through his and let him guide me.

A tall, indecently handsome, dark-skinned man greets us in the hallway. I blink several times, trying to place him. I know this man.

He's talking to me, but my brain is still tripping over itself trying to place him. Then finally, it clicks. "Oh my God! You're Cole Devaney! I'm in love with you!"

"What?" Gus scoffs, making a face. "Ignore her. She's spacing out from exhaustion. Delirious. Nobody loves you."

"I do! I love him." I squeal.

Cole is smiling, his pearly white teeth, dazzling. "It's a pleasure to meet you too…"

"Sara," I offer, almost choking on my own name. Did I die on the boat? Is that what is happening right now? Because I find it hard to believe I am in THE COLE DEVANEY'S house. The ultimate action movie superstar. "I'm sorry, I'm actually not sure how to process this," I say to Gus.

"This is just perfect," Gus jokes. "You know Cole, but you didn't know who I was."

"That's not true. I knew you were famous. I just couldn't pinpoint why. Or how."

Cole laughs, the familiar deep sound has me screaming inwardly. Surreal.

"This is brilliant," he says. "You guys didn't know each other before a few days ago? Honestly, I thought you were a couple. You look so good together."

It's my turn to scoff. Gus says, "Thank you. I know."

I roll my eyes at him. "Funny."

He grins.

"Well, as lovely as it is to greet you both, especially you Sara, I'm up early tomorrow for filming so I should already be asleep, but mi casa es su casa, and all that. My housekeeper, Aline, will be here in the morning. Help yourself to anything in the kitchen. You're in the guest room… er, rooms?" He frowns, clearly confused by our dynamic. Not helped by me still gripping onto Gus's actually very nice arm.

It pains me, but I let go and clear my throat.

I can feel Gus's eyes scanning my expression for clues, so I keep it purposefully neutral. "Yes. Rooms."

Cole glances at Gus before correcting himself and nodding. "Come on then. I'll show you to your rooms."

It's just as well we had our own space for the night because as soon as my head hits the insanely luxurious pillow, my next conscious thought is that I can hear quiet tapping on the door; tapping which is closely followed by Gus's voice.

"Sara?"

I make some kind of undecipherable grunt.

"I've made coffee. Would you like it in there or are you coming down? No pressure but it's already nine a.m. Just thought you'd like to know."

I groan again.

"Sorry?" he asks, laughter in his voice. "I didn't get that. You sounded like a strangled grizzly bear."

"Coffee!" I croak. "Here!"

The door opens. I am not presentable, so I pull the sheets back over my face and mutter a thank you. I hear his footsteps retreating after a mug has been carefully placed beside me, but the door doesn't close.

"Thank you but go away."

He properly chuckles. "I checked the schedule, by the way. The yacht docks tomorrow at ten. But today it's out having a splendid time in the Med. I've made crêpes for breakfast. Yours are staying warm in the oven and there's fresh fruit in the fridge. Cole's housekeeper is called Aline, in case you forgot, and she's literally wonderful." He claps his hands together. "Rise and shine, sunshine. We need to make a plan to conquer Rome today."

"You don't conquer Rome. Rome conquers you." My voice comes through muffled.

"Come on. Up ye get."

I fidget under the duvet. I need a wee. My breath stinks. "Let me drink my coffee and then I'll start using my brain."

"Fine. I'll be in the gym."

When I'm awake, showered and dressed, I venture out into Cole's massive, modern villa. The front half of the building dates back to the 1500s, though it's been beautifully restored, whereas the newer, more modern section at the back of the villa is all sleek lines, with large windows that let in long, warm shadows. I tried looking up how much it sold for online before I eventually drifted off but only came across a similar place on the same street that sold for nine million euros last summer. And that one is smaller. I'm convinced this is all a dream.

The gym takes me a solid ten minutes to find because it's in the basement along with a twenty-metre pool.

Holy shit.

I just remembered I'm in Cole Devaney's house.

Ahh!

I shake myself out of the hysteria, searching for Gus. I find him on one of those weird-looking torture devices with wires and strange apparatus hanging out of it in several directions.

He's wearing a pair of bulky headphones, courtesy of Cole, I assume, so he doesn't hear me stroll in. I keep to the far wall, just out of his sight, watching him lift a large weight repeatedly, his face focused, reddening. He's in a very loose fitted black vest, his toned arms out on full show. His curls are dampened and combed back so that they don't fall into his eyes, and I have to admit there's something kind of... I blow out a steadying breath.

Yeah, I have a problem.

And to add to it, now his hair is out of his eyes his facial features are on full show. He's not devastatingly handsome in the rugged sense like Cole, but he's handsome and muscular in a way that makes my heart race a little quicker.

Plus, he's funny. And funny men have (historically speaking) a way of making my knickers accidently slip a little.

He drops the weight after a round (a set? a lap? a testosterone?), and I almost walk towards him when he starts to sing along to whatever he's listening to, his voice crisp and sharp.

Because, *of course*, he can sing. What did I expect?

And now the fact that I'm hovering back here is awkward.

So awkward. Sara, you are being weird.

He stops singing to focus on adding round things (I think weights?) to a long metal stick. He throws his headphones on the ground and pulls his socks up before lying back on the bench and pressing the bar above his head.

"Sara, stop loitering and come spot me."

Busted!

"Loitering? I'm not loitering!" I could actually perish from embarrassment right here, right now. "Also, I don't know what that means, to spot you, or whatever."

"Stand here," Gus says, pointing to the area behind his head. I do as he says, confused the entire time. "Closer," he adds. "If I can't lift the bar, you just have to slide it back over these hooks here. You never been in a gym before? You look lost."

"Yeah. No. If I'm doing exercise, it's civilised. You know, walking, Pilates, yoga."

"A little closer."

"I mean…" I sigh. His face is going to be indecently close to my thighs. But whatever. I clear my throat, step into place and change the subject. "You have a lovely voice, by the way."

He grunts as he counts in ten reps. He doesn't need me here. He's making very light work of the bar. So, this was a ploy. I am a fool. Once he's done, he sits up, turning towards me with a smile.

"It's almost like I'm a professional singer, huh?"

"Wait, you're a *singer*?" I deadpan.

"You do realise that whole wall there is a mirror, right? I saw you the second you walked in."

"Oh, so that *was* a performance?"

"What? No! I was just enjoying the song."

"Right," I smirk. "So, you just randomly burst into song?"

He snorts like that would be obvious. "Yes. I'm a fucking popstar, remember?"

I shake my head. "You're weird." But really, I'm only teasing him. Which works because he's instantly on the defence.

"Oh. So you're telling me you never sing in the shower?"

"I don't sing in the shower," I say. "I *think* in the shower. It's peak thinking time."

"What do you think about in the shower?"

"Work. Solutions. Family issues."

"In the shower?"

"Yes. What's wrong with that?"

"I don't know. I'm starting to think you're a psychopath."

I shrug. "Rude! You don't think in the shower?"

He bites his bottom lip, leaning an elbow on the wall beside him, tilting his frame slightly. "I've certainly been known to use my imagination in the shower."

"Ew. Gross," I say, turning away from him before he can see my smile.

"I write songs, Sara. Get your head out of the gutter."

"Well go write songs then because we only have one day in Rome and I plan on using it."

"I've been awake since six! It's you who's been lying in like a bloody princess."

"Yeah, yeah," I say. "Get ready and meet me in the courtyard in twenty."

"Twenty minutes, that's all I get?"

I make a comical face as I reach the door. "Guess there'll be no singing in the shower today."

Then I bolt before I can embarrass myself further. Sure enough, Gus is showered and dressed twenty minutes later. He finds me in the courtyard, appreciating the beautiful oleanders. He takes my arm and guides me to the side of the villa.

"Where are we going?" I ask, allowing him to direct me. But before he can reply, I spot a blue and white Vespa and two helmets. He steps up and puts one on his head, handing the other out to me. "What are you doing?"

"Cole said we could borrow his Vespa." He grins.

"Absolutely not. These things are lethal."

Gus scoffs. "No, they're not. Besides, aren't you tired of walking everywhere?" I shift my weight, reluctantly accepting the helmet.

I've never been on a motorbike before, and these past few days I've seen Vespas darting in and out of coaches all across Italy, I'm not sure if I'm ready for the adrenaline rush.

"I am, but I don't... I've never driven one of these before."

"Well, I have. And I know Rome well enough. I lived here for a summer." He takes the helmet and sets it gently on my head. "I'll drive safely," he assures me, pressing it down over my head and fastening the strap. His fingers accidentally scrape against the soft skin under my chin and I glance up at him, my lips parting.

"Shall we?" he asks.

"Ugh, fine. But only because I'm actively trying to be irresponsible and let my hair down."

"Well, your hair *is* down," he points out, climbing on and waiting for me to clamber up behind him. I wrap my arms around his middle, as unromantically as I can possibly muster, before he adds, "Now obviously I don't have my licence on me, but when in Rome, eh?"

"Oh for—" the words get trapped in my throat as the scooter lurches forward, zipping through Cole's front gate and heading up the cobbled street towards the city.

Rome is even more hectic than Naples. It has that "don't stop on the pathway or I will shout expletives at you" rule that exists in central London at rush hour. We jostle along towards the Colosseum, a must-see while in Rome, and I'm unsure whether Gus is breaking all the rules of the road or if other drivers are just irrationally angry, but horns are blaring almost every couple of seconds.

"Fuck," I say out loud.

Gus flinches, peeking at me over his shoulder while we're stuck at traffic lights. "What?"

"I met Cole Devaney last night."

He rolls his eyes, shaking his head. "You fangirled so hard. I'm embarrassed for you."

We continue once the light changes and I have to shout over the engine and wind to be heard, "There's this scene in *The Decider* where he jumps off a moving truck, off a fucking mountain, then parachutes to the bottom – *topless*.

And I mean," I pause for effect, "It's no surprise he has a state-of-the-art gym in his basement. That man has an eight pack."

Gus tuts under his breath. "I've heard he's really average in bed."

"Ha!" I howl. "Did you hear that or is it from personal experience?"

"If I liked guys, I could do better than Cole," he says.

"Mmm. No. You couldn't. He is peak. He is like the male version of Margot Robbie. It doesn't get better. There's not another level of hotness beyond Cole. And I showered, *naked*, in his bathroom this morning," I say, laughing. "How long have you known him?"

"First of all, there are eleven showers in that house so statistically he's never used that one before – I asked. Secondly, he isn't Margot Robbie level hot. You're *deluded*. Thirdly, where was this energy when you met me? And finally, are you telling me you're an action thriller kind of girl?"

"I am!"

He parks up besides hundreds of other Vespas and mopeds, waiting for me to climb off before dismounting himself and taking his hat off, his curls squished flat at the top. He stares at me for a long second. "Hmm. Interesting."

"You didn't answer my question," I say, removing my hat too and fluffing up my hair. "How long have you known him?"

"I was in a film with him six years ago. We hung out a bit. Then we dated the same woman for like three months."

"On purpose?" I gasp.

Gus laughs. "No, of course not. She was playing us. I

was on tour. And she wasn't exactly subtle about it. When it all came out, I was too busy to be wrecked over it, but Cole was furious and tried to knock me out in a fancy club in Mayfair."

"I would've loved to have seen that," I say, already picturing the scuffle.

It's hot.

Gus carefully pulls me out of the way as another moped parks beside us. "I bet you would've. He gave me a black eye and everything. You seriously didn't hear about any of this?"

I can't help it; I smile and shake my head. He seems to care about my opinion which is hilarious to me.

"You got a black eye from Cole Devaney?" I ask, animatedly. "I'm so jealous."

He tilts his head, smiling. He's so onto me.

"Wait. But how are you friends?"

He shrugs. "What can I say, I have a way with words even when I'm being beaten to a pulp. He thought I did it on purpose. He was heartbroken. In all honesty, she was way out of my league, and I'd seen the photos of her and Cole strolling the streets of Rome, but I didn't want to deal with them. I just sort of ignored the whole thing. Until it hit me in the face like Cole Devaney's fist... oh wait..." He gives me a knowing look.

"Ha!"

"I actually do need to keep a low profile here though. Vanessa lives here too, and I can't have people thinking we're in the same city on purpose."

"*Vanessa?*" I ask, shrill voiced. "A *Vanessa* was two-timing you and Cole?"

"Yes?"

"Was she eighty?"

"No. She is the daughter of a very rich old man."

I roll my eyes. "The troubled ones always are."

Gus just snorts and shakes his head.

"What film were you in?"

"It was one of the Jason Bourne spin-offs. It didn't do great in the box office. I thought for a minute my future might have been in Hollywood."

"Oh yeah?"

"I was wrong," he adds.

"Not the next DiCaprio?"

"No. Let's just say I wasn't booked again. Besides they cut all my scenes."

"Ouch."

"Yeah. I decided acting wasn't for me after that."

Without much thought he links his hand in mine, his warm knuckles wide between my fingers. Something about the pressure makes my breathing unsteady. I press my lips together to see how long it takes him to notice, but all he does grin at me over his shoulder.

Later that afternoon, after exploring the Colosseum and strolling through old ruins of the Roman Forum, we hop back on the Vespa and whizz over to Vatican City. As we walk up to St. Peter's Basilica, Gus stops short to eye up the massive queue.

"This could be tricky," he whispers, leaning into me. I nod, prepared to sack it off when I spot an opportunity. A large tour is on the move ahead of us, a man with a strong scouse accent, is holding a British flag and rounding everyone up.

I grab Gus's hand and drag him into the fold. "What the—"

"*Sssh*," I hiss, nudging him with my elbow. "Don't say anything. We'll just follow this tour."

"Sara. I can't go into these buildings with my hat and sunglasses on. They're places of worship. I'm bound to be spotted."

I check the crowd around us. There isn't anyone looking his way, but honestly, nearly everyone is much older than us. I doubt they'll know who he is. And yet, I've seen how tense he gets when he thinks he's about to be pounced on. I sigh. "We can leave if you're really worried. We'll just sneak out that way?"

"No," he whispers. "You wanted to do this. Let's do it."

"I just like basking in the history," I whisper back. "I like to pretend I lived here in a past life."

Gus raises his eyebrows. "In the Vatican?"

"Hey. I might've been an old, bald man in medieval times. You don't know."

We seem to go unnoticed for the first part of the tour. An hour in though, when we're considering sneaking away because it's a little slow for us, the tour guide glances at Gus and I'm pretty sure he knows who he is.

At the end, full of guilt for crashing it, Gus thanks the tour guide and offers to sign something for him. The man is elated but highly discreet. He helps us through the crowds and back to the street unnoticed.

"Hey," Gus says, taking my arm before I can strap my helmet back on. "Thanks for that, that was incredible." He's gazing at me intently.

"Oh, it's nothing! I seized an opportunity."

"Yes, you did," he grins. "Very spontaneous of you."

I can't help the blush that creeps up my neck. Thankfully, his phone buzzes, saving me from the moment. He retrieves it from his pocket, staring down at the screen. For a moment I'm worried I've fucked up, that he's been spotted, and there are pictures of us all over the tabloids. I'm about to ask him when he looks up and smiles.

"Fancy meeting Cole for dinner in the city?"

I tilt my head. "Do you really need me to answer that question?"

Twenty-Two

As soon as I'm back in my room, staring at my limited clothing, I realise agreeing to go to dinner with not one, but *two* world-famous superstars in Rome might've been a stretch.

I don't scratch my head for too long before I'm knocking on Gus's door down the hall. He arrives moments later, freshly damp from the shower with only a towel wrapped low on his waist.

Don't look, don't look, don't look!

I looked. *Obviously.*

"Oh, I'm sorry…" I say, blinking away, heat rushing to my cheeks. "I didn't mean to interrupt. I—"

"Are you blushing?" he asks, surprise in his tone.

"Well, you are practically naked," I point out.

He looks down at himself. I follow his eyes; a light trail of hair starts between the neat grooves of his torso then narrows as it reaches the towel. It doesn't take much work to imagine what's beneath that. I swallow and shake myself out of it.

Why did I come here again?

Oh yes, clothes.

"I have a problem," I say.

"Is it me?"

"No, you're just a *pain*. I don't have anything to wear."

Gus regards me plainly for a minute. "And yet you're not naked," he says, a smile tugging at the corners of his lips.

"Funny." I sigh, letting my arms drop. "Where are we going? Is it somewhere fancy? Somewhere I'll need a dress? I doubt Cole eats anywhere that doesn't have a Michelin star."

"You'd be surprised. He's actually a massive slob."

"Stop shit-talking him to me, it ruins the fantasy."

Gus only chuckles to himself. "Hang on, I'll call him." He heads back into the room and grabs his phone off the nightstand, holding it to his ear. Cole picks up straight away.

"Mate, where we eating?" he asks. I can hear the low drumbeat of Cole's voice down the line. Gus nods along, keeping his eyes firmly on my face the entire time. I try to act like this isn't incredibly intimate and making my heart beat faster than it should be and take slow discreet breaths to steady myself.

Finally, Gus says, "In that case, can I borrow your wardrobe? Our stuff is on the cruise." He nods, hangs up then holds a finger up to me as he closes the door. One moment later he comes back out in a white dressing gown and slippers.

"Follow me," he instructs.

"I doubt I'm going to find anything to wear in Cole's wardrobe."

"Oh yeah?"

"Yeah. For one, he's six foot five."

Gus makes a dismissive sound. "Please. He's pushing six three."

Gus leads me across the villa to where Cole's master suite is, and – to my surprise – Aline is already waiting for us at an enormous wooden door. She doesn't speak much English as she ushers us into what I can only describe as a walk-in wardrobe on steroids. She quickly finds a white shirt and some dark trousers to fit Gus before shooing him away and focusing her attention on me.

She closes the door behind him, so I don't catch what he says as he leaves.

Aline looks me up and down with warm green eyes, nods and guides me to another corner of the room, with mahogany shelves and lit up mirrors. I wish I could ask her how long she's worked here, she has a very gentle, nurturing energy about her. Her first choice, which she holds up against me so I can see my reflection in the mirror, is a long, tight red dress that, quite honestly, intimidates me.

It's beautiful but *way* too sexy.

As if she gets all of this from my facial expressions alone, she nods and takes it back. The next two outfits are the wrong fit. Finally, she pulls out a sleek black dress with a slit up one side. Its far more my style, even if it would annihilate my usual clothing budget, so I try it on.

Despite it being more fitted than I expected, the fabric sheer in places, it gives business sexy. And it's completely my style. I turn to Aline as she's picking out grey snake print heels for me to pair with it. "Why does Cole have so many clothes for women?" I ask, genuinely bemused.

She smiles wryly. "Women guests," she explains. "Girlfriends from past."

I bite my bottom lip and nod at her politeness. I could be severely weirded out right now (and probably should be?!) but as Gus said earlier, when in Rome.

Aline shows me where to forage make-up, hair styling tools and whatever I might need to smarten up. I pinch a brand-new razor and head to the shower, hanging my borrowed dress on the back of my door.

An hour later, I take the main stairs down to meet Gus, hoping he knows where we're going. I spot him first, the white shirt a little long on him and buttoned low but, somehow, he makes it work, especially with the dark trousers he's rolled up at the ankles. When he hears my footsteps, he does a double take, his eyes landing on my waist, then lower to the split, the tease of my thigh.

His reaction sends a thrill right through me. I really wish I would stop reacting this way to him. I keep telling myself that he's a popstar and our worlds do not mesh. Once we're back on the cruise, or back to real life, there's nothing here that can last. It's not plausible. It's not sensible.

Who's to say I'll ever be able to trust again after everything that happened with Mike?

If only my stomach wasn't jittery every time he looked my way. Especially since he's been looking plenty. I'm practically high on the feeling at this point.

He finally corrects himself, clearing his throat and smiling. "You look…"

"Is it ok?" I interrupt. "Not too much? I can wear something else, there were—"

"No, no, don't change, it's—" I don't know why but I don't want him to finish the sentence.

I point at his suit. "You look smart."

It's awkward. I can tell by the press of his lips and the telling glint in his eyes, that he too, thinks I'm being supremely weird about this.

The problem is a compliment from him, right now, would hold too much weight. Which is ridiculous because I never felt like that with Mike but, then again, when was the last time Mike complimented me? I can't honestly remember. I'm not the type of person who needs words of affirmation because if nothing else, they don't feel true. So, in fear of his words installing some kind of panic in me, I drive them away.

He blinks down at himself, presses his lips together in thought, then gestures towards the door. "Shall we?"

It's still light out, but the sun is dropping fast, the city immersed in an orange glow, sharp shadows at every corner. I'm thankful for the slit in my dress, allowing me to straddle the Vespa, as I hang onto Gus, confidently navigating the busy streets towards our destination. My hair beneath my helmet rustles in the breeze.

Fifteen minutes later, he parks us down a narrow street between tall, light-coloured buildings and immediately swaps his helmet for his black cap and sunglasses. He anxiously glances around before taking my hand (an act that's beginning to feel like it's second nature) and guiding me towards the promise of music and good food.

As we turn another corner, we're greeted by a rich aroma of Italian cuisine, fairy lights hung between buildings in a small closed off courtyard with tables and awnings. "Have you been here before?" I ask, since he strides in so purposefully.

He slows a touch, glancing over his shoulder. "Oh yeah.

This is one of Cole's haunts. He's related to the owner, second cousin or something like that. Hence the hat and shades, in case you were wondering. I'd prefer not to be spotted."

I check the surroundings for prying eyes.

"Don't worry," he adds, squeezing my hand. "We'll have a spot out the back."

As soon as we enter the main restaurant a man shouts, "AUGUSTUS!" I almost jump out of my skin but Gus laughs, patting the man on the back and pointing towards a set of stripped curtains behind the bar.

"Sì, sì. I bring you and your beautiful woman drinks right away."

I look at Gus, waiting pointlessly for him to correct this eccentric man but he just smiles, nods and heads towards the curtains, towing me with him. The delectable waft of garlic, basil and onions has my tastebuds watering.

It's not until we emerge from the other side that I feel a sudden wave of nerves. This is it. I – Sara Stirling – am about to have dinner in Rome with a world-famous superstar… and Gus (also world-famous but arguably less cool).

It's absurd. I'm almost lightheaded.

The balcony is a decently sized, private space overlooking a busy roundabout below, surrounded by ancient buildings and beautiful roman architecture. Bougainvillea hangs almost romantically from the floor above and candles are burning on the table set for four.

I almost stumble when I spot Cole and his date.

Gus halts too, blinking. "For fuck's sake," he grumbles, eyeing the blonde woman. "*Really?* Must you turn up everywhere I go?"

The woman, who is absolutely gorgeous, beams at Gus. She stands up to greet us and Gus turns on his heel.

I'm having one of those high-stress, out of body experiences – this will be an ex, or former lover, or something that complicates the feelings I shouldn't even have for this man and just reinforces the fact that this weird little crush (*if we're calling it that!*) is wholly delusional and entirely misplaced – I don't want to hear the next part because, honestly? I've been enjoying this whole adventure, this daydream.

"I'm so sorry," he says. "She does this more than I'd like to admit."

"Who?" I barely croak out, eyes wide like a deer in headlights.

What is happening here?

The woman steps towards me in a figure-hugging green dress, her lips a deep red. She's absolutely stunning and curvaceous in way I could only dream of. She holds out her hand.

"Hi Sara, please ignore him, he's just bitter people prefer my company to his." She sticks her tongue out at him.

What is going on?!

"Keep telling yourself that," Gus tuts.

She pretends he isn't here, "I'm Grace. My brother has told me literally nothing about you, so I bullied an invite out of Cole so I could do what I do best."

Something stupid, like relief, floods me. *His sister.* I could scream, but I actually make a nervous sound instead. It comes out like a squeaky laugh. "*Hi,*" is all I manage.

"And what is it you do best?" Gus interrupts.

She gives him a sisterly smile. "*Intrude.*"

He chokes on a laugh. "Yes. Yes, you do. What are you even doing in Italy?"

She shrugs. "I have a work thing in Milan."

Cole laughs this time. "Just a quick six-hour drive from here." Grace brushes this off, making a face at me like they're all being very dramatic.

"I took the liberty of ordering champagne for us," she says to me, ushering me to the table. I take the seat opposite hers, Gus sliding in beside me.

"Er, thank you," I say, as she fills my glass.

"What are you having?" she asks, nodding at the menu.

"Give the girl a chance," Cole says, giving her a disbelieving glance.

"I'm just excited. This is the first normie Gus has ever dated. Well, since secondary school."

Sirens sound in my head. Must shut this down.

"Oh, we're not…"

But Gus is already speaking too, "She is *not* the first *normal* woman I've dated. What are you basing this on anyway? Normal is subjective."

"We're not dating," I try to add, but nobody is listening.

"You've only ever dated rich people's daughters," Grace accuses.

"Not true! What about Maisy Telling? She wasn't famous when I dated her. The first time anyway."

Cole laughs as Grace sputters. "She's a nepo baby!"

"No, she's not!"

"Her father is Martyn Telling!"

"Who is that?" he asks.

"That guy who wrote that fantasy show about the dragons," she says. "He's a multi-millionaire."

Gus shrugs and blows out a breath. "I didn't know that."

"You didn't talk about her family?" I ask.

To which he sputters a laugh. "What can I say?"

"Oh nothing. I already knew you were a fiend."

"But you like me anyway?"

I give him a stare. "When did I say I liked you?"

When I turn back, Grace and Cole are both sipping slowly, watching our interaction with fascination. Ok, fine. So I'm flirting again. It's just so easy to flirt with him. I could smack my head against the table, instead I sip on my champagne to calm my nerves.

When the waiter comes to take our orders, I keep it simple with a carbonara. "There's no way I'm spending time in Rome and not getting its most famous dish," I say to argue my point but, in the end, all four of us get some kind of pasta.

"Are we going to share though?" Gus asks.

I make a face. "Absolutely not. Why on earth would we share?"

"But how do we re-enact *Lady and The Tramp*?"

"We don't?"

"Such a wasted opportunity."

Grace is grinning at us again. Cole too, but he seems to be entertained by Grace's antics as much as ours. In fact, he's nothing like his characters at all. He's so quiet and morose.

"What was it like being his little sister?" I ask Grace, to pull her attention away from us.

She groans. "It's my entire personality, apparently. But if I try to fight it, it only makes me depressed. Nobody gives a damn about me."

Gus sniffs. "*Please*! Save the sob story, Sara isn't going to buy it. As if you don't reap the benefits."

"I might as well. I might change my name legally to Gus from Just4Summer's sister."

"Sorry if that was insensitive…" I add slowly, but Gus gives me a look that suggests Grace is just messing with me, so I decide to pose a sillier question. "What's the most embarrassing thing he ever did to you?"

At this her face lights up. She flicks her hair behind her shoulders and leans forward with a familiar twinkle in her caramel eyes. I guess the apple doesn't fall far from the tree. When I turn to see what Gus thinks of my question, he looks just as intrigued as I am.

"My twenty-first birthday," she starts.

Gus throws his hands up, shaking his head. "Here we go."

"I asked Jax to kiss me because I knew some of the guests were actively filming us. I thought it would be funny. A bit of drama to throw into the mix. The media and J4S fans were weirdly obsessed with my dating history." She pauses to take a sip of wine. "I honestly got so tired of fighting it, that I just ran with it. I even invited some of the people I knew were involved with spilling my secrets to the press, because they didn't know I knew it was them." She shrugs like she's half-proud of the drama she caused. "Anyway, Jax was a *friend*," she adds, eyeing Gus across the table. He clenches his jaw and looks down at his drink.

"What I didn't know is that Gus and Jax were mid spat about some other girl. Jax didn't tell me. And, well, let's just say Gus intervened. He was yelling, pulling at

Jax's T-shirt, making a whole scene. And yes, I did *want* a scene. But a scene crafted at my own hands. Not my big brother acting all protective at my birthday party. It was mortifying."

I give him a look. "What did you do?"

"I threw a drink at him," he says, his expression unreadable. "I should have punched him though, in hindsight."

"Hmm," Grace mutters. "Gus was so drunk he missed, by the way, and drenched me instead. *On my birthday.*"

"I said I was sorry! And besides, Will dealt with Jax before I had a chance."

Something about this sentence silences Grace, her composure softening. I half expect her to add more to the story, but instead she takes a sip of water and is pleasantly pleased by the waiter arriving with bread to interrupt the conversation.

After we've finished our mains and the table is being cleared, the owner comes in again and starts to converse with Cole in Italian. He invites him to follow him into the kitchen and Gus joins too, checking I'm alright with his sister before he goes.

Obviously, I nod, except I'm instantly on edge as I turn back to her.

She's smiling conspiratorially. "You'd be good for him," she says.

"Oh no, it's not like that, we just met."

"I know."

"Besides, I don't really think—"

"I've never seen him look at anyone the way he looks at you," she says, interrupting me, her tone serious. "I think it's because you remind him of what our childhood was like. We were totally normal. I don't think either of us were designed for the life his fame brought us."

I put my napkin on the table and sit back. "Gus does seem affected by it all."

"He's a sensitive guy, really," she says. "I know he's scared about what life will be like now this is all over. And I also know he doesn't want to hear it, or how much he's actually told you, but it *is* coming to an end. He'll find out soon. Between us, you should be prepared for that. In case you're with him."

I swallow and nod.

"Obviously, he has opportunities, if he wants them. He could make his own music, or act." She laughs. "Fuck. Actually no, not acting. He is a fucking *terrible* actor."

"What do you think he'll do?"

She twists her lips. "Honestly? I think he'd be a good mentor for other young popstars. He's talented. He might perform again. Or he could turn to presenting."

I grin. "He'd be good at that."

"*Right?* He has the personality for it." Although she frowns. "I'm not sure I want to see him in the music industry again though. It's incredibly toxic and takes so much from him."

Before she can say anymore Cole and Gus return. We order desserts, then after, when we're all full and tipsy, Gus leans back, reaching an arm behind me to rest on my chair. I'm hyperaware of Grace, reading my every reaction. She can barely hide her smile. If I knew her better, I'd kick her under the table.

My sisters would like her. She's fiery.

"Right," she says, slapping her palms on the table and standing up. "I'm going to go before the bill arrives because they'll be a super awkward moment where Gus offers to pay and Cole refuses."

"I already paid," Cole responds.

Gus growls good-humouredly. "You mother fuc—"

"See," she says, laughing at me.

"I feel whiplashed."

"Hanging out with Grace will do that to you," Gus says, just as she retorts, "That'll be because Gus is so *annoying*!"

Cole stands to block Grace's escape. "Where are you staying tonight?" he asks. It's almost protective. I glance at Gus to read his expression, but he clearly isn't bothered by their interaction.

"A boutique hotel in Parioli," she says. "Although I appreciate your offer to stay with you, I try not to stay in the same place as my brother, as you know."

Cole nods. "Take my car. My driver will take you wherever you need to go."

I expect her to politely refuse but instead she laughs and says, "Ok." Before she reaches the curtain to the kitchens, she spins on her heel and steps towards Gus, throwing an arm round his neck and holding him close. "I nearly forgot to hug you. Here's some cash. You can pay me back later," she says, stepping back and pulling out a massive wad of euros from her handbag and pressing it into his palm. "And I hope I'll be seeing more of you, Sara." Then she turns again and marches out of the restaurant as Cole calls his driver to explain the change in plans.

Gus leans towards me, his lips almost brushing the shell of my ear. "Are you up for walking back to the villa?"

I turn to him and immediately regret it, my pulse jumping in my throat at his proximity. "Ok," is all I manage to squeak out.

All I can think about, as his eyes track mine, is Grace saying, *I've never seen him look at anyone the way he looks at you.* I swallow that information down and clear my throat, brushing down the invisible dirt on my dress.

Gus throws a helmet at Cole, which he catches with his superhuman reflexes. "Hey, I know you've been drinking, but can you take the Vespa back? We're going to walk."

Cole rolls his eyes good-humouredly. "I'll arrange a taxi to collect me. And the Vespa."

Twenty-Three

Despite it being dark, Rome is surprisingly well-lit. Gus puts his cap on forwards and takes my hand as he guides us back towards Cole's villa, navigating the picturesque streets, stopping to point out the ruins of an old bathhouse or a temple to one of the gods.

"Sorry about Grace," Gus mumbles as we turn another corner, the clip of my heels on the pavement.

"Why are you sorry?"

"She gatecrashed."

"She's ok. I think she just worries about you."

He sighs raggedly, running his spare hand down his nose. "I wish I could've protected her from it all. I was too late to warn her about what this world does to people, and by the time I knew, she had already been flung into the spotlight. And to make matters worse, it was my fault."

"What do you mean?"

"We were on this gameshow in our early years of fame. It was a teen show where you basically dunk each other in gunk. Honestly, it was stupid. And, anyway, they asked us if we wanted to bring family members on to twist it up a little.

Grace was my family member. She's the only sister in the band and, I guess, there were tons of teenage girls out there who wanted to know what life was like being my sister."

"But she embraced it, right?"

He shrugs. "That's what I can never work out. I wasn't close enough to her back then. I was so busy. And then…" He swallows slowly, trying to decide on his next words. "And then I wasn't sober for a while."

"You couldn't protect her," I say. "Because you also needed protecting."

"What I'm trying to say, is she means well. And I guess I understand what you mean when you say you feel like your sisters begrudge you. I know the feeling. I'll live with the guilt of what the media did to her forever. The body image stuff, the time she was papped running away from an ex in tears, the gunk show… I hate myself for it."

"She loves you," I say, because I think that's what he needs to hear. "She wanted to make sure I wasn't using you." When he gives me a worried look, I add, "She didn't ask directly, but she was watching me. You can tell she knows how to spot red flags."

He laughs. "Well, she hasn't warned me off you."

I drop my gaze. "Can *I* warn you off me?"

"You can try."

I chew on my lip, a thrill rushing down my spine.

I've never seen him look at anyone the way he looks at you.

"What's it like?" I ask, changing the subject. "Being famous?"

Gus grins like he's onto me changing the subject, then shrugs as we begin to walk again.

"It's just my life now. I don't give it much thought. And part of me thinks that because it happened when I was still a kid, that I don't really know what normal life is like anymore. Actually, I've really enjoyed spending these past few days with you. You've treated me like an average bloke."

"You're *welcome*," I quip. "And for what it's worth, Popstar, you *are* a normal bloke to me."

He squeezes my hand. "The thing is, I'm not worried about anyone seeing *me*. I'm used to that. By this point, I've had enough adventure that if my team insist on coming to get me, it won't be the end of the world. It's more that social media has made it harder for me to hide away, to escape the attention. Everyone's a reporter these days." He glances over his shoulder as if to make his point. "I'm very aware about dragging you into drama."

"And what drama is that specifically?"

"It's *all* drama. Constantly. If there's no drama, someone will make up a narrative. I do nothing and still get hauled into things." He huffs out a breath. "I, personally, would be thrilled to be seen with you."

"Oh really?"

He smiles softly. "Yes."

"But?"

He looks at our hands, entwined. "But... I don't know if you want the drama that comes with... *me*."

"With you? With being your friend?"

He stops in the middle of a quiet street, moonlight reflecting off the warm tarmac and touches his heart. "You're my friend?"

I burst out laughing, pushing him in the chest with my spare hand. "Shut up!" I step past him, dragging him with me to keep the conversation going. "What kind of friendships did you have with the other band members before it all blew up?"

"Oh, we were thick as thieves. In fact, we actually did rob up the local farm shop when we were fourteen."

"What? *No*," I say, my tone laced with doubt.

He nods. "Got away with an apple each and a stick of celery."

"*Animals.*"

"When Will's mam found out she marched us back down there to apologise and pay them back. Terrifying woman."

"Do you miss those days?"

Gus sighs. "I miss feeling like we were unstoppable. Like our friendship was unshakeable. Unfortunately, the industry has a way of tearing that kind of thing apart."

We're quiet as we pass a group of young adults heading towards a street of bars and clubs, one of whom takes a good long look at Gus. We hasten our pace until we've turned a corner and there doesn't seem to be anyone following us.

"Tell me something," he says after a moment.

"What's that?"

"Why did a woman like you want to get married anyway?"

I groan. "It's embarrassing."

"Well, now you have to tell me or I'll go insane trying to figure it out."

I sigh. "My parents were so in love," I say. "My dad committed to mum for life. I haven't seen him date another woman since. She was his world. I guess that was my inspiration. And, besides, I'm a modern girl, I don't want marriage in the old-fashioned sense. I can support myself."

"I'm waiting for the embarrassing part…"

"I want the emotional stability. I want the part where someone is going to stand before me, in front of all my family and friends, and say they want to live the rest of their life with me, for better or worse. All of it."

Gus gives me a disbelieving glance. "And that's embarrassing to you?"

"It's *soppy*. But I like contracts. I like how you can have everything written down and guaranteed. To me, marriage is a contract." I shrug, keeping my eyes lowered, unwilling to find out whether I'm being judged for my vulnerability.

"I don't think that's embarrassing. I think that's pretty romantic."

I shake my head. "It's soppy," I correct him. "There was so much instability in my childhood. My dad was great and I love him to pieces but he wasn't the kind of man you could cry on. He was too broken himself." We've slowed down again. I can see the ivy-strewn street where Cole lives up ahead. It's like we're both trying to drag this walk out.

"I guess what I'm saying, is I want stability. Or at least I did. Now, I'm not so sure. I feel like I dodged a bullet with Mike and that's a scary thought to have."

"You trusted your instincts. That's impressive. Not everyone trusts themselves enough to do that."

I swallow. "I almost didn't."

We reach the wall outside Cole's villa, a path of moonlight stretching almost all the way back up the street. I pause, leaning my shoulders against it and watch Gus who's more than happy to wait out here too. It's quiet, almost serene – the sound of the city a quiet backdrop. I cross my arms and stare at my feet. "You know, sometimes I wish I had a big sister."

"I could be your big sister," Gus offers. I can't help but laugh, glancing back at him to see that familiar glint in his eye.

I twist my lips. "No."

He acts offended, touching his chest. "Why not?"

He knows why. "Because you're a man. And…"

"And?" He steps closer. My heart pulses in my neck. My body is so game for whatever is going on here, I can feel the adrenaline rushing through my veins.

He knows… I know he knows.

As if he can read my mind, he leans in towards me. I tip my head back and compress a smile.

"What's holding you back?" he practically whispers.

"Apart from the fact you're a stranger?"

He narrows his eyes, waiting for the real reason. "We're not strangers."

"You're a popstar," I remind him. I don't tell him that the thought of falling for him scares me because I have no idea how to navigate a new relationship, yet alone one with someone famous. Someone who could have anyone they wanted.

Gus runs his spare hand down his face and laughs, surprised. "I can't say that's ever been a reason I've been rejected before."

I chew on my lip to prevent a smile. "What are the usual reasons?"

"Mostly my personality," he says, grinning.

I burst out laughing, rolling my head back and smiling at the starry night.

"Fuuuck," he mutters. "You have no idea how much I like making you laugh. It's intoxicating, Sara."

When I allow myself to look at him again, his expression has changed. The usual cheeky glint has vanished and in its place is a parted-lip look of vulnerability. He swallows deeply, his perfect throat working. I run my tongue over my bottom lip thinking about how much I'd like to taste him there.

"Don't look at me like that," I say, staring back at him pointedly.

"Like what?"

"Like *that*!" I say, gesturing at his face. "Like you... *You know!*"

Like you want to ravish me right here in the street, rip my dress from my body and explore every inch of me with your tongue.

He can't fight a smirk, shaking his head. "No, I have no idea. You're going to have to fill me in."

"I'm serious, Gus."

"You are. You're *very* serious, Sara."

I cover my face with my hands, trying to hide my smile and the rising heat in my cheeks. "I can't fancy you," I say, muffled by my fingers.

He reaches forward and peels my hands away, bringing them to his lips and pressing his mouth to them. There's something about the way he runs his warm breath over my knuckles that sends shots right to my core, making me clench my thighs.

It's a promise.

He knows what he's doing.

I tip my head back, ignoring the impulses telling me this is only going to end in tears. That I can't handle this yet. That I'm not ready.

Because my body has entirely different thoughts.

"You can fancy me if you want to, sweetheart," Gus whispers, bringing my hands to his chest and laying them flat as he steps closer, bringing our bodies together. "I'll look after that information. Nobody else needs to know."

My breathing hastens as he runs a hand slowly up my side, starting at my waist, running higher, taking his time. When he traces the underside of my breasts, I almost combust right there on the spot. I'm completely at his mercy.

"Gus," I whimper.

"I'm listening." His cracked voice rumbles by the shell of my ear. "What do you need?"

You. You. You.

"This is a bad idea," I say.

His huff of laughter as his lips graze my neck tells me he only partly agrees. "Then tell me to stop, Sara. Tell me to stop and I'll go." I part my lips but the word never comes. I'm almost certain I'm going to tell him to stop but his fingers brush under my chin, tipping it towards him and it feels so good, as he brings our lips closer, I lose all sensible thoughts.

His wine-soaked breath and perfect, thick lips are irresistible.

"*Fuck it*," I breathe.

I feel his answering groan like sparklers fizzling in my tummy.

"*Fuck it, indeed*," he says, as his lips crash over mine, rough and hungry.

His arms come around my waist, pulling me closer, his lips pressing harder, faster. My hands run higher until they're wrapped around his neck, fingers in his gorgeous curls, tugging him away, pressing him closer, all the time his breathing speaks to me in shattered gasps. And when I open my lips to him and he slides his tongue over mine, I'm rewarded with a solid thigh pressed between my legs. A welcome, delicious friction.

Fuck.

An untethered sound escapes me. I want him to push me harder. Hold me tighter. Kiss me fiercer.

I'm so wanton, so needy, I'm surprised by my reaction.

I want him. I can't have him. I need him.

As one of his hands releases my waist and ventures between us, a finger running lower over the sheer black material of my dress, my breathing ragged and desperate, the gates to Cole's villa creak open.

"Hey, you two keep setting off the security senso – *Oh!*"

The interruption is like a bucket of ice water down my back. I twist out of Gus's grasp and laugh at the wall, turning away from him. I hold a hand to my face. I'm so hot. There's no way Cole won't be able to tell.

I wiggle out of the curve of Gus's body but he takes my arm, attempting to twist me back to him. "Sara."

"Such a lovely evening," I say to them both. *I can't believe we were caught!* "Thank you! But I'm beat."

"Sara…" his voice is urgent as we pass Cole, my arm still in his gentle grip. "Come on, wait up."

I turn and laugh nervously, twisting my arm free once we reach the staircase in the hall. "It's fine, Gus."

He's watching me cautiously from the step below. "I don't think we're finished here," he says. "I think we need…"

I press my hand to his cheek. "We got carried away," I say, like it's obvious. "It's fine. You don't have to worry about me. We're fine. It's fine."

He's shaking his head, a small smile playing on his lips like he isn't sure how to read me now but he lets it drop.

"Night then," I say, my voice too pitchy, spinning on my heels and darting away before he can persuade me to do something insanely irresponsible, like going to his room to finish this whole thing off in detail. Because although I'm outrageously tempted, I know no good can come of it.

I'm already too affected by him.

Twenty-Four

Cruise Location – Rome
Next Port – Portofino
Time of Departure – 18:00 (GMT+1)

My attempt at sleep is fruitless.

I lay there, my heartbeat drumming in my chest until I hear Gus's steady footsteps tread down the hall followed by the quiet creak of his door behind him.

What is happening to me? Why am I being so reckless?

I know deep down that I don't *want* to be with someone famous. I could never handle the public scrutiny. The interference. There isn't a single part of me who would welcome that into my life. I don't want to be a part of that world.

I turn over and groan silently into my pillow.

Breathe. It's not that serious. I've known him for barely a week.

And yet my body is ripe with need. I'm practically buzzing with it. I could sneak over to his room now and let what happens, happen. I'm sure he'd welcome it.

But no.

Ahhh!

Tomorrow we'll (*hopefully*) be back on the cruise and who knows what change that will bring. Who knows how he'll feel once we surface back into the real world.

We should keep it PG. Friendly.

I roll back over and scream silently at the ceiling. I need to cool off and the only way I can think to do that is with a freezing cold shower. I practically crawl to the ensuite, setting myself up on the pristine tiled floor and let the icy water trickle over my body until I feel more human.

In the morning, having managed only a few hours of solid sleep, I shower again and get dressed before making my way down to the kitchen for breakfast. We're heading straight to the port to catch the boat, so thankfully there's no time to linger. Gus comes down, freshly shaven and ready to address last night. My brain is gearing up to spiral but before he has the chance to corner me, Cole walks in to wish us a farewell. He gives me a hug and I take a second to muse on how surreal this whole situation is.

Despite the cruise stopping off in Rome, it *actually* docks in a port almost an hour from the city. The coaches, bringing holidaymakers to and from the tourist attractions, don't return to the cruise until early evening, so Cole offered us his car and driver so we could travel in style and dodge any more mishaps.

I'm careful to avoid touching or looking at Gus, but I can tell he's hyperaware of everything I do. His gaze warms my skin wherever it lands, which certainly doesn't help. It took a solid thirty-minute, freezing cold shower to calm my nerves last night.

And I have things to say today.

As soon as we're alone. I need to insert a healthy dose of reality into this situation because I don't think Gus will be the one to do it.

Except my confidence in my own confrontational style flies right out the window the second I'm sat in the back of Cole's dark car and I'm unable to start the conversation like a normal, adult, human being. Every time I try, my heart rate peaks and the words jumble on my tongue.

"Just say it," Gus says to me after twenty minutes of silence.

I give him a look. "Say what?"

"The thing that's driving you crazy."

"Nothing's driving me crazy," I lie.

He smirks at me. "You've been pulling faces at yourself since we left."

"Fine," I say, sighing. "This isn't a good idea."

"No?" he asks, raising a brow. "I disagree."

"That's because you're *you*," I point out.

"That doesn't feel like a compliment."

"It's just that this can't work. It can't last. You're a famous popstar with an enormous fanbase. You can have anyone you want. I'm going to go back to my reality after this cruise, and you'll go to yours, and there's no way you'll want to follow me. And, well, I won't follow you... That's just not who I am."

"I know," he agrees, his smile fading.

"And so, I don't know if I'm... strong enough for this kind of thing right now."

"I see."

"So, we'll be friends."

Gus doesn't say anything for a disarming amount of time, his eyes tracking mine, running his teeth over his lips in contemplation.

"Ok, Sara. If that's what you want. I won't pretend it

isn't a shame, but I won't pursue this. The next move is yours."

"And I won't make a move," I clarify. "Because of all the reasons I just said."

"Mmhmm," he agrees, nodding. "Understood."

"I'm serious."

"You said."

I narrow my eyes at his suspiciously relaxed response. "Ok."

He moves his hand across the centre console and leans towards me, his lips close to my ear.

"But if that late-night shower is anything to go by, you *will* make the next move and I'm not going to stop you when you do."

My neck gets warm as I turn to hold his gaze.

"I'm not going to make a move," I whisper. I sound so unconvincing; I barely believe my own voice. In my defence, his woody, citrus-scented aftershave is distracting me. That and the tease of his curls falling over his forehead. My fingers twitch to push them back.

Gus nods and rights himself, sitting taller and fixing his collar as he looks ahead.

"Ok."

When we arrive at the port, Cole's driver drops us as close as he can and as we stroll towards our luxury cruise, the giant, pristine yacht, glinting in the sun, I can't help but laugh at the whole thing. Why was I even so stressed to begin with? *Oh no, poor me.* Stuck in the gorgeous Mediterranean with a handsome popstar. *What a chore.* Yes, I've wasted an insurmountable amount of money. Not only for the nights I've missed on the cruise, but all the rooms, the coach trips, the train tickets, the food, the drink and clothes.

I dare not look at my bank account.

That said, I waste no time heading back to my room and lying face down on the soft mattress, absorbing the peace of my own space for over an hour. Next, I wash my face, find my skincare products and do an entire cleanse. I've been using a cheap standard face cream that I found in the pharmacy in Split, but thankfully, other than the slightly burnt nose and dry eyes, my skin is doing fine. Must be all the sunshine.

Once I'm done, I sit on the balcony and fidget with the ties on my soft white robe.

I shouldn't be so twisted with excitement and nerves. It's annoying!

I parted ways with Gus only a matter of hours ago, and yet this excited little buzz keeps teasing me at the thought of seeing him again. I try to shake it off. I am *not* a giddy teenage girl. I do *not* have a crush.

I *can't* have a crush.

I bite the end of my thumb to ease the sensation pooling in my core, and lower, but it only intensifies it. I shake my head. There's no way. I'm being ridiculous. And even if I did think he has a sexy charm about him, a million and more women feel the same.

There's no way we'd make it work. That's that. If I see him tonight, I'll be cordial. I need to pivot. Now I'm back on the yacht, I plan on soaking up every last molecule of luxury and bathing in it.

I head back into the room and, for dinner, pick the sleek black mini dress with a low back that I nearly didn't pack, *not* because of him, it just so happened to be the closest dress in my wardrobe.

I sit myself on the edge of the bed and make a call.

"Hattie," I say, when she answers on the third ring. "I'm in need of some sensible advice."

"Well hello there. And sensible advice? From me?" she asks, surprised. "Nah, if you wanted sensible advice, you wouldn't have called me."

"Ok. I just… I don't know."

"I usually call *you* for sensible advice. What's going on? How is the Mediterranean and the cruise? Is it amazing?"

I fill Hattie in on my mishap adventure, travelling from city to city to city and how I nearly drowned on a fishing boat between Kotor and Bari. She listens, gasping and laughing in all the right places.

"Sara!" she exclaims. "You did this all alone? You actually got on some random man's boat? *Alone?* Who are you? That's wild. I mean, I get it, you've had a weird time of it lately and I guess you're still hurt by… all that went down… Are you doing ok? This is all insanely reckless."

I take a deep breath. "The thing is," I say. "I wasn't actually alone."

There's silence down the line.

"Hattie?"

"Yeah, I heard you. Is Mike there?"

"No! *God.* No."

"Shit. I thought you'd gotten back together for a second there. So, who were you with?"

I frown. "I actually can't tell you."

"Ok…?"

"But it was a man."

"Ok," she says, lighter. "And?"

"And I have complicated feelings about him. I want you to tell me that's insane."

Hattie laughs. "Why?"

"Because Mike—"

"Betrayed you, Sara. Mike betrayed you. You don't owe him anything."

"I know but—"

"Oh, you really thought I was going to tell you to rein it in, didn't you? Do you even *know* me?"

"I—"

"Is he hot?"

"He's... *yeah*. He's hot. But more importantly, he's charming and funny. I've enjoyed spending time with him. Even in the crazy circumstances."

There's a crackle down the line as if Hattie has taken a seat. "Go for it. Fuck his brains out."

"Hattie!"

"Hey, you'd tell me to do the same. If he's up for it and you're two consenting adults, then I say do it. Make him your rebound."

"No."

She laughs again. "Why are you calling me then? If not for permission to be reckless."

"I haven't been reckless in years and I was tougher skinned back then. I was open to heartbreak. Fuck, I actively wanted it sometimes. I enjoyed the pain and excitement it brought me, but life has knocked me down. I can't do that now."

"Ok, then don't. Just flirt a little."

I groan into my palm. She doesn't understand, because

she doesn't know what I'm dealing with. I can hardly tell her who he is, because I know she is aware of Just4Summer. And that will lead to a whole other line of questioning.

I don't know what to say so I just close my eyes and breathe.

"If this guy is flirty and funny and encouraging you to be silly, then let him. Let him energise you. What's the worst that can happen?"

"It could never work."

"How do you know?"

Because I could never be with a popstar. I have my own career and direction in life. I'm never going to be able to follow a man around the world. Obviously, I'm getting ahead of myself, he probably isn't interested in that either. And yet, I can't scramble the words together to explain that to Hattie. "He lives miles away."

"Well, why are you planning your futures together anyway? Stop looking so far ahead, you weirdo. Why not just see how the night goes?"

"I don't know how to do that."

"I know. That's why you're so brilliant. But maybe it's what you need? Remember at uni when you would say, *When I graduate, I'm going to quit drinking, get a kickass job and work my arse off to get the life I want?* And that would be your reasoning for going wild while you could? While you were free?"

"I never said *kickass*. But yes. Sort of."

"Use this holiday to do the same. Use the time. Why not?"

Why not, indeed. I want her to be right. There's an exhilarating buzz building under my skin as if I've just turned a key in a certain part of me. The reckless part. The person who wouldn't think twice about taking what she wanted.

I sigh. "I'm putting on you on video call. Can you tell me if this dress is too slutty?"

"No. It's fine."

"You haven't seen it yet."

"I miss slutty Sara, so I think it sounds great."

After mustering up the confidence to wear a little black dress to dinner, I finish my hair and make-up only to turn around *three* times on the way to the upper deck.

This is silly, I know.

But I'm *so* nervous.

It's wildly out of character for me and it's doing weird things to my body.

The nerves in my stomach reach a crescendo by the time I walk into the restaurant. I have to keep reminding myself to calm down. The hostess offers me a warm greeting and seats me by the window, where I can enjoy the gorgeous backdrop of the Italian coastline at sunset. It's stunning. The lights of the nearby towns twinkle against the silhouette of the mountains behind it.

I'm picking at a warm bread roll when he walks in.

I don't think he spots me right away. He's dressed smart, in a loose fitted shirt only partly buttoned up, sleeves rolled at his elbows and light chinos, his hair once again combed back and gelled in place. It makes him look like a movie star.

I swallow down a sip of wine and savour the taste of it on my tongue.

He's also seated alone.

I try not to look his way but he's right in my line of sight in the middle of the restaurant. I could quickly swap so I'm facing the other way, but I think if I stand right now, he'll spot me and then it would be too obvious.

And besides, I'm hardly trying to avoid him. It's just these weird nervous jitters that have me on edge.

My starter of soup is served and when the waitress walks away again, I find him staring across the room at me. He grins. I bite my bottom lip and take a deep breath.

He mouths something but I can't work out what, so I shake my head.

He mouths it again. I think he says, "What are you having?"

I glance at the bowl and assume it's obvious, mouthing back, "Soup."

He reads his menu. I take a spoonful and close my eyes because this isn't just soup – this is yacht-cruising, five-star, luxury soup, and it might have just ruined all other soups for me, forever. I stifle a groan, covering my mouth.

I feel his smile before I even look. "Good?" he mouths.

I nod, eyes wide. "So good."

"That does it," I think he says before flagging down a waiter. Five seconds later, he's stood next to my table. "Please let me sit with you. I can't bear not to hear your unfettered thoughts on the food."

"What if I'm enjoying my own company?" I ask innocently.

"You're a liar. You think I'm hilarious."

"I think you've confused me with someone else."

"Sara, I'll increase the interest I'm paying you if you don't let me sit with you."

I snort. "You're threatening to pay me more money if I don't want your company? That's a bizarre threat."

"I'm thinking three thousand per cent."

"*Gah*. Fine. Sit down," I say, feigning disinterest.

He takes a seat and rearranges his napkin. "It may be that I am suffering from trauma bonding, but I really missed you this afternoon."

"It's been six hours," I say – mouth full of another spoonful of the soup sent from heaven.

"I know but nobody was mean to me. Nobody rolled their eyes at me. Not even a single jab."

"Sounds awful," I say, trying not to smile.

He leans forward whispering, "I'm not sorry we missed the cruise."

"No?"

"No."

"Why? Because you got to see Naples and Pompeii?"

He smirks. "Yes, Sara. That's why."

"Well, I don't regret it either," I agree, nodding.

"Oh yeah?" His whole face lights up, hopeful.

"Of course. I met Cole Devaney."

His sudden laughter makes the woman behind him jump. He twists and apologises. She clearly has no idea who he is because she simply looks offended.

The waiting staff are quick to synchronise our meals. Once Gus has finished his soup we're served our fish dish. We talk about our favourite parts of the trip so far. I admit I'm missing Roko and his pet dolphin. Gus wonders if the polo he signed for the taxi driver ever made it back to the daughter and whether she was grateful or furious her dad only got Gus to sign his sweaty polo.

I drink slowly, careful not to let myself fall into the same trap as my first evening. A small lump starts to build in my throat at the thought of it. Gus must catch onto my sudden change in mood because he asks, "What's on your mind?"

I blink, lifting my shoulders protectively. "Oh, nothing," I say, trying to brush it away.

"Hey. Come on," he says. "I'm hardly going to judge."

"I'm thinking about the first night. How it felt. That's never happened to me before. I felt out of control." Gus nods but doesn't speak. "I'm sorry you had to rescue me that night," I say.

He frowns, tilting his head. "I'm sorry you were upset. I'm not sorry I found you. I'm glad I could help."

"It seemed like you'd dealt with that sort of thing before."

He nods. "Oh yeah. Panic attacks all over the place in my industry. You wouldn't believe it."

"I think I could surmise, considering the things you've told me."

"As the concerts got bigger, as my fame grew, the pressure took a lot of getting used to. I used to get panic attacks in the middle of the night. The fear of letting people down, the fear of dropping the ball on the rest of the band, it reaches you when the world is silent. I'd have nightmares for days about forgetting to put clothes on and being rushed straight up onto the stage."

"That's a classic."

He laughs, that gorgeous smoky sound. "It's usually just in front of the class though, right? Not Wembley Stadium with eighty-thousand people laughing at you."

I cringe. "*Aww.* Were they laughing?"

"Shut up," he says, sweetly, that vivid glint in his eye. "I'm trying to make you feel better. And yet, here you are, throwing it in my face."

"You love it."

He shrugs like it's a given. His gaze doesn't leave mine as he takes another sip of wine, watching me like I'm his personal evening entertainment. My eyes snag on that shape in his throat as he swallows. It feels like every girl has a weird thing they like in a man. Mine is the throat.

Call me a vampire. I don't care.

I bite my lip, unsure where to go from there. Between talking and eating, we take so long, the restaurant is almost clear, the music louder, the lights low, once we're finishing up. Gus suggests we stroll the top deck and take in the views.

As we reach the doors, we take our shoes off as instructed.

We stroll slowly, doing a perimeter, the smooth, cool decking under our bare feet, bumping into each other gently as we drift closer. We don't bother putting our shoes back on as we head to my room, Gus insisting on walking me back. Other than a few guests ambling at the bar still, the cruise has gone silent, the guests preparing for another busy day of sightseeing in Portofino. Which reminds me...

"I'm booked on the food and wine tour tomorrow."

Gus leans on the wall outside my door. "That sounds incredible."

"I certainly think so. Are you booked onto anything?"

He shakes his head, lips pressed together. "I came back to about a million messages. My team are stressed about a few events I have coming up. So I promised to do some things for them tomorrow."

Disappointment fills my veins, and I want to slap myself for it. "I'm sorry you have to work."

I'm sorry I have to go on a dumb tour without you.

He reaches out to tuck a loose strand of hair behind my ears, his fingers lingering. I drift a step closer, inviting. I relish the way my nerves feel whenever he touches me. He sucks in a breath, dropping his hand.

I can smell the red wine on his lips. I want to taste it too. The thought rushes down my spine and pools somewhere deep and wanting.

"Nope. Your move, remember?" he says, voice low. He blinks quickly, leaning back. I bite my tongue. "I'm sorry about tomorrow. But I know Monaco well. Can I take you on a personal tour?"

I swallow, righting myself and taking hold of my bedroom door. I want to say something witty, keep him on his toes but my brain isn't firing at all. So, I nod dumbly, then nearly fall into my room as I lean into the door and it opens faster than expected.

Gus reaches out to grab me but I right myself quickly.

"Balls," I hiss.

"You ok?" he asks, humour lacing his tone.

"Good night," I whisper, conscious of the other guests sleeping.

He winks. "Sleep tight, sunshine."

Twenty-Five

Cruise Location – Portofino
Next Port – Monaco
Time of Departure – 16:00 (GMT+1)

The next day is filled with wine and bread and olives and anchovies and so much delicious food they have to practically roll me back onto the boat.

And although I dress up again for dinner, Gus is nowhere to be seen. For a moment, I wonder if he's left the cruise all together, and it suddenly occurs to me that I don't even know what room he is in, or how I'd contact him. It's not like we exchanged numbers.

After a lonely dinner, I head back to my cabin for a moment and send Dad a message to see if he's free. I like to check in on him at least once a week and I'm conscious it's been slightly more than that.

"Why, if it isn't my jet-setting daughter!" he says once he answers.

"How you doing Dad?"

"I'm grand," he says. "Making some beans on toast for dinner."

"Not again."

"What do you mean 'not again'? I haven't had this in four days. Last night was a jacket potato."

"And what topping?" I ask, already knowing the answer.

"Mind your business," he huffs.

"It was beans, wasn't it?"

"So what if it was? Arrest me."

"You need vegetables, Dad," I scold.

I hear him pick the can off the side and slide his reading glasses on. "It says here that a tin of baked beans contains one of your five a day."

"Ok, good," I say. "What are your other four?"

"I had potatoes at lunch."

"Do you mean crisps?"

He grumbles something unintelligible.

"What was that?" I nudge.

"Are you really calling me on holiday to harass me about my dinner?"

I laugh. "No, not necessarily. I was calling to see how you were."

"Ah, a welfare check?"

"Have your other daughters been kind to you since I left?"

He makes a dismissive sound. "They're too busy for their poor old father. Abby popped in but only because she left her clarinet here."

I press my lips together, mildly frustrated with my sisters. Even Abby. They have a tendency to assume I'll pick up the slack with Dad. Not that he's a burden so much but he is lonely and sometimes I wish he could find himself someone to love again.

I catch up with him about what he's been watching on TV and how the new recruits are getting on at work. He tells me about the roses in the back garden which are in full bloom. I tell him all about Dubrovnik. Well, not all about it. I miss out some key elements.

And when I hang up, with him insisting he's keeping me from things. I decide I can't stay in the room all night.

I spend the evening alone, strolling along the deck, staring at the incredible views as we head towards Monaco, the rocky, greenery of Cape Martin in the distance as the sun drops behind me. The truth is, there's an ounce of relief in me that he's not shown today. Maybe he's realised I'm right and that nothing good can come of us flirting.

All that lays ahead of us is a trail of broken promises and shattered hearts.

I'm too sensible to get involved with a popstar. I've made a stable, safe life for myself. So much so, that I was able to leave Mike just like that and stay on my own two feet. I had a house, a decent salary and a bunch of friends who were mine and not his.

Then again, I wonder, as I listen to the yacht coasting over the waves below, if that was the problem. What if I was so focused on myself, on my career and my family, that I pushed Mike away? What if I was the reason he cheated? What if all the cruel things he complained to her about me were true? I *was* hard to be around. I *was* uptight.

But even thinking it, it doesn't sound right.

Someone who truly loved *me*, would love *all* of me, surely?

I think about the heated kiss back in Rome. The way I haven't laughed and flirted with someone as much as I have with Gus this past week, maybe ever! What if I ignore that feeling and it's the biggest regret of my life?

What if I already screwed it up and I'll never see him again?

Ugh. I groan at the navy sky, now littered with stars as the sun fully tucks itself away. Fine. I'll make a move. Maybe. If I see him again, I'll consider making the next move.

Because I want to. Because I enjoy his company. And because maybe he's exactly the sort of thrill I need to escape this safety blanket I've created for myself, tossing all the fun and excitement from my life.

So, at breakfast the next morning, I'm nervous that I'm about to be horribly disappointed. I eat a bowl of fruit and yoghurt alone, sipping on my coffee waiting for him to arrive. I'm maybe on my fourth mug – I've lost count – before he arrives, striding into the room with purpose, searching for me. His shoulders relax the second he spots me, his tense facial features easing.

"Good morning," he says, that familiar grin returning to his lips. "Are you ready for the best tour of your life?"

I'm embarrassed by how relieved I am that he's still here.

But first, I have to address the elephant in the room. "Was everything ok, yesterday?"

A shadow crosses his face, but it's gone so fast, I can't be sure.

"Oh yeah. I'm the last amenable band member according to my team. The others have gone awol. They thought I'd disappeared too. Which I *did*, but we won't tell them that. They just wanted to check in; ensure I'm prepared for what's next in the schedule."

"Oh, really? Like what?"

He makes a cynical tutting sound I haven't heard from him before. "A book with my name on that I haven't read. A whole bunch of interviews with podcasters to talk about life in the band. *Well...*" he laughs, blinking, "To *lie* about life in the band. And then other things too… It's all waiting for me as soon as I'm back."

I can't fight the frown. "I'm sorry."

He shakes himself out of it. "Don't worry. It's just my reality." He points at the splash of coffee I have left in my mug. "You mind?"

"Oh no. Go ahead. I've had enough to keep me wired all day."

He gulps the rest down and clears his throat. "I'll have both my phones with me going forward, but my main one is turned off. I've saved my security team's number in my contacts on this one," he waves his burner phone at me. "I've been instructed to tell someone I'm with that if there's an emergency, you need to dial this number. They'll ask you for the codeword."

"That sounds serious."

"I told them it's Roko." I know he's trying to diffuse any tension.

I smile. "Ok."

"This counts for you too. Worst case scenario they're linked up with local police and can make sure you're safe."

"Gus, I feel like you received a bollocking."

He half-smiles, half-cringes. "You could say that." Then he sighs. "Shall we go?"

Gus wears lighter clothing in Monaco than he did when we were walking the streets of Croatia, Montenegro and Italy. I wonder if it's because his team know he's here, so he's less concerned about being undercover. But now *I* have this sense of being watched, being followed. I want to ask him about it and yet I don't because he's relaxed again, his smiles flowing freely, his laughing light.

He explains he's taking me to one of the key tourist attractions and I follow him blindly when he stops and says, "What do you think?"

I blink. "What do I think about what?"

He nods his head towards a road with high metal barriers. "Well?"

"It's a road."

His lips part, his face disbelieving. "Tell me you know what Formula 1 is." Not a question, a demand.

"The car racing thingy?"

Gus gasps. "Don't mess with me."

"What do you mean?"

"You seriously don't follow Formula 1?"

"Well, I know it's about cars that go fast and men who wear skimpy cat suits. Is that a crime?"

"No," he laughs. "So I guess that means you don't know how famous this bend is?"

"There's such a thing as a *famous bend*?"

"Well, when you say it like that… honestly, you're ruining it for me. This is the Fairmont Hairpin Curve."

"Are you serious right now? I have dodgy ankles. It's a million degrees out and you made me walk all the way up here to look at a bend in the road?"

"*A famous bend in the road!*"

I shake my head and laugh, exasperated. "I refuse to accept that's a thing!"

Gus is gobsmacked, looking between me and the bend, gesturing with his hands. "I can't believe you don't get it. It's *the* bend."

He's not being serious. "Gus…"

"Sara…"

"Oh my God, is that guy proposing at a bend in the road?" I whisper, pointing at the couple behind us. The man gets down on one knee as a line of classic cars vroom up the hill towards the sharp hairpin.

Gus touches his heart. "Romantic."

"It's a fucking *road*."

"It's a *famous* road," he mutters, his tone laced with humour as he tows me away by the elbow. "Let's leave them to it before you ruin the moment."

After that we hop in a taxi to the Monaco Cathedral, then take a leisurely stroll through Old Town (because Gus knows this is where my heart truly lies) and take our time admiring the fancy yachts. Once we've exhausted ourselves and my bloody useless ankle is starting to complain, Gus says he's taking me to his favourite bar. At first it doesn't look like much, a tall building with yellow painted walls and a staircase that goes up and around the apartments out front, but once we reach the top, I realise we're on a rooftop bar with views across the city and out to sea. A lovely breeze blows through the tables, which are shaded by mismatched awnings.

The barman greets Gus with a familiar handshake.

And because there's hardly anyone up here, besides a few locals, Gus suggests I find a table I like, then returns a few minutes later with an espresso martini for me and a beer for him. "I assume you like caffeine in your cocktails too?"

"I do," I say, with a pleased grin. "Especially when it's early afternoon. So, have you been here a lot? You seem so familiar with the place."

"I come here for the Grand Prix. It's usually a lot busier."

"I bet. Lots of vroom vroom people."

"That *is* what they call themselves," he jokes.

"Where do you usually stay?"

He fidgets as if the conversation catches him off guard. "A yacht."

"*A* yacht. That's very specific. Do you own the yacht?"

"No. I am not *own*-a-yacht rich. I am *borrow-a-small* yacht rich. At least, I couldn't afford the big one that I stayed on."

"Was it a friend's?"

He wrinkles his nose, sliding down in his seat as if my line of questioning makes him uncomfortable. "Another ex."

"Oh. I see," I say, brushing it off. "Another rich girl, then."

He sighs. "Her dad is, yes."

"*Oh.*" I nod, taking a sip of my cocktail. It's not like it's any of my business. I should probably have done more research on him. I'm sure this information is available to anybody who wants to look for it. "I think you might you have a type." I'm sort of teasing him but I'm also sort of hoping he proves me wrong.

"Her dad owned a team."

"A football team?"

His eyes sparkle like I'm the most amusing person he's ever come across. "You remind me of who I used to be."

"Yeah?"

"Yeah. I wouldn't have considered someone owning a team meant an entire Formula 1 team before all this either. It wasn't even in my realm of understanding. I thought it was a treat if I was getting a takeaway on a Friday night."

"You mean your ex's dad owned an entire Formula 1 *team?*"

He nods slowly, a smile teasing his lips.

"Yeah. I couldn't even fathom what it's like to have that kind of wealth. Was she nice at least?"

"Rain was beautiful. She was clever, creative and insightful. But she was also manipulative, controlling and kind of scary to be honest."

I put my drink down, my face falling. "I'm sorry you had to deal with that."

He runs a hand through his hair. "Yeah. I think part of this industry is accepting powerful people want to have access to you. And when you're in a difficult contract like the one I was..." He groans. "The one I can't currently escape from. You start thinking that maybe if one of those really powerful, rich people might just love you a little, maybe they'll help you. Maybe they'll see you're struggling."

I feel an ache run down my spine. "I had no idea."

"I guess signing something with as little understanding as we had at sixteen was a poisoned chalice. Then again, Callum and Will have managed to scarper. Jax has disappeared. Please explain to me how I'm the only one still being held to a wall by my throat?"

I sit up, rolling my shoulders back. His usual jokey tone has vanished and instead I'm seeing genuine concern in his eyes. "Are you serious?"

He shrugs. "I'm not meant to tell you."

"Ok..."

"I want to."

I nod. I'm no lawyer but I sit in contractual meetings daily. What would I advise a client in this situation? What would I do? "I know you're not really asking for advice. I don't want to overstep but... If I was you, I'd want to know how the others managed to escape without legal repercussions."

Gus frowns at the table. "My team keeps telling me they can't reach them. So maybe there will be?"

"Nonsense. They'd find them, right? Track them down?"

"I guess?"

"Have you officially told them you wish to terminate the agreement?"

He cringes. "I shouldn't be telling you this."

I smile, trying to ease the tension. "Who am I going to tell?"

He holds my stare for a lingering moment then wilts as if he's come to an unfortunate conclusion. I don't know why, but it stings a little. As if he's decided he can't trust me just yet. "I'm sorry to say I've been stung too many times not to know better."

"I understand," I say, because I do, even if I'm now horribly embarrassed about overstepping.

"You've been more helpful than you know," he says, as if he can read my mind. "I'll take on board what you've said."

"Can you reach the others? Maybe they'll be able to tell you what they're doing?"

"I don't know if that's a wise idea, right now," is all he says and the conversation moves onto the weather as the wind picks up, a wall of clouds gathering above the sea.

I'm three espresso martinis down on our stroll back to the cruise. Thankfully, the barman brought us olives and bread so I'm not too tipsy, just a little light on my feet.

The yacht is docked until early evening so there's no rush to get back. That said, small, warm droplets of rain keep splattering on my arm and face. Gus looks up and sticks his tongue out like a child trying to taste the rain.

I snort. "How old are you?"

"Mentally or physically?"

"Age doesn't work like that."

He grins. "Oh, it does. We already know you were born fifty-two."

"I haven't aged a day since birth."

"Come on, let's get back before we get soaked," he says.

At that exact moment, I swear I hear someone shout "Gus!"

We both pause in our step, looking over our shoulders. Tension runs through his fingertips laced with mine. I don't like it, I want to protect him from that feeling.

"IT *IS* HIM! IT'S GUS!" an American woman shouts again.

Gus squeezes my hand and begins walking briskly towards the narrower lanes of old buildings near the port.

"What do we do?" I whisper, just loud enough for him to hear.

"Stay calm."

"Ok. But what do *I* do if they catch us up?"

"Just stay nearby. And follow my lead."

"Should I call your team?"

"*No*," he says too sharply before calming himself and saying, "Please don't do that... If you do, I'm going home. And I'm not done with this yet." The look he gives me makes my blood fizz. Although I'm certain he means he isn't done with the holiday, part of me, *the deluded, romantic part*, wants it to be about us.

God, I hate that part of me. She's so irresponsible.

A deep mix of fear and excitement rips through me, probably fuelled by the adrenaline of escape but maybe not, maybe it's something else. Maybe I'm in more trouble here than I know.

As the footsteps behind us get louder and quicker – *fuck, how many of them are there?* – we get faster too. A half walk, half jog, my ankle hissing in pain.

There's a deep, grumbling from the dark cloud that's breezed in over the city and, as if out of nowhere, the heavens open. A cloak of rain sweeping over us like a paintbrush.

The dry city streets aren't designed for this much water, and before we even reach the end of one alleyway, narrow, whizzing streams of water gush either side of us.

The footsteps don't stop though. We're still being followed.

Another crack of thunder and Gus is pulling me towards a house with a covered door frame. My hair sticks to my shoulders, my hat floppy with the weight of the rain. There's barely any shelter at all, so he positions himself so that his large frame is keeping me dry, his back and head still being drenched from the downpour. But he leaves enough space between us as if he's being cautious of not overstepping again.

The next move is yours…

I appreciate it. I don't like it.

I fist some of his T-shirt in my spare hand and tug him closer, pulling him off-balance, his chest pressing me into the door. His head drops, his gaze flicking between my eyes and lips, his soaked hair, dripping onto my forehead and running down my nose.

One drop finds its way to my lips and instinctively I lick it off.

His breathing deepens, his pupils expanding.

Our pursuers get closer. They slow, their footsteps on the cobbles quietening, but I don't think they know we're tucked around the corner, or they'd already be on us. I can feel Gus's heartbeat hasten against my palm. I want to put him at ease. I want him to know that I'm not the kind of person to throw him to the wolves.

He can trust me.

When one of them checks around the side to get a better look, I whip my sodden hat off and hold it behind his head.

His eyes haven't left my face. I think he's waiting. Waiting for me to make a decision or confirm we're safe? I can't tell.

I peek around him to see if they're still there.

The street is clear.

"I think we've lost them," I whisper.

Gus doesn't reply. But I don't think he cares about them anymore. And now I'm this close to him again, the feel of his firm, solid body propped against mine, I'm not sure I do either. I can only think about one thing as I watch him run his teeth over his bottom lip.

Kiss me.

Except, I already know he won't. Because I stupidly told him not to.

Now why did I do that?

Something really sensible about our lives and going separate ways.

Ah, screw it!

I press my lips to his in a hasty, chaste kiss. I pull back, half-expecting him to take it as permission, but instead he stays statue still. Is he ok? Did I read this completely wrong? Maybe he's worried they'll return? How deep is his trauma?

"I'm sorry," I say, feeling his solid, tense body beneath my fingers as I run them over his shoulders, hoping to settle him. "I'm sorry, it's just us." His heart rate hasn't slowed, his breathing somehow even deeper. I lean back to check his expression.

His lips are parted. "You call that making a move?"

"I'm sor—" I start to apologise again but before I can finish, Gus's mouth is on mine, hungry and pressing. I gasp, grabbing him for support as he manages to bring himself even closer, his hips holding me in place.

I taste his breathy groan as I open to him, his tongue sliding with mine.

My heartbeat is now racing as fast as his, hands roaming lower. I'm feverish with need. With the rain still hammering down behind Gus, I'm heartbroken to be interrupted when the door I'm leaning on is ceremoniously opened and an angry old man starts yelling at us. Luckily, Gus was already supporting my body from getting pressed too hard against the door, his hand on the frame, so I don't fall.

"Pardon," Gus says, cringing, that glint in his eye telling me he finds this hilarious and then before I know what's happening, my hand is enveloped in his and we're running in the direction of the yacht again.

The torrential downpour only adds to the hilarity of our situation.

We hop a raised curb to access the path along the portside but it's like jumping a brook. I miss, dipping one foot in and slipping.

"*Bollocks*," I hiss when it feels like an explosion has gone off in my ankle.

I slow, reaching down to grab it. Before I can get there, Gus swoops me into his arms and carries me the rest of the way.

Twenty-Six

The attendants are quick to fuss over us as we barrel into the lobby of the boat, wrapping us in clean white towels. I take a seat on a leather sofa, finding I'm somewhere between 'ouch this hurts', 'why is this so surreal and funny?' and 'man, I'm out of breath'. A first aider practically dives on me to treat my ankle, twisting it this way and that.

"Does that hurt?" he asks.

"A great deal," I respond, straight-faced.

He frowns, trying to read me. "Is it injured?"

"Yes."

"Have you injured it before?"

"Many times."

"What is wrong with it?"

"It's useless," I explain. "I might as well have it chopped off."

Again, he frowns, clearly not reading my humour at all. "I don't think that's necessary."

No shit.

"Well, that's good news," I say, finally smiling so he doesn't think I'm completely insane. In all honesty, I don't surround myself with people who are big on sympathy and receiving so much attention for an ouchy ankle makes me uncomfortable. I would like to go and be in pain all alone now.

Especially because I'm suddenly freezing. The air-con is usually a treat in the centre of the yacht but with the layer of rain across my skin, I find myself shivering. Again – more fussing. You'd never get this level of service in a Premier Inn.

I laugh again at how ridiculous this attention is. All we've done is run through a rainstorm in Monte Carlo.

I've survived far worse and will again.

I search the room for Gus but he's already leaving, phone to his ear, he looks me over with darkened eyes, waits for me to nod that I'm ok before heading towards his room. An assumption, of course, since I'm not sure where he's staying. And why would I?

"I'll just go grab a shower and I'll be fine," I tell the staff, hoping they'll release me, except the first aider, a tall Italian man about the same age as me, and a female attendant from behind the main desk, insist on walking me to my room, my arm slung around the man's shoulders.

My overbearing helpers linger at the door and for a worryingly long minute, I wonder if they're going to stay and watch me shower. I practically shove them out the door then slide down it into a seated position to examine my swollen ankle.

I run my fingers over it, a bruise already forming. "You know you work really hard at making me seem like the damsel in distress that I am very much not," I mutter.

"What was that?" my ankle replies, except of course it's the nosey staff outside my door.

The temptation to scream "BUGGER OFF!" is a hard one to swallow down.

Instead, I crawl away from the door and into the bathroom, switching the water on so they know I'm not talking to them. Once I'm done with my shower, cautiously leaning on walls in case my traitor ankle might betray me again, I lie face down on the massive bed, damp and exhausted.

And then I scream into my pillow because… *what the fuck am I doing!?*

The kiss replays in my mind. I track the decisions that led us there, pressed into the doorway of some unsuspecting poor old man's house. It's like I've lost my calm head. I did it. I made the next move. Now I'm on this rollercoaster and even though I'm a little scared and a whole lot exhilarated, I don't want it to end.

I roll over onto my back, my breathing hastened, my heart heavy in my chest, pulse beating in my throat.

I can't ignore the pressure in my core. I close my eyes when an image of him kissing his way down my stomach flashes into my mind. *Fuck.* What even is it about this man? He isn't my usual type. But then again, what is my type? I was with Mike for five years. And he was sensible and yes, a little boring at times. But safe. And that felt like my type then. I wasn't going to waste my energy on a risk. *Little did I know.*

Before Mike, it was *all* risks and heated crushes.

I brush it from my mind. Irrelevant.

Gus is desired by thousands of women. He's followed everywhere he goes. His fame is such, that he might never escape it.

He's a risk.

A risk I can't mitigate.

And if the way my heart is crashing about in my chest at the very thought of taking it further with him is anything to go by, I know, despite how my friends and family see me, that I am horrifically breakable.

The sensible part of me would *never* take that risk. The wild part has her toes over the edge, ready to plunge herself into whatever danger this adventure poses. Screw the consequences.

I bite the end of my middle finger. I feel like the version of me at university. The one who let herself off the leash for once. The one who realised there was nobody watching who could be influenced. No one who needed her right in that moment. Letting her hair down wasn't going to hurt anyone.

I release my middle finger from between my teeth, letting it run down my chin, neck and front, lower... I close my eyes and imagine it's Gus. I bite my lip so hard I swear I might draw blood. When I reach my clit, I press down on it, squeezing my thighs together.

There's something about him. He has that fire in his eyes. The confidence.

That's when there's a knock at the door.

I search the room for something to pull on but in a rush, between my ankle nearly giving up on me again (*blasted useless joint*) and all my clothes tidied away, I wrap the towel tighter and carefully slide off the bed.

I open the door half-expecting it to be first aid man again.

But no. Gus is right there, arm resting on the doorframe. Face so close to mine I can feel his breath fanning across my nose.

His warm eyes flick lower for the briefest of seconds, his gaze trailing along the line of my towel, before finding my face again. He does that secret smile, the one he's trying to hide. I chew on my bottom lip, crossing my thighs.

"Can I help you?"

A notch forms between his brows. "I don't know. I can't remember."

I will not laugh. "Oh really?"

"Yes."

"You must've come here for a reason," I say.

He blinks. "Probably."

"I would invite you in but…" I shrug like it's obvious.

He breaks and lets his smile consume his face, uncrossing and crossing his arms again. Is he nervous? "I'm sorry. I didn't mean to interrupt you."

"Interrupt me?"

He laughs. "Yeah, you know, from being… naked?"

"How do you know I was naked?"

Gus runs his tongue over his teeth and nods, looking away down the corridor like he's trying to recalibrate. Half a second later he pushes away from the doorframe, stepping back and swinging his arms. He can barely look at me.

"I think I was going to ask you for dinner. It's that dance thing tonight. I was going to skip it. You know? Since I'm here alone. But now I sort of don't feel like I am."

"I'm not much of a dancer."

"You don't have to be. *I am.*"

"I love how you're asking me for dinner, but all the food and drinks are already paid for."

"Yeah, but I'm paying you like ten thousand per cent interest at this point."

"*No*," I playfully whisper. "That's so unnecessary."

"Is that a no?" he asks, clutching a hand to his chest. "You don't want to dance with me?"

I pretend to think it over, wiggling a little to hold the towel up that keeps slipping. Bloody thing is in on whatever flirty game this has become. "Fine, I guess," I say. "I can do dinner."

He nods. "I like that dress. You should wear that dress."

"This is a towel."

"I said what I said."

"See you in an hour," I tell him, shaking my head and closing the door while I'm still holding my composure together.

An hour, as it turns out, isn't enough time. I'm scrambling to get my dress on at the last minute, careful not to get any make-up on it as I pull it over my head. I've gone for a white and yellow striped summer dress that should keep me cool on the top deck where the dancing takes place. Paired with my favourite bra, my tits look epic.

I don't care. I've come too far not to dance in the flames.

I pair it with some easy-to-kick-off leather sandals, knowing that after dinner we'll be barefoot on the deck and do one final check in the mirror. This will have to do.

The knock comes as I'm fiddling with small hoop earrings in the full-length mirror. My dress has discreet pockets which I slide my phone and room key into before heading out the door.

Gus waits, leant once again against the wall. I let my eyes consume him, curls left unruly tonight, a loose-fitted black shirt with sleeves rolled up and smart chinos. He tilts his head, taking me in with that lopsided grin. It's as I get closer that I notice how extraordinarily good he smells.

I don't even hide it, breathing him in. "What are you wearing?"

"Lovely to see you too."

"I don't subscribe to social norms."

He laughs; the sound does something unholy to my belly. "I know."

"You smell like freshly cut grass and bonfires."

"Funny. I was going for *old man gardening on a lovely summer's day*, actually." I roll my eyes as he holds his arm out for me to take. "Shall we?"

"Where are you taking me?"

"It's a surprise."

He pretends to change direction from the restaurant twice, where, if we hadn't been stranded in Split a week ago, we would've spent every night eating dinner alone. Maybe this would've never developed, and I wouldn't feel like I'm on the precipice of throwing my heart directly into the fire.

It's the most I've felt in years.

The safety net I created for myself has been incinerated.

What am I doing?

The waiter greets us. The tables move every night so that each party gets a chance to sit by the windows or out on the covered decking at the back. "Tonight, we're doing social seating."

We both smile, Gus with genuine intrigue, me, totally forced, because *what the actual fuck* is 'social seating'? Is this Wagamama? There's a bloody good reason I never go there. I am nothing if not proudly unsociable towards strangers.

As if he can sense my reaction, Gus squeezes my arm closer towards his body, towing me along to the table where I scan ahead to see quite how badly our evening is about to be ruined. Except we're shown to a table of four where an old couple are seated already. The moment they realise we're joining them they're straight on their feet to greet us.

"Ah, you're the pair from the first night," the lady says and suddenly I remember her. She thought we were a couple, right? Back when I thought Gus was a rude arsehole.

She's pinned her silver hair back into a tidy bun, her face crinkling when she smiles. She hauls me away from Gus, who finally releases me, and hugs me before I can so much as take a breath.

"It's lovely to see you again," I say. Then again, how drunk was I the last time we met? Maybe I should be mortified.

Gus shakes the hand of the old man, who then reaches across the table to shake mine too, except he brings my hand to his mouth and kisses my fingers. It's wholesome.

Would be creepy if he wasn't an old man.

We finally sit as the waiter takes our drinks order.

"I'm Edith," the lady tells me. "And my husband is Paul."

"I'm Sara," I say.

"And your husband?" she asks, smiling. Does she not...? I press my lips together but let it lie since it might be embarrassing to remind her. Besides, Gus doesn't fill the gap for me, just tilts his head and smiles for me to continue. He can tell I'm too socially awkward to make her feel bad. So, I say, "That's Gus."

"Sara and Gus," Paul says. "And what a gorgeous couple you are."

"Thank you," Gus replies. Because of course he does. He reaches over the table and slides his fingers with mine. It's familiar in a way that spreads from my palm to my core, heating me throughout, especially when one fingertip strokes the sensitive part between my ring and middle finger.

I roll my shoulders back. I'm in so much trouble.

"Where are you two from?" Paul asks.

Gus sucks his bottom lip in, eyeing me. I feel like this is peak entertainment for him. I'll let him have his fun. "The Cotswolds," he explains. "Near Tetbury."

"A lovely part of the world," Edith says.

"What about you?"

"Surrey," she says. "Do you know of Godstone?"

Gus nods politely. "I've definitely heard of it."

"We've lived there for fifty years," she says. "Wouldn't change a thing."

Paul hums in agreement as our drinks are delivered. "What is it you two do?" he asks us.

This time I answer before Gus, his lips parted in readiness. "I work in business. And Gus is in a band."

"Oh, how interesting. What kind of business?"

"It's corporate. We help companies negotiate high-risk procurements."

"Fascinating," he says, before turning to Gus. "And you dabble in music?"

I nearly choke on my first sip of wine at the way Paul brushes Gus's band off as a hobby. Gus handles it exactly as I knew he would. "I absolutely dabble."

"And what about you two?" I ask to keep the conversation moving.

Look at me, being friendly, socialising with strangers. Must be whatever I've caught from Popstar these past few days.

Edith and Paul spend the next twenty minutes walking us through their entire career history. The depression only starts to wade in when I realise that they got incredibly lucky with the property market, buying young and building equity. Paul was a postman for thirty years and Edith only worked a year before becoming a full-time mother. I suppose they can't be blamed for their own luck.

"When did you marry?" Paul asks.

Gus looks at me as he says, "Actually, this is our honeymoon."

Edith gasps. "Well, no wonder you both look so loved up. What made you pick this cruise?"

"We've been craving adventure," he says, and it isn't a lie.

"I can tell you two are going to be married for a long, long time. You're so handsome," she says, reaching out and patting Gus's hand.

"Now, now, Edith, you're going to get me in trouble with your husband."

Paul laughs. "She'll do and say what she likes either way."

"And you're beautiful," she says to me, squeezing my hand. "You'll have the most stunning babies."

I choke on red wine.

I give Edith a look. "I don't know if we're ready to talk children."

In fact, I laugh because she has no idea how far away we are from talking about children. Contraception, maybe.

Old people really don't give a fuck, do they?

We chat all the way through the five-course meal and sometime around the main, I slide one shoe off and reach between us until I find Gus's leg. His breath catches when he feels my toes on his shin.

I leave it there throughout the course and when dessert arrives, I let my leg drift higher all the way up to his knee. At this point he turns to me slowly, his stare a challenge, his eyes darkening as I press my toes into his thigh.

When the meal is over, a band starts up on the deck outside and many parties, including Edith and Paul, are quick to rise from their seats and head out to dance but we remain seated, gazes locked.

"You're being very mean to me," he mutters.

I raise an eyebrow. "Is that so?"

"It is, yeah. But I like it. I think it suits me."

"Me being mean to you, suits you."

"Dangerously so." He runs his tongue over his bottom lip, his stare unwavering. "I think you know why I'm still sitting."

Yes. I do. "Would you like me to remove my foot?"

"No."

"Would you like me to move it higher?"

"Yes."

"Really? In here?"

He smirks looking around. Most people have left the room now, the music louder as they clear tables. "I think we'd better go and dance, don't you?"

"No."

"No?"

"I am *not* a dancer."

Gus stands, gently placing my foot down, before repositioning himself discreetly and offering me his hand. "Sara, please do me the honour."

"Ugh."

He chuckles. "Exactly the reaction every man wants when he asks a woman to dance. Shall I word it differently?" He leans down closer so that he can speak quietly. "Sara, sunshine, you've given me a raging boner and now I'm going to have to hold you very close to cover it up while I sway you around the deck."

"The *what?*"

"The dick."

"That's what I heard." I fake a sigh, placing my hand in his. "*Fine*, I'll dance with you. But only because you're desperate."

Twenty-Seven

The five-piece band play slow, romantic music, which is the perfect soundtrack when the backdrop, as the evening sun lowers over the horizon, leaving the sky a warm yellow, is the breathtakingly beautiful French coastline. Tonight, we're anchored not far off the coast since it isn't far to travel in the morning to Cannes. The boat is still, the sea calm, the colourful buildings and bright lights of Nice glitter in the distance.

Gus walks me out to the dance floor and spins us before I've even had a moment to register what he's doing. I find myself flush against his chest, one palm pressed between my shoulder blades, the other on my waist, fingers splaying, grazing the peak of my bottom. I've instinctively slung one arm around his neck; the other holds onto his tanned, solid bicep.

He's strong and steady, a relief since I have a total lack of coordination. Not to mention the useless ankle that could buckle at any moment.

His face is so close to mine, those light brown eyes almost golden in the lowering light, that all it would take is for me to press onto my toes and we'd be kissing again. And as if he has the same thought he allows himself to look at my lips.

He fights that smile. "How are you doing Mrs Kenwood?"

I snort. "Big of you to think I'd take your name."

"You're right. I'd change mine. What's your surname?"

"Stirling."

"Mr Stirling," he says, trying it out. "That makes me sound quite official."

I smile. "You enjoy letting people think we're together, don't you? Is it a favourite pasttime of yours? Fake dating your female friends?"

"We're not friends," he says without pause.

"Ouch."

"Friends don't play footsie."

I bite my bottom lip and look away. "I shouldn't have done that."

Gus spins me again, supporting my weight, careful to make sure my balance is sound.

"Do you really live in The Cotswolds?" I ask.

"Well… I own a house there. My sister looks after it at the moment. I'm barely ever at home."

"*These great men are never at home*," I say, finding myself incredibly funny.

"I don't understand."

"Pfft."

"Should I understand?"

I nod. "Yes. But don't worry. I'll let you off for now."

He leans back to get a read on my face. I think he wants in on the joke but it's one that has to be earned. He swallows and I watch his throat work and ache to kiss him there. To taste his skin. He smells so inviting.

"Come on," he says, taking my hand and leading me away from the dance floor. I follow him, my bare feet pattering against the slick decking. He leads me down two floors where we find a quieter spot at the back of the yacht. The water is close enough from here that you can hear the peaceful slapping of it against the sides.

I'm feeling just a tad tipsy, when I lean against the railings to feel the wind rustle through my hair.

Our gazes are caught by another yacht passing by. It's sleek, black and pretentious. We wave because it feels funny and other cruises and yachts passing have done so. The people on board this one though don't even acknowledge us, but we carry on, laughing at ourselves being entirely fucking blanked by billionaires.

"You know, my mum humbled me so much growing up that when I first started getting money, I felt really guilty," Gus says. "They made us talk to financial advisers. And all I could think was, why the hell are you telling me how to make that money into more money? Surely, I just, you know, get a fancier bank account? It's like once you've got it, all you're meant to do is make it into more."

"Aww. Poor wealthy Popstar," I mock, pouting.

He reaches over, carefully pinching the front of my dress. His fingers don't even graze my skin, but I feel it everywhere, a small electric current rippling at the surface. I bite down hard on my tongue.

I can't have him. For so many reasons. This can't work.

I'm not even remotely emotionally ready for him. I was a runaway bride just over two months ago. The most I can offer him is a rebound

But the teasing thought of him on top of me, the weight

of him everywhere, the feel of his hair in my hands.

Ahhhh.

As if he's reading my mind, he steps closer, planting one hand either side of me, trapping me against the railings. "When are you going home?"

"After Barcelona. Why?"

"We could stay in the city for a few nights. Just us."

"Don't tease me."

"I'm serious," he says, his face so close I have to tip mine back, feel the warmth of his breath brush against my nose. His expensive aftershave, the woody, citrussy smell surrounds my senses.

"Pfft. You're *never* serious."

"I might be. When it comes to certain topics."

"And what are those topics?"

"You."

I swallow, feeling like my world is spinning. One word. *You.* It rolls through me like the first sip of a rich whiskey. But if we're being serious, I need to lay the groundwork. "I don't know what I have to give right now. I'm pretty depleted."

"I don't want to take anything from you, Sara."

My voice comes almost like a whisper. "What *do* you want?"

"To give."

I can't fight the breathy laugh that escapes me. "What does that even mean?"

"I reckon you can use your imagination."

I can. It's *very* busy. It's working up all kinds of delicious scenarios. "I'm worried I only have space for a rebound right now," I say. I don't want to mislead him. It sounds like he's had to deal with that before. I won't let it be me.

It's his turn to swallow, his eyes tracing the line of my lips, his apple bobbing. "I just want to be whatever it is you need. And if that means a rebound, I'll take it for now."

We've gotten even closer. His nose grazes mine. One of my hands drops the railings and fists in his shirt to steady me.

"Gus," I whisper. I don't even know what I want to say. I feel like I need to push him away, to recalibrate my mind and yet all I can think to do is pull him closer.

He drops his head, grazing his lips down the side of my face, gently running them over my jawline and lower to the groove of my collarbone. I sigh, tipping back further. I want to get higher. I want to wrap my legs around him, so I shuffle upwards.

But the top bar I was searching for isn't there.

I've got it horribly wrong.

I release his shirt, scrambling for a bar.

Gus's hands are quick to reach for me, but my body has already tipped too far back.

I'm fucking falling.

Typical.

The squeal that leaves my lips is feral. There are frantic footsteps from the deck below, but I'm already gone, slipping through Gus's fingers like I'm made of something slick.

Twenty-Eight

It's far enough before I hit the water that I feel that weightlessness in my tummy. Then comes the splash, the disorientation. I feel like I've been slapped from head to toe, my skin tingling. I swim upwards, the water burning in my nose. I surface, gasping for air.

I try to right my hair covering my face with one hand while using the other to assist with treading water. Something blocks what's left of the evening sun. I look up to find Gus diving in after me.

I squeal again, turning my face away to avoid getting splashed.

He resurfaces fast, his body warm as he pulls me to him. "Are you ok?" he asks, breathless.

I laugh, gurgled. It's ridiculous. "*Yes. Oh my God.*"

"You essentially did a twenty-foot backflip."

"I was showing off."

"Then I'm impressed."

"You dove in after me."

He shakes his head to get his hair out of his eyes. "Of course I did," he says like it's obvious. With one hand around my waist, he's keeping himself above the water pretty much with the kick of his legs alone. He runs his thumb over my cheeks, lips, chin.

I gasp against him.

I think he's going to kiss me by the way he's leaning in. My heart rate rises, my breathing coming short and sharp but then we hear shouting from the deck and the crew are throwing us a lifebuoy to grab hold of.

Gus nudges me to take it first as we're slowly hauled back onto the ship, climbing a dangling ladder which is surprisingly tough going, especially with a soaked dress clinging to my skin.

Once I'm back on board and being fussed over, I can't stop laughing. I'm unsure whether it's the adrenaline or the fact that I could've died. I mean, this ship is more like a yacht, so the deck we were on was only about twenty feet above the water, but still, the slap of the water as I hit it certainly stung.

Gus takes a towel and apologises to the crew members. I'm still too stunned to stammer anything, holding onto the towel now wrapped around me with one hand at the front of my neck while he grabs my spare one.

"Follow me," he orders, striding through a storage room full of brooms and strong cleaning products. He's definitely lost, looking for the staircase but styles it out. We emerge into the main lobby, other guests staring at our drenched hair and clothes, our frantic need to be alone.

We stride up three flights of stairs and by the top of them the adrenaline has worn off and I'm panting again. "Was the lift out of order?"

"I wasn't waiting for the lift."

I laugh, exasperated. He turns to find me out of breath. Taking pity on me, he crouches down and throws me over his shoulder and I can't fight the breathless giggles that escape me.

He takes me to his room. As he lets me in and places me down, I realise I've been wasting far too much time worrying about the fact that Gus is a popstar, when I could've been sharing the suite of dreams. It must be four times the size of my tiny cabin, with glass sliding doors at the rear plus a massive balcony with gorgeous furniture including a hammock.

What the hell!

I realise we've paused. I turn to him. He's watching me carefully.

"Did I rush this?" he asks.

"What?"

"Racing you up here?" he breathes, his chest rising as heavily as mine. "Look, Sara, I've never met anyone like you. You're so sure. So strong. You've made me less afraid to step away from everything I know. You've shown me there's a world beyond the band. I don't think you realise what you're doing to me."

I laugh. "It's only been a week."

"It's only been a week," he agrees, dropping his shoulders and stepping closer. "In only a week you've shown me I'm more than a popstar. I'm a brother, a friend and if nothing else I'm absolutely hilarious."

I fight the smile. "Your sense of humour is average at best."

"I needed you. I needed this." He returns to me, frantic mouth on my neck, lips, throat, earlobes. I gasp as he walks me backwards until my body flops down onto a plump, cool leather chair. Gus kneels before me, leaning in closer, tugging me towards him.

I lace my fingers into his hair and pull on his sodden curls.

"Do you want this?" he whispers against my throat as he lets his hands wander lower, over my waist, my soaked dress slick against my skin. Gus runs his tongue over my collarbone.

I probably taste salty.

I don't care.

Fire is whirling in my veins, setting every part of me alight. I want to be devoured by him. "I want it. I want you."

"Good girl," he mutters, sucking a nipple over my dress as he runs one hand up and over my front then back down the middle, splaying fingers to touch as much of me as he can. "Fuck, I'm obsessed with your body, Sara. It's all I can think about..."

He pauses, pressing a kiss to my belly, moving lower. His long, strong fingers run over my thighs, squeezing and pressing them upwards so I'm forced to bend my knees, leaving myself exposed for him.

I gasp again as his mouth travels, his right hand releasing my thigh, leaving behind little imprints, as he strokes me over my lace-trimmed knickers.

His eyes dart back to mine as he teases me in exactly the right spot. I hum as the heated sensation races up my spine.

I swear I feel it in my ears.

His lips return, nudging the material out of the way as he runs his tongue over my clit. He nudges one finger inside of me, that bitten-off groan escaping him again. "Look at you. You're so ready," he breathes. "Is this all for me?"

I feel like I should be embarrassed but I'm not.

His warm tongue runs over me again and I curve my back reflexively. I usually take a minute to settle into it, but the hazy, brilliant sensations are already rocking through me. He adds a second finger, finding my biting point, massaging it so that every time his tongue finds my clit, I swear I'm going to come undone.

And then he takes it away, adding to that swell, that pressure.

I roll my head back, lift my thighs. I couldn't serve myself more freely.

I tug on his hair. *Here*, I think. *Put your head here. Kiss me here.*

But he's too strong, too focused. Instead, he uses his hand around my thigh, to tug me closer to his mouth and I watch him practically feast on me, mouth open, eyes on me, a daring look that has my core coiling.

I release his head to run my fingers over his toned, rigid back and he returns his focus to my clit. It's unfair. If we're doing this, and it appears we most certainly – *ahh* – are! Then I want time to explore him too.

He ups the pressure with his fingers, and I curse at the ceiling, unbothered that there could be prying ears on the yacht. I hope they enjoy the performance. Gus's lips venture away from my centre, pressing damply on my inner thighs, nibbling there so I can't help but squirm.

"Sara, you're too close. I'm not done with you yet. You're doing so well."

"*Please*," I whimper.

"Beg again and you're going to finish me."

This girl loves a challenge. "*Please*, Gus. *Please*. I want you to make me come."

He groans, dropping his head onto my stomach, kissing me there, breathing me in. He uses his tongue like a brush, licking all the sea water from my body.

"*Please*."

He huffs a groan, kisses lower, slower, teasing. When he finally reaches my clit again, he doesn't hold back, his fingers work me until I'm swollen and gasping for it. He sucks, kisses, licks and bites until I'm tugging his hair like it's the only thing stopping me from floating off into the sky.

"You're delicious," he says as he works his body between my legs. We kiss there for a moment until he laughs, fidgeting uncomfortably. It occurs to me that he's still wearing his wet chinos.

"I need to change," he says, kissing my nose. "Wrap your arms around my neck."

Well, ok.

I'm nothing if not a whore for a bossy, sexy man. I do as I'm told, as he slides his arms underneath me and scoops me up. He places me down on the bed, still soaked through and kisses me softly.

"I'm going to get dressed. Be good and stay here."

"Yes, sir."

Barely two minutes pass and he's back, topless, dry sweat shorts and a pleased glint in his eye to find me still lying exactly where he left me.

I'm aware the sheets will be damp from lying in them but I'm also riding the steadying waves of endorphins, my limbs heavy and lazy.

He offers me his hand to help me stand. I take his lead as he pulls me into the ensuite and slowly helps me out of my dress. It lands beside me in a damp thud. He carefully unhooks my bra, eyeing me like I'm about to stop him. I'm not. Then he hooks his finger under my knickers, dragging them down my legs, supporting my balance to step out of them.

There's something beautifully intimate about the way he wraps an arm around my bare waist now, pressing my body into his as he turns the shower on behind me. He steps out of his shorts too and I fight a smile when I realise he didn't put any boxers on.

Prepared.

He moves me under the water, shampooing my hair, turning me to face away, careful not to let the water into my eyes. He runs his hands over my body, feeling me, positioning me. My heart races. I think he's going to take it further.

He's hard and hot against my back. I want that part of him. I'm almost rocking forward, ready. But he doesn't take anything from me. It's all given as he kisses along my shoulder, nipping at my earlobes, massaging my scalp. His spare hand slowly works my clit, thumb circling, until I'm coming undone again, whimpering at the tiles.

"Turn around," he says afterwards. I do as I'm told. He's beautiful naked, all strong lines of muscle under freshly tanned skin. "Do you want to touch me?"

Adrenaline has me in its clutches as I step closer to him, running my hands over his chest, taking my time feeling over the ridges on his stomach. He's so firm and smooth except for the hair there that provides a delightful texture under my palm. Once I have his warm cock in my hand, he curses, pinching his eyes tight.

He presses his hands flat against the tiles behind me to balance himself as I increase the pressure. He runs his lips along my collarbone, humming low and crackled. "You're so good." And moments later. "I'm going to paint your hand."

I run my mouth over his chest in return, kissing and gasping against him as his body tenses around me. And just as promised, he finishes, pressing his forehead on my shoulder, coating my fingers.

He grabs my face in his hands and kisses me after; my body squished between him and the damp wall. We remain like that until the hot water runs cold. It's the perfect way to shake us out of the moment. We clean ourselves again, dry, then collapse onto the bed, sated and calm.

It doesn't take me long to doze off, but as soon as I do, the dream starts. I don't know how long I've been going around this roundabout, alone in this cold car, but my tears are coming hard, and I can't stop repeating Mum's name. I'm so tired of doing this. I want off this ride.

"Please just stop!" I yell at the steering wheel, closing my eyes and letting go. Maybe crashing will release me. Maybe that's been the answer all along. What if I just keep steering around and around and it never lets me off?

I hear the wheels spin. A screech from the tyres.

But I don't crash.

"You're ok, Sara," I hear. "You're not alone."

My conscious mind knows it's not part of the dream and yet I'm not ready to step out of it. A warm arm encircles my waist, pulling me backwards, lips press against my shoulder.

Moments before I wake, I see the car hurtling off the side of the road, slamming into a tree but I'm not in it. My body is on the outside, looking in.

I gasp, half-choking awake.

"It's ok," he whispers, sitting up with me as I pant out breaths, trying to ground myself again. One of his hands smooths circles on my lower back as he kisses my shoulder. Normally I'd be embarrassed but with Gus, I know I'm safe. He understands.

As the dream drifts away and I come back to myself, I press my face into my palms. "I'm sorry," I say, my voice muffled.

"Hey," he scolds gently. "You're not allowed to apologise."

"I just... It felt worse than usual." I turn to read his face, but he only looks concerned. "I think... I think something changed."

A notch forms between his brows. "Want to talk about it?"

I shake my head. I never want to talk about it again, in fact, I don't even want to talk. Instead, I lean across and kiss him like it hurts not to. Because right now it *does*. He runs his thumb over my cheek, soothing me, like he knows this kiss is feral but he's happy to help, happy to be of use.

Once I'm calmer, he presses me back into the pillows, turns me away from him before bringing my body flush with his. I finally fall back to sleep knowing that even if I find myself in that damn car again, he'll wake me, and I'll be ok.

Because I'm not alone.

Twenty-Nine

I sleep in Gus's room that night, lose track of time in the morning and have to rush back to mine – wearing his clothes like an absolute hussy – to shower and change in time for the tour of Cannes. After the drama at Monaco, Gus decides to stay on the yacht. He doesn't want me in any kind of danger and the risk of him being hounded by fans is too high in an area where he's been known to frequent.

I take this as my opportunity to do some last-minute gift shopping.

My favourite part of the tour is strolling through the narrow streets of Le Suquet and feeling as if I've been immersed into another time with its provincial charm and tiny, privately own trinket shops. Restaurants spill out into the narrow alleyways, covered tables becoming obstacles. Everywhere I look there's so much more colour – the shutters, doors and walls painted in a mix of pastels.

After consuming my weight in macarons at a quirky café in our free time at the end of the tour, I buy another box and return to the cruise with a forbidden hop in my step. I haven't been able to stop thinking about last night.

I keep getting flashbacks of his tongue doing unseemly things and having to bite my lip and breath steadily.

When I board the yacht again, I head back to my room, not wanting to seem too keen. Anyway, he's probably dealing with important popstar things – whatever those are. Maybe he's taken my advice and finally reached out to one of his band members.

To kill a few hours, I end up sunbathing on the sundeck in my skimpy, black bikini, opening the thriller novel I bought with me, for the first time since I arrived. There are a few people milling about the jacuzzi out here but it's a serene atmosphere with soft European pop music playing in the background. I'm barely through the first chapter when I hear him clear his throat from behind.

Because I'm adept at playing hard to get, I pretend not to notice him, flicking a page. And so, imagine my disappointment when I hear his footsteps retreating. I peek around my sunbed, my sunglasses sliding down my nose.

He's so onto me.

Leaning against the bar, he watches me with that amused half-smile.

When he returns, he places a fresh fruit smoothie on the table beside me, takes a seat on the neighbouring sunbed and leans across to grab my book.

"Hey!"

"You weren't reading it anyway."

"I was!" I lie.

"How was Cannes?"

"Beautiful."

"She is."

I glance at him, but his expression tells me nothing. "I got you a present."

He raises an eyebrow. "Oh?"

I lean down to my bag beside me and pull out the cardboard box of macarons, handing it to him. He doesn't take it right away as he's been distracted by the way my body was twisted, giving him a full view of my arse.

"You, Sir, are not very subtle."

He takes the box. "I'm not trying to be anymore."

"What do you mean *anymore*?"

"You think I haven't been distracted by you this whole time?"

"This *whole* time?"

"Come on now. If I wasn't famous—"

"*You're famous?!* You never said."

"—you'd be way out of my league."

I laugh, tipping my head back. "What a load of crap."

"You don't think so?"

"No. I don't. I think you're trying to woo me."

"Did I not already woo you?"

I shrug, pushing my sunglasses back up my nose. "No comment."

"Thank you for the gift," he says. "How much was it?"

"I'm not telling you because you'll try to pay me back."

"If it isn't money you want, I can repay you in other ways."

And that's how we end up booking room service from Gus's suite.

Thirty

The next day, Gus joins me in Toulon as we follow a historical tour of the city. We stroll along at the back, taking in the sights as Gus captures copious amounts of photos. I even listen, as instructed this time, letting Gus boss me about, walking ahead in my denim mini dress, sun-kissed hair tumbling around my shoulders as I hear the click of his camera.

He's once again wearing dark clothing with his blacked-out sunglasses and sun cap pressed low over his forehead. I watch the way his body moves, the flex of his muscles, the way, even though people don't know who he is right now, they're caught on his aura, eyes flicking in his direction.

It's so damn hot. I cross my thighs. Bite my lip.

He gets up from his low position; camera still pointed at me. He moves slowly like a tiger on the prowl. I'm leant against an old building unable to take my attention away from his lips, consumed by his lazy smile.

We're given thirty minutes of freedom from the tour to grab some lunch before we get the cable car up to Mont Faron. I pick a small café with an array of fresh pastries, and we sit at a table tucked into a shadowy spot.

I'm one mouthful into my pain au chocolat when Gus's main phone lights up. I don't catch the number before he grabs it, but I do watch the way his face runs through a myriad of emotions, see how he squeezes his chin, tension returning to his shoulders.

He glances at me. "I've got to take this."

"Ok," I say, nodding.

"Will you be ok? I'll go back to the yacht."

"Oh. Sure." I work hard to hide the disappointment on my face, forcing a smile as he rises from the table and strides back down the busy street, phone already placed to his ear.

I finish my pastry and coffee just in time to join the tour again. I check behind me to see if he might catch us up but when there's no sign of him, I queue with the rest of the tour to ride the cable car.

I hold onto the handle as we slowly rise in the very hot, cramped metal box, looking out over the view. I try to spot him on the yacht waiting elegantly in the port. But I don't see him.

I take my phone out to snap a photo like the rest of the tourists. The views really are magnificent. Except I notice a message from Millie.

Check this out! It says with a link to an article.

Heartbreak As Just4Summer Break Up

Following a statement by the band themselves, Will, Callum and Gus have officially announced that Just4Summer have split for good. It comes after a twelve-year stint of major success, following six albums, ten number ones, three sold-out world tours and even a hit, most-watched documentary following their career.

DuckEgg Records CEO, Nigel Burns, said, "We know this news will bring Just4Summer fans a lot of heartbreak. But every good thing must come to an end at some point. On behalf of the whole team at DuckEgg we want to thank Will, Callum, Jax and Gus for their time in the band and for the music they gave us."

Fans around the world will be reeling at this news…

I don't finish the article.

"Fuck," I mutter, receiving dirty looks from the elderly women sat beside me. "Sorry," I say. "*Fuck!*"

Now I'm up *here*.

And he's down *there*.

No, no, no.

I've never felt more frustrated at the snail pace of anything in my life, not even the damn coach between Split and Dubrovnik. It's infuriating as I push myself through the crammed-in tourists, much to their displeasure, so I can be the first out when we reach the top.

Once the doors open, I frantically search for the queue to get back down. The tour guide is yelling something at me, but I don't register. All I can think about is Gus down there on his own, agonising over this announcement. Did he know? He looked so heartbroken when the phone rang.

I should've guessed.

"*Excusez-moi*," I say to the man running the cable car descent queue, trying to remember any crumbs of GCSE

French that I can. "*J'ai une… Er… Urgence.*"

Thankfully, he takes pity on me, allowing me onto the cable car about to head back down the mountain. I leap on, ignoring the groans of those queuing behind me. Once it's moving, there's nothing to do but tap my feet and stare at the breath-taking scenery of Toulon below and stunning French Riviera beyond that.

I find a scrunchie in my bag, roll my hair into a bun and secure it.

At the bottom, I run as fast I can in sandals, with a dodgy ankle and a tight denim dress that keeps riding up my arse, all the way back to the ship. Arriving breathless and sweaty, I head straight to his suite and knock.

He doesn't answer.

I knock again.

Nothing.

I sigh, pressing my head against his door. Maybe he isn't in there. What if he's left? I should take the hint, but instead, I try again.

"Gus," I call out, half-choked from running. "It's me. Let me in… I just…" I sigh, trying to win my breath back. "Are you ok?"

I nearly give up but then I hear movement behind the door.

"Please, Gus. I just want to check you're ok."

Moments later, the door opens. Luckily, I had one hand propped on the frame or I'd have fallen face first into his suite. He looks tortured, eyes dark, lips parted. I haven't seen this version of him and it does something exhilarating to my core. My heart beats faster, heavier. My toes curling. I want this man beyond questionable doubt. He swallows, that gorgeous ridge in his throat flexing.

I reach out and run my hand over his neck, trail my thumb over his apple. I step closer. His breath catches.

"I want to make you feel better," I whisper, pressing my lips to his tense shoulder.

"It's over," he says, half-choked.

I kiss him again, working my lips up to his chin. "I know. I'm so sorry."

When my mouth runs over his jawline he snaps, a ragged-pained sound escaping him, pulling me into the room, pushing me back against the closed door and crashing his mouth over mine. I feel the pressure all the way down to my toes. His hand cradles the back of my head to protect it, his fingers in my hair.

I can feel adrenaline rushing in my veins.

I want to distract him. I want him. I need this.

I twist from beneath him, stepping further into the room and spin to face him. He watches me, curious, a slight slant to his lips. I think he wants this distraction as much as I need to make him feel better. And despite his mood, I can see his wonderful energy bursting out of him too.

If his eyes could smile…

"Ensuite," he orders, lifting his chin in that direction.

I laugh, nervously. "Make me."

He doesn't move for an unnerving moment. My breathing is coming quickly like I've been sprinting. It was barely a jog from the cable car.

"Is that what you want? You want to play?"

I nod, determined. Then I squeal as he strides toward me, long, quick steps. He grabs at my waist, but I evade him. I plaster myself against the full-length window that looks out to sea. You can't see through it from the other side, so I know we're truly alone.

He smiles at me now, laughing and shaking his head as if he can barely believe this is happening himself. This big, funny, silly, gorgeous man.

"Fuck. I really like you."

I make a sound somewhere between a laugh and a sigh.

"Look at you," he says, barely able to comprehend whatever it is he sees in me. I can't imagine. "Come here."

He leaps again, and although I hop away, this time he's successful, trapping me in his firm arms and throwing me over his shoulder. I struggle a bit – got to make him work for it – but he has me in his grasp now, squeezing us through the door to the ensuite and placing me back on my feet.

He kicks the sliding door closed with his foot, not wanting to remove his hands from my sides. His strong fingers press almost painfully at my hip as he spins me to face away from him. We stare at each other through the mirror above the sink for a long second. He grazes my cheek with his fresh stubble, and I feel the sensation in my toes.

Our gazes lock in challenge.

"Now, are you going to be a good girl and do as you're told?" he asks, his hard, warm body pressing my hips against the cold sink.

I can't even speak. So, I nod, biting my lower lip.

"Hold onto the sink," he instructs, moving his hand up my spine slowly until he finds my low messy bun. He tangles his fingers in it, tugging. I feel the pressure directed straight from my scalp to my core, clenching my thighs in response. "Did you tie your hair into a slutty little handle just for me?"

Nope. Can't run with hair in my face. But again, I nod.

He encourages my body forward, bending me at the hips so my butt is pressed into his crotch. I can feel the solid length of him through his shorts. But he keeps my head up so I can't look away. He nips on my shoulder, bare skin on show. He runs his tongue up to my earlobe and pulls on it, a devilish glint in his eye.

"Shall I take you like this, gorgeous?"

"*Mmm. Yes. Oh fuck.*"

He uses the hand on my hip to venture lower, cupping my butt, testing the material of my knickers before brazenly trailing his finger through my middle. His pained groan echoes off the tiles. "You're always so ready for me, aren't you?"

I nod, still chewing on my poor little lip.

He pushes two fingers inside of me then immediately retracts them. It's utterly cruel.

He pats me on the bottom, stepping away. "I'm going to go and grab protection. If you move from this position, there'll be consequences. Do you understand?"

I can't help the nervous laugh that escapes me before returning to my straight face and nodding sternly. He tugs again on my bun, pulling my head to the side to kiss me full on the mouth, his tongue pressing against mine, damp fingers grazing my cheek.

Then he's gone, leaving me in suspense.

I stare at myself in the mirror, my hair already messed up, my lips swollen, lipstick smudged. It's a moment of realisation that Mike never played with me like this and I know it's because he wasn't fun enough to try. He probably never even knew I'd be into it.

And maybe that's a little bit my fault.

Gus takes longer than necessary, leaving me to stew, to wait in anticipation.

When he returns, he leans on the doorframe, his shoulders blocking the light, staring at my body for a long moment. Then his gaze flits back to mine in the mirror. "Take your knickers off."

I do as I'm told, watching as he deftly rolls a condom on. I nearly turn around, the desire to touch him again is stronger than I'd like to admit.

He gives me a warning look. "Look in the mirror."

I bite my lip, turning back.

"Still want this?"

I nod.

"Good."

He works his hand back into my bun, pressing his lips firmly between my shoulder blades so I have to grab the sides of the sink to stay balanced. He uses his foot to push my legs wider, so commanding and sexy. I swear I could come just from this action alone. His big, lean body bends over me as he works his cock over my middle.

I hum, closing my eyes.

"Open your eyes. I want you looking at me. I want to see you take me."

And the second my gaze locks with his again, he thrusts inside, gasping into my neck. I throw my head back, but he repositions me again. As he begins to move us, whispering endearments, he runs his fingers over my front, pressing them against my tummy until he ventures lower.

He doesn't hold back, no teasing, no waiting. His thumb grazes my clit and stays there, working into a rhythm until

I'm practically humming with pleasure.

"I'm going to need you to come quick for me, sunshine," he pants.

He tugs on my hair again, driving into me, working his thumb harder until I'm gasping at us in the mirror. His lips are parted too and seeing him come undone for me, the desperation in his eyes, the vulnerability, it builds so quick, I swear it could blind me. I grip harder onto the sink, collapsing forward, breaking eye contact.

"*Gus*," I whimper as the release finds me like a flare spreading to every cell in my body, sparkling.

Almost instantly, I feel his teeth press softly into the skin at my neck as he groans, shivering from the release.

We must be still for a few minutes, breathing heavily, Gus's thumb making small circles between my shoulder blades, his other hand on my stomach, holding me to him. Finally, he rearranges himself then lifts me like a doll and carries me back to the bed, laying me down, trailing kisses everywhere, brushing his lips over my belly button then blowing on it, making me squirm.

He sighs, then looks up at me through the unruly curls that have fallen over his eyes. "Sara, you're an excellent distraction. The best."

I run a hand through his hair. "Are you ok?"

"I'll be fine," he says. He releases my bun from the scrunchie and plays with my hair, making me shiver.

"What are we, Sara?" he asks. "It's only..."

I sit up a little when he pauses. "What?"

He sighs. "The band is over. But this lifestyle... It's not going anywhere. At the start of our adventure, you said you could never be with someone famous. Is that still true?"

"I don't know." I flop back down so I don't have to look at him.

Gus moves to sit up, pulling me with him. I find myself pressed against his chest, listening to his heartbeat. "Don't say any more," he says. "I want to keep hold of this moment for as long as I can."

And so I don't.

Thirty-One

Our final stop is in Barcelona. I pack my bags after breakfast and feel bizarrely bereft at the thought of returning to reality. I hand my suitcase over at the desk. The cruise company arrange for it to be delivered to the airport so that I'm free to explore the city without hauling it around with me.

We chose not to disembark at Palamos, the penultimate destination because we didn't want to risk ruining our last full day together on the cruise with him being spotted, followed and harassed.

Gus meets me in the lobby, and we stroll the city streets, shopping, taking photos, eating and drinking. It's a bloody hot day and I'm grateful for my hat and the copious amounts of Fanta Limón I've drunk since we arrived. I've got a loose pair of denim shorts on, white sneakers and a flowy blouse. Gus, on the other hand, is dressed in his usual disguise of dark colours, cap and sunglasses.

He takes a seat on a nearby bench while I stroll round a couple of trinket stalls again, spying for last-minute gifts for my sisters. They're little sparrows like me. They like small shiny things they can put in small, adorable boxes. I pick up a few cute rings and a pretty gemstone.

Once I've browsed all the stalls I join him on the bench, sitting beside him and leaning on his shoulder. He smiles down at me but there's a ghost of something behind his eyes.

"What happens after today?"

I swallow, glancing at my crossed ankles. "I thought we weren't going to talk about it."

"It feels insane to me that I've seen you every day for the last fortnight. At one point, you were my lifeline. And now, it's just going to crumble into nothing."

I look up and find him already staring. I sigh, nudging him with my elbow. I don't know what to say. I don't know how to tell him that I've loved this time but my very sensible brain tells me this is a holiday fling and all these feelings, this intense ache in my chest will all melt into nothing in a matter of days. I can't say it, because my heart doesn't believe it and I don't want to hurt him.

I think he senses it anyway, letting out a slow sigh. He places a hand on my thigh and smiles sadly. He glances over my shoulder. "The city is busy," he says. "Do you remember what I said about the burner phone and my team?"

I nod. "Call the number saved under security."

"And the codeword?"

"Roko."

"Good. Yeah. I have a feeling. I'm pretty sure I've been spotted already. And with everything going on, there'll be speculation about where I am."

I tense, searching the sunny square for dangers. Gus squeezes my leg again. It's not that I'm ashamed to be seen with him, of course I'm not. How could I be? It's more that I have no idea what the damage of being seen with him right now would be to my world, my sisters, my dad.

"What are you doing after today?" I ask.

"I guess I'll go home and start the process of kicking my bratty sister out of my house."

"Will you be ok?"

He drops his head. "I've got lots to keep me busy." Which isn't really an answer, but it's something.

At least he'll be busy. He'll forget about all of this within days. I swallow as the pain of that thought lodges itself in my throat.

I don't want him to forget me.

I don't want to go back to my lonely apartment.

I don't want to *only* be in his wildest dreams.

To distract myself, I jump back to my feet and brush myself down, even though nothing even fell on me. Gus blinks at me.

"Come on. Let's get to the Sagrada Familia before we miss our slot." The cruise booked us specific times to meet there, organising the final tour of our trip before I'll take a taxi back to the airport, my flight leaving later tonight.

We stroll side by side. He takes my arm and loops it through his. And I'm not sure if it's because Gus has specifically brought it up and I'm now more aware, or whether I was simply completely blind before but I'm certain there are eyes tracking us. Or more specifically, Gus.

Groups of young women. A few men. There's a middle-aged lady too, who I'm convinced is following us with her phone out filming.

And it doesn't become an issue until we arrive outside the basilica, staring up at its magnificent architecture, when we're essentially parked here like sitting ducks. A blonde girl, with a Spanish accent, marches up to Gus.

"Is it *you?*" she says, her face disbelieving. "It is!"

And like some kind of superpower, I watch him turn it on. Suddenly he's a famous popstar. He takes his sunglasses off, hanging them on his T-shirt, then he grabs something from his back pocket and places it in my palm without even looking at me. It's his burner phone. I step away but watch the situation unfold. He'll want to see the basilica. Maybe she'll go and…

Another person comes up to him. He signs a leaflet she's given him. The Spanish girl asks him to sign her white T-shirt.

I glance around me to see if anyone is taking any interest in me. But no. I'm a nobody. Of course. What did I expect? They wouldn't look at me and see a woman worthy of Gus from Just4Summer. It's laughable really.

As more people huddle around, asking questions about the band splitting up and taking selfies with him, I realise I have no choice but to call his team.

My chest is tight as I open the phone and find the number. It rings once before a stern voice answers. "Yes?"

"Hi," my voice is shaky. "Yeah. Erm, *Roko?*"

"Sara," a gruff voice responds. "Did he tell you to call me?"

"I don't actually know who you are." I frown. Should Gus have told me that? Despite him briefing me on this exact scenario, I feel so unprepared. "But yes. We're at the basilica in…"

"Barcelona. I know. What's the situation?"

"He's surrounded by fans."

"We're two minutes away," he says, his voice softening as if he can sense my tension. "Stay on the phone."

I do as I'm told, listening to the engine revving, indicators clicking, then the sound of car doors opening and slamming shut. When I spot two large men, dressed in dark shirts and black trousers, striding towards Gus, I experience a wave of nausea.

Is this it?

Do I even get to say goodbye?

I suck in a sharp breath as they reach him. I've stepped away so much now that it feels like I'm only spectating. I hang up the phone and drop it into my bag.

The bodyguards are polite to his fans but carefully untangle him, guiding him back towards the car that's been abandoned by the side of the road.

It's like watching a stranger. I can't comprehend that the Gus I've been with for the last two weeks is the same one being treated like a royalty now. He stops to speak to his bodyguards, but they continue to encourage him towards the car.

He shakes his head, clearly irritated with their insistence to leave.

Before they can push him in, he pauses, searching the crowd. He leans on the open door. Some of the people in the crowd have followed him. There are so many phones out, filming. I swallow thickly.

And when his eyes find mine, I don't know what to do. I stand there numb.

Gus nods towards the vehicle as if inviting me in.

I shake my head subtly.

I feel like an absolute coward.

But it's asking too much. He's asking me to step into the spotlight. And I'm not ready for that.

Because I never intended to join him past Barcelona anyway.

I barely know the man, not really. The rational part of me is already clocking this whole situation as a romantic, summer fling. It's only… I've had them before and they've never felt quite like this, like we're threads in a rope being unravelled and torn apart.

What good could come from extending this goodbye?

His stare holds mine across the crowd for the longest moment. He looks like he wants to run to me. It looks like he wants to say something he's forgotten.

But, instead, he smiles sadly, nods and does one final wave before climbing into the car. Once the door is closed, I realise there's no changing my mind. It's like a wall has been built between the time that we've had together and the super celebrity who is so far out of my reach it blows my mind.

For a moment, I think I'm going to cry.

But I'm too good at evading tears, too practised and it passes.

Because I'm a grownup.

I am rational.

This will all pass.

And so, I join the queue for the Sagrada Familia like nothing happened.

Thirty-Two

When I arrive home in the middle of the night, the air is noticeably cooler in England.

I decide to watch *Pride and Prejudice*, the Keira Knightly version, *obviously* – mostly so that I can pine after Matthew Macfadyen and his sexy sideburns – but end up falling asleep there on the sofa, only woken again by the morning light pouring through my open blinds.

I take a shower and then make myself a coffee, contemplating what would be best to do with my final day of annual leave when I see a message from Dad asking me to call him when I get a moment.

He answers on the first ring. "Hello, darling."

I smile but hearing his voice makes me wobble. A tiny part of me wants to tell him everything, to reveal all the messy feelings that are making my head and heart ache. And yet, I know I never will. Because it's not who we are, even if I want it to be. "Hey, Dad."

"How was your holiday? Millie was sharing the photos with me."

"It was…" I take a steadying breath. "…like a dream."

"You deserve it. I know you don't tell me anything because you're worried this old man won't be able to handle it but I'm not stupid. You've had a tough time. And you needed a break."

I try to brush it off. "Yes, old man. It doesn't stop you from being nosey though. What's this call really about?"

He clears his throat and takes a moment to find the words. "Well… Since you asked. I've been looking for my cufflinks."

I make a face, not that he can see it. "And?"

"And I can't find them anywhere." He sounds flustered and I wonder how long he's been sat on this. Probably not wanting to interrupt my time away.

"Dad, did you call me to help you find *your* cufflinks in *your* own home?" I ask, trying not to laugh at him.

"Yes, yes, I know. I'm useless. But I have a thing. And I need them."

"A thing?" I press.

"Yes."

"What thing?"

He rattles out an irritated sigh. "If you must know, I have a date."

I bite my lip. I almost play with him some more, but I can feel how hard this is for him to share with me. And I understand, because it's hard for me too.

"That's great, Dad," I say instead, a tear escaping.

I blink it away because I don't want him to hear it in my voice. Something about knowing he's ok with moving on and trying to be happy, finally, after all these years, overwhelms me.

"They're in the shoebox box under your bed," I say eventually.

"Well, why would they be there?" he says, gruffly.

I laugh. "You put them there, silly man."

"Never. This was one of you four messing with me."

"Alright, alright. Yes. We tidied up and organised your house on purpose just to make you mad."

I listen to him rattling around his room until he finds the ones he's after and thanks me. "You'll come for dinner at the weekend, won't you? I'm going to do a barbecue. It would be nice if you could all be there to meet Sandra."

"Oh, she has a name!" I say, knowing it will wind him up.

"She's very nervous. You'll tell the girls, won't you?"

He means he wants me to inform my sisters of his news and it's so second nature to me now I can't help but agree because I just want him to be happy, even if it does mean taking on some extra baggage to see it. It's not like I have a whole lot else to do.

I agree to his terms, begging him to make a salad so that his new girlfriend doesn't think he only eats red meat and baked beans (he does) and then say farewell so I can crack on with the rest of my day.

After the call, in a weirdly high mood, I head to the seaside, taking a long blustery stroll down to the Marina and back. I almost pop into a shop on the seafront before remembering I'm almost definitely skint until payday. Sighing, I open my banking app to check my financial situation and nearly walk straight into someone going the opposite way. The number showing on my screen can't be correct.

"Holy shit," I hiss, holding a hand over my mouth.

My bank account has fifty thousand pounds in it.

The transaction says it came from a Mr A Kenwood.

I panic, swiftly closing my phone in case anyone walking past might see and judge me for being rich.

Bastard.

I told him not to pay me any interest. And this is more than interest. It's a massive chunk of money that he probably barely thought twice about.

My breathing is rapid, my pulse beating in my throat. I take a seat on a bench and give myself a moment before a seagull starts to eye me from the armrest at the other end and I feel harassed.

"I don't have any chips. Bugger off you beady-eyed bastard."

The one skill every Brightonian must learn is how to speak the language of the huge, aggressive seagulls here.

I swallow roughly, getting up from the bench and walking across the crunchy pebble beach towards the rough chop of waves, crashing and retreating against the shore.

The fucking seagull follows me.

It's just as well as the rest of the beach is quiet this fine Monday morning, because other than a man in speedos warming up for a swim, I'm alone and on the verge of tears.

I'm tired of fighting my emotions. Something about knowing he's thought about me since yesterday has me welling up, my cheeks becoming damp. I use my long sleeves to dry them, but it just gets worse.

Ok, this is fine.

It's ok.

I can cry about him a little. I'm probably in shock and feeling overwhelmed by the sudden goodbye and also the potential implication of this money in my account. Is this it, then? Is this some sort of payment for my company? Does it not mean anything more to him than that?

No.

Of course not.

In the end, it was my decision not to pursue this. And he never hid his plan to pay me back in an obscene way.

Besides, it's the right decision. I could never make it work with a popstar. Honestly at this point, I'm wondering if I could make it work with anyone. I throw my head back and stare at the sky, the sun bright in the middle of the day.

I made the right decision.

I did.

Time will prove that to me. I'll never forget what we had, but I'll move on. And if not, I'll just keep telling myself that until I believe it.

Thirty-Three

What I never considered, as the weeks fly past, is that Gus would be hard to escape.

I guess, before, I barely knew of Just4Summer. Sure, I heard them on the radio. It just didn't register like it does now. I didn't become weak at the knees, have sudden breathlessness, and experience heated visions replaying in my mind whenever their songs came on.

Now, I see him *everywhere*.

My social media algorithm is bombarding me with J4S clips and slow, horny edits of the man I'm still having to fight out of my dreams.

It's cruel.

The world is a cruel place.

But it's not just that. Whenever something popular comes to an end, unfortunately often a celebrity death but this time the breakup of the band, the world wants to consume that thing in bulk. So everywhere I go now, whether the shopping centre, the supermarket, even at work, I hear his music, pretending I'm not hyper-focusing on his solos. I know all the bloody lyrics to their popular hits at this point.

I'm basically a superfan. I've been recruited.

I must *never* let my sisters find out.

He's even on TV. The usual news cycles ignore actual worldwide catastrophes and issues, to instead air J4S's breakup conference, where they've forced the three remaining boyband members into a room with microphones. It hardly seems worth it either. They clearly have nothing to say to each other, the spark in their eyes extinguished. They answer the questions with short and quippy responses without any emotion behind them.

I pause on a closeup of Gus.

It was just a fling, right?

Those moments we shared. The way fate forced us together. It was just a fluke.

The chemistry between us – he'd have had that with anyone.

I have to believe it or I'll go insane.

The weekends are the worst, when things are too quiet in my apartment. So, this week I call my sisters over for lunch, since they all live in Brighton too, because I want a distraction and some company.

I know Millie will come for free food.

Abby is too kind to say no.

And Gemma won't want to be left out if we're all here without her.

When they arrive, we sit around the breakfast bar, tucking into the roast dinner I've served them.

"There's no way you cooked this," Gemma accuses, pointing her fork in my direction. "Do you even know how to use that oven?"

"Excuse me!" I scoff. "I *can* cook."

"Yeah. *Sure.* But she didn't," Abby interjects.

I faux gasp at her, surprised she can stoop so low.

She laughs, mouth half-full. "Sara, the Deliveroo man was leaving as I was walking down the street. And besides, the oven is still cold, and the takeout containers are in the bin."

I take a sip of my drink. "Well, bugger."

They all find this very funny. It's in a moment of quiet afterwards when we have our mouths full that I realise Millie is blasting music from her phone and Just4Summer are playing. I roll my eyes. It's the song about hot summers that go on and on and on. It's annoyingly good and I can't believe I didn't discover them before.

I don't bring this up, however. The subject matter feels too close to the bone. *Still.*

Instead, I ask about my sisters. They tell me what they've been up to over the last few weeks, but I swear they keep glancing at each other, like there's something happening here I'm not privy too. As the eldest sister, I'm immediately suspicious.

And to make matters worse, the music just keeps switching to more J4S songs. In fact, this is their Best Of playlist on Spotify. I should know, I've listened to it enough at this point. It almost seems deliberate, but I can't imagine why it would be.

It's just that Gus's voice seems to reverberate right through me, right to my core. I'm losing my appetite and there's apple crumble and custard for dessert.

Dammit.

Gemma scoffs whilst reading something on her phone and I look up to find them all typing away. *Are they using the group chat that I'm not in?*

"Alright. What's going on?" I demand.

Millie glares at Abby. Gemma groans at Millie. Abby sighs defeatedly.

"*Seriously.* What am I missing?"

"I'm just going to say it," Millie blurts out, raising her hands.

"*No,*" Abby says. "Let her come to it on her own. When she's ready."

"She's never going to do that, Abby. She doesn't share things with us. She never has."

"*What?*" I mumble.

Millie shrugs. "You think you're better than us and it shows."

"I... don't..." I say, shaking my head slowly, entirely confused.

"It's actually kind of disrespectful at this point." Gemma puts her fork down and gives me a reproachful stare.

"*What are you talking about?*"

"If she doesn't want to tell us, she doesn't have to," Abby adds.

"You're right," Millie agrees. "She doesn't have to share her dirty secrets with her little sisters. But she *does* have to accept she'll never be in our group chat."

"What are you bloody talking about?" I huff, throwing my hands up. I feed them for free and this is what I get. Honestly, they wonder why I am the way I am.

"Fuck it. I'm just going to show her," Millie says.

"Show me what? What is actually happening right now?"

Millie scrolls through her phone before holding the screen towards me so I can see what she's showing me.

Ah. I see.

It's Gus and me strolling through Monaco, hand-in-hand. I have my big hat on so unless you knew me well, you'd never recognise me. Unfortunately, my sisters do know me quite well so it doesn't take me long to realise why they're annoyed.

I feel like I'm busted.

Am I busted?

I don't know what to say. Because is this even a crime? Why am I not allowed to keep secrets from them? This all feels a little unjust, so I hold my head up as I face them. This doesn't prove anything anyway. That *could* be someone else. Could be. *It isn't.* But it could be for all they know…

Millie snatches the phone back and scrolls again.

This time I'm shown a deeply pixelated photo of Gus and me laughing at a small restaurant in Old Town, Dubrovnik.

Then Gemma adds to the evidence, showing me a photo taken from on the yacht. Gus is spinning me on the dance floor, Edith and Paul smiling at us adoringly in the background.

Well, ok. That's undeniably me. I'm going to struggle to squirrel out of this one.

"So?" I say, eyeing them. "What do you want me to say?"

"*SO?!*" Millie scoffs, finally putting her phone down.

Abby's eyes go wide. "So? *Sara.*" She says my name like she's about to put me in a timeout.

Gemma shrugs like she's unsurprised but still disappointed by my response. "Told you. She doesn't air her dirty laundry with us."

This gets my back up. "Hold up. Gus is *not* dirty laundry."

There's a collective gasp. "SO, IT'S TRUE!" Millie shouts. They're all staring at me, gobsmacked.

"What do you want me to say!?" I ask, gesticulating. "We hung out a little. *So what?*"

"Sara, Gus Kenwood doesn't just *hang out* with random strangers. Also, his fans have done the math. You guys missed the cruise. There's this big social media search for the blonde girl in all the photos. They're hunting you."

I scrunch up my face. "*Hunting* me?"

"Yeah. But don't worry," Gemma says, waving her hand dismissively. "They'll never guess it was you."

Millie nods, snorting. "Yeah. You're safe."

"Wait?" I blink rapidly, completely and utterly shocked by this revelation. How long did they know? How long have they been keeping this from me? What if someone actually worked out who I was and harassed me in the street?

"What do you mean?" I demand, fiddling with my hair. "I'm so confused. Who is *hunting* me?"

"Gus's fans," Millie says like it's obvious. *Oh, yeah, like duh.*

"But why?"

"Because you're not with him now. They want to know what went down. What happened, obviously."

"Obviously," I breathe. Except it isn't obvious to me at all. I shake my head. "No. I need more detail. Tell me why."

"Because, Sara, some people are powered by gossip. And you know what really hurts? When those people don't even get to hear from their own sister that they had a romantic summer fling with the most beloved popstar ever." She means her. She means I hurt her feelings by not revealing this intimate, painful information about myself to her right away. I can't help feeling that's unfair.

And besides, "You said you preferred Jax."

She points at me across the table. "Not the point. I have been sat on this for weeks. Abby told me not to say anything. It's bad enough that I've lied to my friends, telling them it wasn't you," she flails her arms around dramatically. "It couldn't be Sara. Oh *no!* She's too uptight and goody two shoes to go and have a fling mere months after absconding from her wedding. And, of course, if it was her, she'd obviously tell her own *sisters*. Right? *RIGHT?*"

I part my lips to defend myself, but nothing comes out.

The truth is, I've been waiting for all those feelings I harbour for Gus to fade away. Like Millie said, *it was a fling.* How could it be more? It was fourteen days… How deep can my feelings honestly be? I'm being horribly dramatic. He'll find someone famous, someone who understands his lifestyle and he'll move on.

That can't be me.

"Do you all feel this way?" I ask, checking my sisters' expressions one at a time.

Gemma nods. Not really surprised there.

"Abby?"

She cringes. "It's just… Well…"

"Oh my God. You guys think I don't have secrets?"

"No. We're sure you do," Gemma says, twisting her lips. "But you don't share them with us. You never tell us anything juicy. Which, when you were with Mike, wasn't surprising."

Millie snorts. "Yeah."

"Wait. What do you mean by that?"

"He was boring," Abby says.

I gasp. "Abby!"

"He was. He made *you* boring too."

"Why didn't any of you tell me?"

"Because you act like you've always got your shit together," Millie says. "It's gross and annoying. It's hard to keep up with, always comparing yourself to your perfect eldest sister."

"And you wouldn't have listened," Gemma adds. "Look. We know you'd do anything for us. We *know* that. But the reason you're not in our group chat is because you'd probably judge us for the things we confess in there."

I scoff. "As if! I want to know your gossip. Wait? So, it wasn't set up for you three to bitch about me?"

"We do that too," Millie says, rolling her eyes. "But no. It was set up to tell each other the stupid shit we do."

"Sometimes it feels like you're more our mother than our sister," Abby interjects.

Her words are like little daggers to the heart because, yeah, that's exactly how it feels because that's exactly what was needed for so long. A breath lodges itself in my throat and I find myself unable to respond. I think about all the tantrums I handled. All the times, when I was also on the way to school, I had to deal with one of their meltdowns or forgotten homework, or last-minute shop runs for food tech because Dad would already be at work. I think about all the childhood I gave up for these three and wonder if any of them are even grateful.

"Yeah," I say finally. "That's exactly how it feels for me too. Because you know what? You needed a mother figure. All of you did. And I did the best I fucking could! So, I'm sorry if you feel like you can't *relate* to me as a sister these days. But I feel the same way about all of you."

They're quiet, absorbing my outburst as I pretend to cut the roasted parsnip on my plate. Then, when nothing is said, I sigh, get up from the kitchen island and make myself a drink so I can turn my back on them.

I can feel them bickering silently behind me.

After a moment, Abby gently says, "Sara? We're sorry."

"Yeah. Same," Gemma says, half-heartedly.

Millie doesn't say anything because she's the youngest and Abby already spoke for her. I laugh into my cup, exasperated. I guess at least it's better than crying. When I turn back to them, they're all looking at me, wide-eyed and apologetic.

"Yes," I say finally. "I spent a lot of time with Gus from Just4Summer while I was away. *Things*," I shake my head, heat warming my cheeks, "*happened*."

"Did you sleep with him?" Millie asks. Because, of course, when all is said and done, that's the real juice. It's all that matters. Even if it's none of her business and I'd never ask the same of her. The fact that she readily gives up that information is beside the point.

I raise my shoulders and twist my lips. "Maybe." But they continue to stare. "Fine. Yes. Yes, I did."

All three of their mouths pop open, their jaws practically on the floor.

"But you're not allowed to tell anyone!" I warn, pointing at them.

"I shagged my window cleaner," Gemma says. Which... *Huh?*

Millie covers her face. "I gave one of Dad's cadets a

blowjob behind the Portaloos at the summer fundraiser."

"Millie!" I exclaim. "That's aw—"

She holds up a finger, pausing me mid-sentence. "Before you judge, Gemma's window cleaner is in his *sixties*. Oh, and the rule is you *can't* judge."

"And I had a one-night stand at some randomer's house after clubbing a few weeks ago and he paid me a wad of cash because he thought I was hooker," Abby adds. "Apparently the going rate for a shag is two hundred quid."

Millie and Gemma both start chuckling at Abby whose cheeks have gone an alarming shade of red.

"Ok?" I don't understand why they're telling me this.

"Now you have dirt on us. So, your secret is safe."

I laugh, unsure what to do with that information. "I don't know if that's how it works."

Millie holds her hands up, as if I'm overthinking it. "Well, it works for us."

"I've added you to the group chat," Abby says, smiling. "*Sister.*"

After that Abby helps me clear the plates into the dishwasher as Gemma and Millie work out how to reheat the apple crumble I also ordered from the local pub.

We finally sit down again, spooning our deserts.

"So, was he good?" Millie asks, a cheeky glint in her eye.

"At dancing?" I ask, innocently.

"Sure. Naked dancing."

"Millie. I'm your sister."

"*Come on*, Sara," Gemma goads.

"I'm not telling you guys that. What I will say... is he was fun to be around."

"I bet he was!" Millie squeals. "So, you're really not speaking to him anymore?"

I shrug like it's of no importance and not physically hurting my heart every time I think about him, like I missed something, like I left my person behind. "No."

"Why not?"

"Because he's a famous popstar. He lives in a different universe to me. It would never work." It's so matter of fact. So honest. And yet, so damningly horrible to say out loud.

The three of them share a look as if they can read me.

"Ok. I'm going to be a bitch for once," Gemma says. *When is she ever not a bitch?* "You're self-sabotaging. You lead this perfect little life. And yes, you have a fab career and earn a good salary. Look at you and your gorgeous apartment, all fucking independent and shit. You almost had the perfect, boring man. You would've had perfectly boring children and lived a dull, but safe life."

"Fuck me. Say what you really mean, Gemma!"

"I *am*. I'm being completely honest."

Sarcasm often evades her.

"So what?" I ask. "Are we just back to roasting me every time we hang out? I know you think I'm uptight, and stressy, I'm not an idiot. You've told me enough times. But have you ever stopped and thought about the fact that I lost a mum too? That I was still a child. I was *fourteen*. I wanted to be carefree. But carefree isn't how you manage to keep your life on track. I have to be steady, so I am here and ready to help you out, help Dad out, when or if any of you need me."

Gemma swallows. Millie looks at her bowl. Abby is

fiddling with her spoon.

"We're adults now," Millie says, her voice small. "You don't *have* to be there for us."

"Is that why you're not speaking to Gus?" Abby interjects. "Because you're worried being with him would send your life off track?"

I shrug. I feel like that oversimplifies the issue. Because it's more than that. There's fear there too. There's a lack of belief in myself which I sometimes disguise as needing to be steady. "Partly. I don't know. It just... He's a very famous popstar."

I don't know why I need to explain that further.

"A hot one," Millie says. "Who really liked you. You can tell by the photos. He was *down bad*. That's why they're so keen to find out who you are. He hasn't looked at many girls like that."

"I—"

"You can afford a little off track," Gemma says, rolling her eyes. "It will make us look a lot less scatty if you're also a little scatty. Honestly, you'd be doing us a favour. Go mess up your life a bit. Do some dumb shit."

Millie nods. "Yeah. Fuck it. You've worked so hard. You're too..." She gestures to all of me and doesn't finish the sentence. Good. Great. Love that for me. "I'll admit, I almost didn't recognise you in some of those photos. You were smiling so... big. And you seemed so relaxed."

"I was on holiday."

She gives me a look. "That's not why."

I focus on finishing the excessive amount of custard that Millie poured onto the crumble. Just4Summer songs are still playing from her phone, albeit quieter now where she's turned it down to talk. It's hard to ignore that my sisters all go silent whenever he's singing too.

I can't. It's a fruitless, pointless conversation. I drop my spoon into my bowl. "It's all irrelevant anyway. I don't even have his number. He has to change it all the time for security reasons."

"Then slide into his DMs," Millie says, like it's obvious.

"What does that mean?"

They all roll their eyes at me this time. "You spend *way* too much time in that corporate job surrounded by old men."

So, we're back to roasting Sara. Yay!

"Oh!" I say, a thought suddenly occurring to me. "I actually do have something. Wait here."

I head to my room, searching for my hand luggage from the flight home. It's the same bag I carried around Barcelona. I cleared most of it out weeks ago when I let my sisters sparrow through the trinkets and random bits and bobs I found in different cities. I dig my hand in and take out the cheap burner phone Gus handed me.

I think part of me has purposefully forgotten it was there.

I try to turn it on, but the battery is dead.

I storm out to the kitchen yank Millie's phone out of the charger and switch it for his.

"Hey!" she says, snatching hers up and holding it to her chest. "Careful with that."

I use the moment to fill the jug of water and offer it round the table when I realise I haven't dug into this conversation even nearly enough.

"Which cadet did you suck off at the fundraiser?" I ask

Millie. "And please tell me he was one of the adult ones."

She sticks her tongue out. "Obviously! Dad only trains the adults now. He was like a year older than me."

"He was hot to be fair," Gemma defends.

"Doesn't excuse the Portaloo situation."

Millie nods. "Trust me, I know where you're coming from but... It does. He had a very nice..."

"Hose?" I offer.

We all burst out laughing. Abby dribbles red wine down her chin and has to grab some kitchen roll to clean up.

"And you!" I say to Abby. "When did you become a hooker?"

"I'm *not* a hooker. It was because I wore Millie's dress."

"Hey! That's *never* happened to me."

Gemma sniffs. "That's because they think you'll do it for free."

"So gross. I can feel the feminism leaking from our bodies." I shake my limbs as if to prove it. Then I glance at Gemma. "Did you pay for your window cleaning or..."

"No. He's taking me out on a date next week." Not even an ounce of shame. In fact, she looks pretty pleased with herself. I wish I had that much confidence when it came to letting my hair down.

"You realise your old man thing is very strange," I tell her.

She nods, gulping back more wine. "I'm *very* aware. I don't know what it is. There's just something about them..."

"You're such a bunch of skanks," I joke, throwing an arm around Abby and kissing her hair. "I'm so embarrassed we're related. But I love you."

At that moment, the burner phone lights up, turning itself back on. I practically launch at it. It takes five minutes to fully wake up and load to the home screen. We're all poised in anticipation. I feel a bit weird looking at somebody else's phone until a message pops up that clearly reads: *Hi Sara.*

Ok... So, I'm pretty sure I can open it without feeling guilty or like I'm evading his privacy. And besides, he gave me the phone. I'm probably overthinking this. Definitely overthinking.

Even so, I turn my back on my sisters to read it without their prying eyes.

I open the message, but it takes a second to load because there are large attachments.

Thirty photos to be precise.

The message reads:

Hi Sara, I don't know where you are now or what you're doing but I hope you receive this message. Amongst all the sights we saw together, the history, the architecture, it was you I noticed. You became my muse.

I wanted to share these with you. I want you to know how incredibly beautiful you are. I want you to see you how I saw you. The two weeks we spent together mean more than you'll ever know. I still think about you all the time.

Whatever happens. I'm so glad you came. I'm so glad to have met you.

Gus x

I try to hide the message but it's too late, my sisters are

all over me. Millie is literally on the kitchen island on her hands and knees so she can read the message.

"Call him!" Millie shouts. We all jump. She clears her throat, tucks her hair behind her ears and tries again. "Call him!" she echoes, slightly quieter this time.

I'm still scrolling through the photos. I didn't realise I'd laughed so much. Or smiled like that. He's got me up close and off in the distance, totally unaware he was even taking pictures of me. There's some of us together on the fishing boat, him staring at me, then me staring at him, then us both locked in each other's eyes. It was before we'd even kissed. I snigger when I remember the way Roko came between us.

Gemma would've loved him.

"You look so good together," she mutters. Why does she always sound so resentful?

"You do," Abby says. "Oh my God. I think he fell for you."

"No. He's also a photographer. He enjoys this stuff. And he's really good at it," I explain. It's not that. Can't be that. Won't be that.

All three of them give me an exasperated look then in unison shout, "CALL HIM!"

"No!" I say, getting out of my seat and escaping their clutches. They don't follow but their gazes don't leave me either. "It doesn't... He doesn't... It can't be... It's too soon... I just." I rub my forehead.

"Have you run out of excuses yet?" Millie asks, raising an eyebrow.

"Ugh! Fine. You're the most annoying people on the planet."

I clutch my chest. My heart is beating way too hard. This is absurd. But maybe this is how it is meant to feel. Maybe it's meant to be a little scary. Maybe that's how you know.

I dial the number and hold the phone to my ear.

Thirty-Four

The line is dead.

It doesn't even dial. Just beeps at me like I'm rude for having the audacity to try. And I have to agree. What was I even thinking?

Why does it feel like I'm on the verge of tears?! I drop my arms to my side and say, "Well. Guess that's over."

When I turn to my sisters, I find all three of them on their phones.

"He's in London," Millie says without looking up.

"Yep," Gemma agrees. "Book event. Signing until four p.m. It's a biography of their tour."

"Tickets only though," Abby says, pursing her lips.

Millie nods. "Get dressed. We're going book shopping, bitches."

Gemma wrinkles her nose. Abby woops.

"In *London*?" I ask.

"Yes," Millie replies, giving me a look like I'm being dumb.

"Right *now*?"

"Yes! Get dressed!" she says, shimmying me into my room.

I slide into a flattering dress and pair it with some ankle heeled sandals. Fifteen minutes later, we're marching up the hill towards Brighton station. Thirty minutes later, we're on the fast train to London. And an hour later, we're filing into the busy, sweaty underground enroute to Piccadilly Circus.

I haven't said much this whole journey, partly because Millie hasn't shut up, but also because I've been trying to work out what I'd say to Gus even if I did see him. We probably won't. I haven't got tickets, and I've seen first-hand how his security is with him.

"What do I even say?" I ask them when we're all crammed into the tube, Millie's face so close I can count her freckles.

"Don't ask me," she says. "I'm useless with men."

"You could say you want to see him again. I'm sure he'll be thrilled to hear from you," Abby adds.

I huff. "I should've called Hattie."

"Ugh her boyfriend is so hot," Millie says.

"Freddie? He *is* hot," Abby agrees.

I click my fingers. "Can we focus please? I've never actually asked someone out before and I'm nervous."

"Never? What a humble brag..." Gemma croons.

I ignore her. "What if it's awkward? What if he's moved on?"

They all collectively agree that I shouldn't worry. I should ignore my head and listen to my heart. So, fine. I just wish the thought of seeing him again didn't make my stomach feel like it's trying to backflip.

We arrive in busy Piccadilly Circus and run round the corner to find the massive Waterstones, only to be greeted by a queue that winds all the way out of the shop and up the side of the street for as far as we can see.

All these people came to see Gus.

The man I spent two weeks with.

The man I was very intimate with.

All these women (and some men) *want* this man.

Love this man.

"This is waste of time," I say. *God.* My heart is beating so hard. "There's no way we're going to get to see him. Not with that queue."

"Pfft. This is nothing," Millie says. "You should see the queues I've skipped in Ibiza."

Gemma snorts. "Yeah. If needed, Millie can shag a security guard."

"That was Magaluf."

I give them a look. "You actually…?" I shake my head. "You know what? We share genes. It tracks."

"HEY!" Abby shouts beside me. I grab onto Gemma in surprise. Who is this person and what has she done with my darling little sister? "WHO WANTS TO GIVE UP THEIR TICKET FOR TWO HUNDRED QUID? *CASH.*"

"What the actual fuck, Abby," I hiss.

"If I'm going to pimp myself out, I'd rather spend the cash on something I care about. Plus, I didn't want to put it in the bank in case HMRC try to tax me and ask where I got it from…"

"I don't think they're too worried about…"

"I'll take it," someone in the crowd says, stepping towards us. A big bloke with tattoos all up his arms holds out a book with a ticket poking out the top like a bookmark. "I didn't want it anyway. My girlfriend made me come. If you want to queue with her – she's over there." He points to a dark-haired woman who looks conflicted about being left to queue alone.

"How much was the ticket originally?" I ask the man.

He scratches his forehead. "Twenty quid."

"Right. Good. Great."

Abby fishes the cash out of her bag. It's even been folded neatly into a brown envelope. I need to pay more attention to her. This is probably drug money. "I don't know if I want to spend your hussy money," I tell her as she hands it to the man.

He gives us a strange look.

"Think of it as charity," she says with a smile.

"That doesn't make me feel better."

But after a few rough nudges from them, I find myself in the ridiculous queue to meet Gus. I remember him saying he hadn't even read this damn book. I doubt, from the excitable conversations I'm overhearing, that many of the people queuing plan on reading it either. It's more of a memento for meeting him.

The queue moves slowly. My sisters message to tell me they've gone in search of a pub and to keep them updated. Once we're in the building and up the first staircase, I finally regard the book with the band's faces on. They look younger here, up on stage at a concert. Gus always had his signature hair, but he's gotten better at styling it as he grew up. It looks sexier now than it did back then.

I open the book and peruse the images. There are photos of them at Madame Tussauds next to their wax figures. On the London Eye. Performing at Glastonbury. There are photos of Gus and Jax together, hugging. I wonder if they skirt over their fall out in the book or pay reference to it.

There's a whole section about ex-girlfriends which I choose to skip. Then there's that performance at the Kid's Choice Awards – the one that made them famous in the US. The cover of "Girls Just Want To Have Fun" lit up the room. I'm ashamed to say I've watched it almost every day since I arrived home. Gus stands at the edge of the stage in only denim dungarees, leaning into the crowd and getting them to sing along.

His aura is unmatched. He wonders how fame happened to him. He says he never understood it. But just one look at him and it's obvious.

He's a superstar.

It must be an hour before I spot him and I'm still twenty or thirty people back. There's at least a few hundred after me. I have no idea how long he's agreed to sit there and sign books.

He doesn't see me. Or at least, I don't think he does.

He's dressed casually, in an unbuttoned shirt with a plain white T-shirt underneath. His hair has been left to its own devices but it's hard not to see the exhaustion in his face. Of course, he works hard not to let any of this onto the fans. But I can see it. His smile doesn't quite reach his eyes like it did on the cruise.

It suddenly occurs to me, with only one more girl ahead, that this is unfair on him. *What the fuck am I doing?* I try to turn around but the event staff usher me forward.

"If you want your book signed you have to go now. We have lots of people to get through," the woman tells me, exasperated.

She's fed up. I don't want to be her problem. I've worked retail and it sucks. Especially when customers are arseholes.

I turn back towards the table.

He's staring at me, lips parted. It takes everything in me to step up and hand him my book.

The notch between his brows tells me this was unexpected. I get it.

"Hi," I say, breathless.

"Hi." He blinks then glances at the book. "Shall I make it out to you? What's your name?"

I swear I feel my heart dislodge in my chest. He's playing it like he doesn't know me. This is so much worse than I thought it would be.

Everything suddenly hurts. I want the floor to open and swallow me whole.

I decide not to let him know how affected I am. He glances behind me at the people waiting. He doesn't want to see me or be seen with me. I knew I shouldn't have come.

"Make it out to Millie," I say.

His eyes catch on mine, confusion bubbling across his features. "Sure."

He writes quickly, closing the book and handing it back to me before I can so much as smile. "Did you want a photo?" he asks.

But I'm already stepping away, whiplashed and fucking embarrassed. I shake my head before I hear him ask the same question to the woman after me.

I swear I don't take a single breath until I'm back outside the building. And then I'm marching away, gasping for air, trying to force the impending tears away with painful gulps.

I don't know where to go. All I know is I can't get away quick enough.

What a fucking idiot.

Why did I let my sisters persuade me this was a good idea?

The first tear escapes me, rolling slowly down my cheek, as I hear, "Sara!" being called from behind.

Thirty-Five

I spin on my heel.

It's him.

Gus is sprinting towards me, a member of his security team hot on his heels. He stops when he catches me up, close enough to touch. I'm clutching the book to my chest, tears falling from my eyes. It's not a good time.

What does he want?

He takes a steadying breath. "What are you doing here?"

His words are almost accusatory. It's like a dagger to the chest. I press the book even closer as if it can protect me.

"Sorry, I shouldn't have come," I say, turning away from him.

"Sara, stop," he grabs my arm. "I'm just confused, I wasn't expecting to see you, I'm just… surprised." He frowns, and it takes every ounce of self-control not to embrace him.

"I'm sorry, I—"

"You told me you couldn't be with someone famous." He takes a deep breath. "I didn't know how to react to seeing you. But I don't want you to think—"

The burly man I recognise from Barcelona, dressed in a tight black T-shirt stops beside him, tapping him on the arm. "*Gus!* What the *fuck* do you think you're doing!?"

"Give me a second, Carl."

"You can't run off like that. We're in central London."

"Carl!" Gus yells. "Give me a second!"

Carl holds his hands up, eyeing me as he steps back to give us space.

"I shouldn't have come," I say. "I don't know what I was thinking."

"Right." Gus laughs, exasperated. "I don't know what to think either. I don't know what to do. You're here. But you're embarrassed to see me?"

I can't help looking around for spying eyes. It's bad enough knowing some of his fans have been trying to track me down. *Hunting me.*

He notices, tensing. "Tell me to go, and I'll go."

I don't say anything. I don't want him to go. I also don't want more photos of me online. More speculation.

"What am I meant to do with this?" he says, gesturing at the space between us. "You don't reply to my message. I haven't heard from you at all. You didn't join me in Barcelona. What do you want from me?"

"I don't know," I say, voice shaky. "I'm confused. My sisters persuaded me to come and see you. They thought... but..." But I don't know what to say. That we stood a chance? That it might be romantic?

Carl clears his throat, pointedly.

Gus runs a hand through his curls and groans. "Right. I have to get back."

I nod. "Yeah."

"Bye, Sara," he says, shaking his head. "For the record, this is seriously fucking confusing."

I know.

Because I can feel my pulse beating in my throat and words are evading me. My breathing is choppy, and I need to hide before another panic attack steals the last of my composure.

"And read the book," he adds assertively.

As Gus walks swiftly back towards the bookshop, I escape too, deciding to head home without waiting for my sisters. They'll understand.

I'm on the tube heading south by the time my tears really hit. Nobody looks my way as I attempt to hide that I'm crying uncontrollably. One man moves seats to get away from me but mostly everyone else minds their own business.

Once I'm on the train back to Brighton, I take the book out. When I open the page my heart stops for a beat.

He didn't sign it.

He left a phone number and a note.

Sara, I'm not signing this for someone else. Please call me.
   Gus

My brain scrambles. I'm still wiping tears away. There's no way I can call him. I don't even know what to say. I know what I *want* to say. Deep down, the voice from my heart has lots of words to describe how I feel. The voice in my head, however, is telling me to tread carefully.

But where has that ethos ever gotten me?

Instead of calling, I send him a message with my address in it. If we're going to talk, we need privacy. And if he really does want to talk, he'll come find me.

I don't hear from him all evening.

My sisters on the other hand nag me for updates in the group chat. When I send them a thumbs down emoji and a short message to say I'm home, they leave it. Probably pitying me. Or not. The rascals. I'm sure they're enjoying their night out in London.

After a light dinner, I climb into my pyjamas, brush my teeth and get ready for bed. It's nearly midnight by the time I start turning the lights off. My eyes are dry from all the crying, and my chest is tight from the breathlessness.

My head hits the pillow and then the doorbell rings.

Thirty-Six

I creep through the apartment in silence, barefooted.

It's late, and I leave all the lights off as I sneak up to the door and check through the peephole. My body reacts so fast, I find myself clutching my chest.

I open the door.

Gus waits on the other side.

He looks tired, his curls array, a takeaway coffee and box of chocolates in hand.

I don't know what to say to him so I just stare.

He half-grins. "You have no idea the trouble I went to in order to find a coffee at this hour. But I guessed you weren't the flower kind of girl."

He's right. "I hate watching them die."

He nods, like that makes sense. "Can I come in? Before I'm spotted?"

"It's midnight," I say, eyeing the road that is currently deserted.

He takes a step forward. "It's just an excuse. I really want to come in."

I open the door wider, then switch the lights on. He's still in the same outfit from earlier. Has he come directly from the event? My mind is racing.

He steps over the threshold and I shut the door behind him, showing him into the living room. He offers me the coffee and I accept it, unable to hide a smile.

"It's decaf," he explains.

"Phew," I say, taking a sip. "Er, this is my place." I gesture vaguely.

He sighs happily. "It's so intensely you."

"Thank you?"

"It's definitely a compliment."

I take a deep breath, trying to ground myself again. "Can I get you a drink?"

"No," he says. He looks like he has so much to say but doesn't know where to begin. "Thank you. But no. I won't stay long, I know it's late."

A wave of disappointment rolls through me. "Ok."

He opens his mouth then closes it again, placing the box of chocolates on the coffee table. "I'm sorry about earlier."

"No, please, I'm the one who should be sorry. I let my sisters whip me up into a frenzy and then ambushed you."

"Why?"

"Because they're like that. They get all excited about things…"

"No. I meant, why were *you* in a frenzy?"

I swallow, feeling a knot form in my stomach. "They got it in their heads that I stood a chance with you."

"Did they?" he asks, not giving anything away.

"Yes. But I realise now that it was a stupid thing to do. You had hundreds of people queuing to meet you today. And then I just crashed your event. I'm nobody. I had no right—"

"Stop it, Sara," he says, shaking his head. "You're not nobody. You're very much somebody. You're the beautiful blonde everybody keeps pestering me about. You're the one who rescued me, not just in Croatia, but from myself. You helped me escape it all, and you gave me the best gift of all." His eyes hold mine, so intense, so clear. "You let me be myself. Sara, I haven't stopped thinking about you since Barcelona. I don't think even a minute passes where I'm not thinking about you."

"Well, imagine how it's been for me," I say, finding his statement funny. "You're *everywhere*! I couldn't escape you even if I tried. I haven't been able to go anywhere without hearing your music or seeing you on TV."

"I'm not sorry. In fact, I'm glad," he says. "I was so worried you'd moved on, that you'd just put aside our time together. It was killing me."

"Me too," I whisper. "I worried about that too."

"Sara," he says, taking a step towards me. "Where does this leave us?"

"Do you have a car waiting for you round the corner?"

He nods, chewing his lip. "I do."

"What if..." my voice trails off.

"What if what?"

"What if... I want you to stay? What if I'm not ready to give you up?"

"Then I can stay," he says. He watches me, holding his phone in his palm. "Should I do that?"

I groan, spinning away. "I want you to stay. I do. I'm just so scared, Gus. I don't want to lead you on. I might not be able to handle this. What if I can't?"

He releases a long breath, nodding as if he's figured me

out. "I get it. You're worried I'm going to fall too hard. That I'm going to hold you to this relationship and blame you if it all falls apart. Am I right?"

"Maybe not even *you*. Maybe other people will do that. Maybe I will."

He smiles. "And you're way ahead of yourself. All those things you're thinking, those are future things. Be here now, in the moment, right now."

I swallow. "Stop figuring me out. It's annoying."

He steps closer. "What can I do to reassure you?"

I wrap my arms around myself. "I think the thought of being with you, of the scrutiny, is *so* terrifying that I've tried to put you out of my mind. But I miss you. I miss your smile, your energy, your laugh. I miss it all. I want to be around you."

"Sara—"

"Let me get this out," I put a hand up, making him wait. "I want to try. Because I think if I play this safe, I'll never forgive myself, even it does eventually break my heart."

His smile broadens. He dials a number on his phone. "Yeah. Go home," he says. He hangs up, places his phone down then before I can gather my thoughts, my back is pressed against the wall.

The adrenaline hits me so fast, I lose all train of thought.

His hands work through my hair, lips crushing mine as we gasp into each other. It starts out calmly, until one nip here, one scratch there, and suddenly my legs are wrapped around his waist and he's running his hands up under my pyjama top.

"Wait," he breathes, dropping me back to the floor. "Wait. We haven't talked this out. I just. I had to kiss you. It nearly killed me earlier, having you that close and not being able to touch you."

"I felt the same. I've been so in my head about this. About us. I'm just so scared I'm not strong enough to handle all that comes with being with you."

"And I hear your concerns. They're mine too. But you're selling yourself short. You're one of the strongest people I've ever met. You've dealt with so much and yet your focus and dedication to the people you love is so wildly beyond anything a weak person could offer. You have to know that."

There are tears in my eyes that I blink away. "It doesn't feel that way, but what I *do* know, after not seeing you, is that I very much don't want to do that again. I missed you, Gus. I missed you in a really embarrassing, totally insensible way."

"Please can we practise at you being mine?"

"Gus, I *am* yours."

He brushes his nose against mine, kisses me deep and slow. "You were right, by the way," he murmurs.

"About what?"

"About the contract. Today was the last time I represent the label. The last time I'm Gus from Just4Summer."

I gasp. "What happened?"

"My agent didn't have my best interests at heart. I had this massive bust up with Will and Callum at the conference. I was so tired of them shrugging this all off their shoulders without any consequences. Turns out they'd switched to a new agency. They have lawyers on the case. And so, I've done the same." He breathes out, a smile consuming his lips. "I'm free of it. I can do whatever I want to do now."

"What will you do?"

He laughs, his hands squeezing my buttocks. "You, I guess."

"Shut up. Be serious."

"I am."

"*Gus.*"

"But that's the beauty of all this. I don't have to decide just yet. I can write music. I can sign with another label, maybe. I'm free. Maybe for now, I need this time to review me. Who I am. What I want from life. I've barely had any time to do that free of other people's opinions and directions."

"I'm so happy for you," I say, running one hand over his face and through his curls, tugging gently at the back of his head so I have free access to gorgeous throat.

Our lips graze once, twice, then before I know it we're all hands and teeth and lips and wanton sounds. I'm not subtle about my needs, unbuttoning his shorts and taking him into my hand, hot and smooth.

He groans and it tastes like lust. If only I could bottle it.

We scramble backwards towards my room. I guide Gus through the dark to the bed where he sits on the edge and pulls me to him.

"If we're doing this, I need to grab a…"

I can't wait. "Are you clean?"

"Yes. I'm tested. There's been no one…"

"I'm on the pill."

"Sara," he mutters, pausing me, his hand strong at my waist. "Are you sure?"

I press against him, testing his strength. He's unmoveable. Stubborn. "So sure," I breathe into his lips.

He releases me carefully as I use him to press my knickers

aside and slide onto him. He moans and I throw my head back as I begin to bounce, enjoying the stretch, the ache.

"Sara, I *swear*," Gus mumbles into my skin, his voice cracked, as he sucks on my neck, pulling my waist into him. "So tight. So good. I don't think I'll ever have enough of you."

And we fall apart right there, Gus holding me to him like he promised, keeping all the pieces of me together for another night.

And maybe, hopefully, every night after.

Thirty-Seven

"**H**appy Birthday!" I sing. "*Well*, you're thirty in Thailand anyway. What time is it there?"

Hattie laughs down the line, her familiar emo music playing in the background.

"It's just gone five. I'm not even ready yet. We're leaving in two hours."

Hattie's birthday is New Year's Day and our friend Sam's birthday is New Year's Eve. It's a whole thing. Every year I've known them, they've celebrated it together and I've always been there, along with our other friend Priya. In fact, this is the first time since we were eighteen that I haven't celebrated New Year's Eve with them and for a moment I experience a sinking feeling.

Am I homesick?

I look out of our beachside shack and stare at the moonlit beach, the sea sparkling. Gus is strolling along the water, his naked silhouette dipping his toes and glancing back to see if I'm joining. The fireworks have settled down at the resort now, leaving a serene charm.

Nah. I'm exactly where I want to be.

"How's Thailand?" she asks.

I sigh, happily. "Totally remote and very quiet."

"Love that for you. Does that mean you've had lots of privacy?"

"Yep. *Lots*. I think some of the staff recognise him but we're staying out of the way. We've barely left…"

"The bed," Hattie finishes for me.

"The shack… But sure."

The past couple of months have been a total whirlwind. I've been trying to juggle work while sneaking away to different houses, hotels and city breaks, trying to keep our relationship under wraps. Dare I say, it's been fun. Almost exhilarating.

But we're not stupid.

I know that at some point we're going to be spotted together again and I'm going to have to accept whatever that means. Because the alternative is not having Gus. Grace has been laying the foundations publicity wise, pressing secrets into the right palms, as she puts it, and tells me that the storm will feel bumpy at first but with all PR, something else will take the spotlight before you know it and then we'll be forgotten about.

"Well, next year," Hattie says, "Gus is coming to our party."

"Agreed. I'm very sad to miss tonight. Have a special birthday and mess Sam's hair up for me because I'm not there to do it myself."

"It will be a pleasure," she says. "Right, go and enjoy yourself. We'll catch up when you're back."

We hang up and I head out to join Gus. I've been in this bikini most of the day, dipping into the sea, sunbathing, a spa treatment then back in the sea again. It's been dreadful, as you can imagine.

Gus has taken a seat in the sand, hugging his knees. He glances back at me and although I can't see his face, I can imagine his secret smile. His curls have been unruly since we arrived and he's been blaming it on the sun but really, it's because I can't keep my hands off them.

I slowly peel my bikini top off which makes him twist some more, using his hand to lean backwards. Then, because I love his reactions to my body, I push the bottoms down too, working incredibly hard to make stepping out of them look sexy and not clumsy.

By the time I've reached him, Gus is on his belly reaching out to my ankles like a touch-starved man. Something he is most certainly *not*. Especially this week.

He tugs on my leg so that I can't help but collapse beside him, and he rolls on top of me. His hands brush my hair back from my face, his lips trailing kisses down the side of my neck.

"Have your friends forgiven me for stealing you away?" he asks.

I shrug. "Are you kidding? Hattie is very happy about this situation."

"She is?"

"Obviously she is completely heartbroken and beside herself that I'm not with her."

"How couldn't she be?" Gus jokes.

"But she loves that I'm being reckless."

"Mmm." Gus presses a kiss to my lips. "You are being very reckless, look at you. Naked on the beach."

"We have this beach to ourselves. You've been naked for hours. Nobody will see."

"You're right. This isn't reckless at all. We should up our game," he mumbles, running his hand down my front and pressing on my clit, kissing my neck until I'm gasping into the starry night sky.

And I have let loose a bit. I'm back to my old, wild self. But… "Fuck. No. This is totally illegal and we do not need that PR."

"You say that but whenever one of us got arrested back in the day, especially abroad, our sales would increase."

"Beside the point," I say, squirming from underneath him and bouncing onto my feet. "We have a beautiful beach shack right there." I start heading towards it, picking up my discarded bikini as I go. I hear him puffing behind me and then he sprints past, racing me back to the bed.

"Hey!" I complain, adrenaline hitting me in the best damn way, grabbing his arm and half-racing, half-tackling him to the shack, hitting the bed in a jumble of sandy limbs and lips and hands. He kisses me, his curls falling over his eyes.

"Thank you for putting up with all this. I can't say the next year will be any easier."

I run my fingers over his face, pinching his chin. "Good thing I *like* you."

He raises an eyebrow. "Only like?"

"And that's pushing it to be honest. I think you're bearable. I'm only with you because your…"

"I know, my massive—"

"—Cotswold house."

He laughs. "Exactly." He drops his head to kiss my collarbone and whispers, "But also, I'm horribly, frighteningly, never leave me, I'd go to prison for you, in love with you," he says. "Even when you're mean to me to compensate for your huge, beautiful, unmanageable feelings. But don't worry, we can keep that between us."

I can't fight the smile. "I hate how much I love you."

"It's inconvenient for you, isn't it?"

"Is it," I quip, "But it's a burden I'm willing to accept."

He laughs into my neck, rising above me. I run my hand down his front and guide him into me, enjoying the ragged sounds he makes. Then, there's nothing more to say, because we're both exactly where we're meant to be.

Epilogue

Eighteen months later...

"I have a confession," Millie says, bursting into the room where we're getting ready. It's our final moments to get our hair and make-up right. I've had more mirrors and a desk brought into the main bedroom so we can sit side by side.

"Oh God," I mutter. "Do you have to confess right now? We're pretty busy if you can't tell?"

"I think I do. Partly because we'll be in the ceremony in an hour and I can't lie once it's started."

"Why not?"

She shrugs. "Religion, probably."

"*Right...*" I give Gemma and Hattie a look waiting for them to intercede but they both stare at Millie with intrigue. "Go on then."

"When I was fifteen, I did a voodoo love spell on Jax, and I think it went wrong. Maybe it confused your DNA with mine or something like that? And maybe I wasn't clear enough about which J4S member I wanted to fall in love with me. And now it's happening to *you*. Not me, sadly. I just thought you should know."

I glance at her reflection behind me, guilt and concern all over her face. "I'm so glad you told me that."

She smiles and nods. Good. One sister is happy. Now to check on the other two.

And yet, I realise Millie's confession needs further scrutiny. Because – *what the hell?* "But just so I understand. How is it relevant, right now, today of all days?"

Gemma snorts. We've become a lot closer over the last year. Sometimes she's even on my side in these moments when Millie is making absolutely no sense whatsoever. Unfortunately, she's also gotten an eye load of Gus's security lead – a muscly, fifty-year-old bald man, named Carl, who, as I've explained to her several times, is a hardworking professional and she is not to pet him. Basically, her desired trifecta.

"Well, obviously, if I got it wrong and now it's happening to *you* then you deserve to know. Especially if the spell backfires."

"I hear you," I say, nodding, trying to pretend to respect her quirks. I remember her doing the voodoo stuff when she was a teenager. She used to pick random herbs (see also: weeds) from the garden, mix them in a bowl and blast music in her room while chewing on popping candy. I assumed she'd figured out it was all hocus pocus by now, but maybe not. I watch her considering the situation in the mirror.

"So what?" I ask. "Should I break it off with Gus? Just to be safe? You know, in case he doesn't know the last two years have actually been due to the effects of the voodoo spell you got wrong when you were thirteen?"

"I was fifteen. I'd mastered the skill much better by then."

Gemma tilts her head. "And yet you think you got it wrong."

"All I'm saying is—"

"You're nuts," Abby interjects, coming up to stand beside Millie. I told them this time around they could wear whatever they felt like. I wanted no airs and graces. No perfect wedding. No drama. No expectations.

I wanted a whole party of happy people being unashamedly themselves.

And they do look like themselves. Relaxed and comfortable in their own style.

Millie is pouting behind us. "None of you are taking this seriously."

"No, I am!" I say. "Get Gus on the phone, I'll let him know it's over."

"You're being facetious."

"*Millie*, careful with those big words, you might hurt somebody," Gemma quips.

"Whatever. I'm just trying to make sense of this whole situation. It doesn't feel that long ago that you were trying to marry another man."

"Thanks for bringing that up today," I say. "I was worried nobody would."

"*Millie!*" Abby scolds.

But she continues. "Then suddenly you were dating the famous popstar. You buggered off all summer and winter, travelling almost every weekend, to go somewhere fancy with him and now you're doing this whirlwind wedding. I'm sorry if you two are just totally chill with it, but I'm freaking out a little."

I make a face. "Why are *you* freaking out, Millie?"

"There are celebrities downstairs. They're *everywhere*."

"Yes, they're Gus's friends."

"This is a huge moment for me."

I take a deep breath and spin to face her. I take her hands and make her sit down so we're eye to eye. "I'm so glad you're here and we've spent the last couple of years becoming closer. Don't worry, I don't subscribe to voodoo..."

"You should, it's very serious."

"...because I'm... I don't know? Normal. And I'm not nervous about this. I know it feels like a whirlwind, looking in from the outside, but it feels right to me. To us. I've never felt like this about anyone. Ever. Even when we argue, even when it feels like he's the most annoying man on the planet, I have no doubt that I want to tolerate him and love him for the rest of our lives. And I am confident he feels the same way."

Gemma hums. "Yeah. He definitely tolerates you."

I swear Hattie kicks her under the table.

"And loves you," she adds.

"He's calling *again*," Hattie says. I spin back to see his name lighting up my phone.

"Ah, look at that. I can break up with him. Thanks for the heads up, Millie."

Hattie is fighting a smile; her fizzy hair brushed back into an explosive bun. I'm still in my casual, loose clothing as I grab the phone and head into the walk-in closet that's attached to our room for privacy.

Once things got out about us dating publicly, there was a buzz of interest in me for a few weeks. Work found it tricky to navigate when fans were waiting in the lobby to speak with me about Gus. And it took some getting used to, being papped when we went for our Sunday morning walks down the seafront. And yet, with all these things, they moved onto a new big topic.

But since Gus has been unemployed for the past year, he's been able to flex to my schedule. We've travelled at weekends and during my annual leave. I've helped him navigate the rocky waters of his future and enjoyed listening to him create music for other people whenever I'm with him.

And when we're not travelling, we're at his beautiful home in Tetbury – which is now mine too, I guess. It's all modern and tidy inside, but externally it's an ancient Cotswold barn with massive glass windows and doors where the entrance used to be.

It's totally my cup of tea.

Essentially, I have fallen in love with more than one thing these past couple of years.

When I peer out of the window at the long lawn at the rear of the house, I can see the garden is filling up with familiar faces. We said we'd keep it a small affair, but of course, my extended family is massive, and Gus's mother is intense. Not to mention Grace's social circle that we had to consider for some reason.

I answer his call. "Are you still doing this?"

"I am," he says. "This is the last time though as I fear I'm close to being attacked by my auntie."

"Isn't Carl around to protect you?"

"Probably. He's always creeping about."

"How can I help you, Augustus?"

"I want to tell you, I love you. And I'm here. And I know there are *way* more people than we originally planned. And

I know your dad is only seconds away from coming up to the bridal suite to make you cry. But I'm here. And I'm staying. There's pretty much nothing in the world you could do now to change that."

"On that note. You should know, Millie has just confessed our love may be due to a failed voodoo experiment that she messed up in her teens."

Gus blows out a breath, but I can hear his smile as he says, "Well, thank God for that. Will you thank her for me."

I laugh quietly, hoping they're not all listening in at the door. "I love that you're putting me at ease, but I'm pretty sure this is bad luck."

"I thought you didn't believe in luck."

"Well, maybe you've changed me."

"I wouldn't change a single thing about you."

There's a knock on the door and I'm distracted for a second. Hattie yells at me to get off the phone, it's time to go for photos and I'm not even in my dress yet.

I laugh. It's time.

"I've got to go. Apparently, there's this event today that I can't be late for."

"I better not keep you then. One final question."

"Go on."

"What you wearing?"

I snort, rolling my eyes. "You'll have to wait and see."

"Hurry up, sunshine. Come and sign this contract with me." The most important contract I'll ever sign. No negotiations required.

I hang up and take a deep breath. My final moment of peace before the chaos unfolds. I step out of the room, and we work as a team to get me into my dress. Not that it's needed since this wedding dress is far less dramatic than the one from last time.

It's a simple A-line satin gown with no sleeves and a sneaky slit all the way up one thigh. Once it's on and Hattie has rearranged my hair to fall naturally around my shoulders, I smile, feeling completely and unapologetically like myself.

I decided as well that we'd all stroll together. No specific order. No organisation. The bridesmaids will walk down ahead, grasping their flowers, followed closely by Dad and me.

When I reach the lawn, it all comes together in a daze. A massive rose-covered arch has been set up at the end of the aisle for the vows to take place under, and the outskirts of the field next to the garden has been purposefully left as meadow grass, wildflowers and butterflies scattered like a dream.

I greet guests near the back and smile at Will's daughter, Olive, her dark hair styled into tight ringlets that hug her round face, who comes over for a cuddle before everyone is told to stand for the bride. Hattie is the first bridesmaid to walk down the aisle, followed swiftly by my sisters.

And then finally, it's my turn.

Acknowledgements

AS A FAN of pop-rock from a young age, I was so excited to pitch this series because some of my favourite childhood memories were of my parents driving me to HMV to stock up on the latest albums, posters and magazines. *Glad You Came* is the first in a series of four romcoms that are my ode to British boybands. I know everyone says this about their own era, but I honestly believe some of the best pop music came from the early noughties and it will never be beaten.

A special shoutout to Busted because they were my first true love – I'm still so proud of myself when I went to the Busted vs McFly tour in 2025, that I could recite all the lyrics to their backlist songs because I had their albums stuck on repeat for many, many years.

All that to say, I'm endlessly grateful to be here, writing acknowledgements, for my third book. I know what a privilege it is and it fills my heart with warmth to know there are people out there who still want to read my stories.

Of course, this book wouldn't even exist if it wasn't for my brilliant editor, Aubrie Artiano. Thanks for your editorial guidance, support and everything you do to champion my books. Thanks to Shannon, Holly, Sophie, Yas and Pippa – you're always on hand to help and do such a wonderful job of supporting and promoting my books. *Team Aria is a dream!* Thank you to Anna for copyediting – your feedback is vital! I am always amazed by how blind I am to my own mistakes. Thanks to Gemma for designing this absolutely stunning book cover. And to Lorena for the most beautiful artwork.

As always, thank you Safae, my wonderful agent. Where would I be without you? Thank you for humouring me when I send you bonkers manuscript ideas that I come up with at 2am. Our catchups always make me smile.

A massive thank you to my hype crew! To my early readers, Anna, Kay, Steph and Lauren. The more I write, the more sensitive and worried I become about every single word. You are on hand to settle my nerves and throw encouragement my way whilst also providing me with excellent feedback and insight. You are amazing! As always, thanks to my mum (who is still my first reader on every book) – your feedback is biased but I love it anyway. And to my writing/reading friends! There are so many of you! I don't even know where to begin, but you hopefully know exactly who you are. I'm sorry for my confusing voice messages. Thank you to Eli for your wonderful social media support. I'd be lost without you.

Thank you to my family! I wrote a long passage about how grateful I am to all of you, especially my husband and son, because writing takes me away from you quite a lot, but I realised I tell you every day. Even so, THANK YOU!

And, finally, thank you to authors who inspire me. Thank

you to the readers who read and buy my books – you are the reason I get to continue. And thanks to everyone in the Booksta/BookTok world who shouts about and promotes my stories. I adore you!

THE JUST4SUMMER SERIES
WILL CONTINUE IN

ALL ABOUT YOU

APRIL 2027

'Bursting with sparkling wit and crackling tension'
Catherine Walsh, bestselling author of *Snowed In*

AN UNEXPECTED
OVERNIGHT

WORK
TRIP

WHAT COULD
GO WRONG?

CHLOE FORD

Discover the hilarious enemies-to-lovers rom-com from Chloe Ford

They say you should keep your enemies closer...

For Fliss, the prospect of a team building work trip fills her with dread. Mostly because she cannot stand her pushy colleague James, who often attempts to derail her brilliant plans. But when the two arrive in the Scottish Highlands, they find themselves facing a unique challenge: their boss has abandoned them in the middle of nowhere with only one tent, two sleeping bags and a few protein bars.

Cut off from the outside world, the pair are forced to put aside their differences to weather the unpredictable elements of the Highlands and get home. As they set out on a journey across miles of rugged wilderness - pushing each other to survive and testing their physical and emotional limits - they remain fully aware of their boss's manipulative plan to orchestrate a hook up between them.

But even with only each other for company, Fliss and James stand firm in their resolve: they won't give in to any romantic notions. Or will they?

Available to buy now

About the Author

CHLOE FORD grew up in rural Sussex but is now based in South Gloucestershire. She has an affinity with all things country, from riding horses to muddy walks. Her love for writing began at secondary school when her English teacher would set a writing task for the whole hour. An avid reader, she started sneaking Mills & Boon books out from under her mum's bed as a teenager and hasn't stopped devouring romance books ever since.

Thanks for reading!

Want to receive exclusive author content, news on the latest Aria books and updates on offers and giveaways?

Follow us on X @AriaFiction and on Facebook and Instagram @HeadofZeus, and join our mailing list.